D1433904

THE SNIPER

By Willo Davis Roberts:

THE SNIPER
ACT OF FEAR
THE JAUBERT RING
EXPENDABLE
WHITE JADE

THE SNIPER

WILLO DAVIS ROBERTS

PUBLISHED FOR THE CRIME CLUB BY
DOUBLEDAY & COMPANY, INC.
GARDEN CITY, NEW YORK
1984

All of the characters in this book
are fictitious, and any resemblance
to actual persons, living or dead,
is purely coincidental.

Library of Congress Cataloging in Publication Data
Roberts, Willo Davis.
The sniper.
I. Title.
PS3568.O2478S6 1984   813'.54
ISBN 0-385-19277-0

Library of Congress Catalog Card Number 83-40139

THE SNIPER

PROLOGUE

The watcher crouched in the deeply shadowed doorway, mouth-breathing as shallowly as possible, waiting. The wait was not long.

The old woman came as she had come on previous mornings to the dumpster in the alley behind the supermarket. The aroma of gin drifted across the narrow space. Disgusting, the watcher thought. No loss to anyone when she was gone.

She moved heavily and slowly, as if her feet hurt. She wore a shapeless dress of indistinguishable color, with a Salvation Army coat buttoned across her sagging body. Her hair was matted and uncombed, protruding in gray wisps from beneath a dark felt cap.

She moved with purpose to the green metal dumpster, raising the lid to peer inside. Carefully, she began to make her selections.

A few lettuce leaves, a pair of brown bananas, a loaf of bread, something the watcher could not identify, which the old woman lifted to her mouth and chewed with apparent relish.

She gave a small, triumphant cry, and lifted herself on tiptoes to reach farther over the rim of the bin, stretching for some item just beyond her reach.

The watcher inhaled deeply, exhaled, and squeezed the trigger. The sound seemed loud in the confined area, but it attracted no attention; traffic moved noisily by only yards away, and no one opened the back doors of the adjoining buildings.

The old woman hung there for long seconds, one hand grasping the dumpster rim, before she slid silently to the asphalt surface of the alley.

The old woman didn't move. No blood appeared around the hole in the back of her coat, at least none that the watcher could see.

After a moment the watcher sighed and stepped out of the doorway. Within a matter of seconds, the alley was empty except for the old woman on her face in the litter beside the dumpster.

1

The alarm buzzed shrilly in her ears, and Jane Madison groped for the button to turn it off, groaning. "It's Saturday, isn't it? I don't have to get up!"

She lifted her head, then groaned again and buried her face in the pillow. It *was* Saturday, wasn't it?

"Janie? You up?"

A freckled, twelve-year-old face was poked around the edge of her bedroom door. "Hey, remember? Today we're going to go and see Uncle Addison's house."

Why hadn't she remembered to turn off the alarm last night? Now she'd never go back to sleep.

"You're going with us, aren't you? Mom thinks you are," Teddy informed her. "If it's worth a lot of money, maybe we can buy a new car, and I can get a bike, and—"

"If it's worth a lot of money, it would never have been left to *me*," Janie said, giving up and opening her eyes. "Uncle Addison would have taken it with him. Don't get your hopes up, Teddy. More than likely, it's falling apart. Uncle Addison probably didn't fix the roof or the plumbing all the time he lived in the place."

"Well, let's go see anyway before we give up, OK?" Teddy Madison had gray eyes and brown hair and freckles, much like his sister's.

Janie rolled over and stretched and stared up at the ceiling. Saturday. Two days a week she got away from the office where she worked for that creep Dickson Zeller, and one of the pleasures of not going to work, aside from not having to dodge Dickson all day, was being allowed to sleep late.

"Come on," Teddy urged. "You can have the bathroom; Mom's out."

"OK," Janie said. "I'm coming."

What was the appropriate outfit, she wondered, for inspecting an inheritance from an uncle you'd never known, even though he lived in the same city where you'd grown up, because he didn't like children?

Of course, there was no reason to take it personally, her mother had assured her. Addison Hamer didn't only dislike children. He disliked everybody.

"How come?" Teddy had asked, incredulous.

He was repeating the question now as Janie came out of her bedroom, buttoning the shirt which she had decided was suitable, with jeans, for the inspection tour.

"He must have liked *somebody*, sometime," Teddy insisted.

Muriel Madison was a pretty woman in her late forties. Except for the fact that there were touches of gray in her brown hair and that she weighed fifteen pounds more, her resemblance to her daughter was remarkable. She divided scrambled eggs between the three plates on the kitchen table and pushed the jam jar toward her son. "If he did, I don't remember it. He was your father's only uncle, but he never came to family gatherings."

"But Aunt Beatrice lived with him, didn't she?" Janie slid into her chair and wondered if they'd ever be able to afford bacon with their eggs again. "Didn't he even like *her?*"

"I doubt it. Poor Bea. I'd have hated to be at Addison's mercy; he didn't know the meaning of the word."

"Why would she live with him, then?" Teddy wanted to know.

"He always supported her. After she was widowed, I mean. She married a man Addison didn't like—naturally—and they never had any money. When the man died, there wasn't even any insurance, and Bea went to live with her brother. She never complained, but I suspect he made life miserable for her."

"Why'd she stay there, then? Why didn't she go out and get a job the way you did, Mom?"

"I don't think she ever held a job in her life. Women of her generation didn't, Teddy. In those days females kept house and raised families; Bea never had any children, and I suppose she wouldn't have any idea how to support herself. She was close to seventy when she was widowed, I think."

"Maybe Uncle Addison wanted a housekeeper for free," Janie speculated, sipping coffee. "What did Mr. Nunnally say about her, Mom? She's still living in the house now, isn't she?"

Curtis Nunnally was Addison Hamer's lawyer, and he had notified them of Janie's inheritance. All he'd told them about the house was that it was large and old. Addison's money had been left to a grand-nephew on the East Coast, and the house was a minor share of the estate.

"If we'd been able to persuade him to invest his money instead of sticking it into a safety deposit box," the lawyer had remarked dryly, "there would have been considerably more of it. Unfortunately, he didn't trust banks or investment counselors."

Muriel took her own place and ate her scrambled eggs with dry toast, a token effort at losing a few pounds. "Yes, Bea was still there when I talked to Mr. Nunnally on Thursday. I think he indicated that she'd be going into a nursing home, though."

"Poor old soul. Well, let's go get this over with. I won't be surprised if it's one of those houses you read about, inhabited by an eccentric who filled it with newspapers. Still, it's presumably inhabitable, which ought to make it worth a few thousand. What do you think, Mom? You want to try to buy a house, if there's enough for a down payment on one?"

Muriel stirred Sweet 'n Low into her coffee. "It would be wonder-ful if that happened, but from what the lawyer said, I can't be too optimistic." She sighed, a habit that had grown since her husband's death nearly a year earlier. "If one of us doesn't get a raise pretty soon, I'm not sure we can even keep this apartment. I hated to tell you, but the notice came in the mail yesterday."

Janie put down her fork. "You mean that Mrs. Talley has raised the rent *again?* How much this time?"

"Twenty-five dollars a month."

There was silence around the breakfast table except for the crunch of toast. Damn, Janie thought bitterly. She frequently considered quitting her job at Zeller and Markham Insurance because Dickson Zeller was so obnoxious to work for, but jobs were hard to come by right now. And the only way he'd give her a raise was if she decided to "be nice to him," as he put it. That would be the day.

If the rent was going up, they'd have to find some other source of income. There wasn't enough slack in their present budget to cover any increase in the rent at all unless they just stopped eating.

She thought of the little pile of manuscript pages that grew, ever so slowly, on the table beside her typewriter in the bedroom. She'd wanted to write a book for kids for as long as she could remember, but there was so little time. She'd attended a writer's conference in Tacoma a couple of years ago and learned there that very few people got rich writing for children. But they did make *some* money, and a few thousand would help, at least temporarily. She daydreamed of making enough so that she could not only tell Dickson Zeller what to do with his job, but to allow her mother to quit working, too.

Not that Muriel disliked her job. As a matter of fact, she loved being ward clerk at the hospital a few blocks away. She liked the people and the sense of doing something worthwhile. It was only that Janie knew that her mother missed having time to do the reading and the sewing she'd always enjoyed, though Muriel seldom mentioned this.

Janie rose and carried her dishes to the sink. Maybe, she thought, just once, they'd have a stroke of good luck. Maybe this house would turn out to be worth something after all.

They took the bus, because they'd sold the car six months ago when they couldn't afford to renew the insurance on it. Even working for an insurance company didn't help enough to enable them to maintain the middle-aged Ford ranch wagon.

Luckily, Muriel could walk to St. Joseph's Hospital, and Janie had only a twenty-minute bus ride to her job. The primary hardship, aside from not being able to drive out into the country on weekends or visit out-of-town friends, was in the matter of hauling groceries. They took the bus for that, too, for the only neighborhood market was too expensive to use regularly.

Someday, Janie told herself, things would get better. Maybe when she sold her book and got a lot of money for it and the books she would write after it. That was as likely as Harry Bowers getting rich selling insurance and offering to marry her and support her. Not that she wanted to marry him, but it would be rather nice if it occurred to him, considering the fact that they'd been dating for over a year.

The bus left them off half a block from the address Curtis Nunnally had given them. It was a part of town Janie'd never been in, and she looked around with her customary curiosity.

It was a middle-class neighborhood, with a few small businesses and large, relatively old houses. Most of them were in a good state of repair, some showing fresh paint and small, neat lawns. No one had yet gotten around to cutting down the maples and oaks that were pushing up sections of sidewalk, so on this spring morning Relton Street was attractive, with sun touching pale green leaves and daffodils.

Janie felt her spirits rising. "Which one is it? Number twenty-two forty? This side of the street, it would be."

"Probably that ugly brown one there," Teddy offered. "With the big front porch."

It was, naturally. Trust Addison Hamer to paint it whatever color he could get cheap. Still, Janie thought when they stood directly in front of the house, in spite of its paint the place looked sturdy and in good repair.

"Maybe we could live in it ourselves," Teddy said. "Wouldn't it be cheaper to live in a house we own, rather than an apartment? And I could have a big bedroom, instead of that broom closet I'm sleeping in now."

Muriel stared up at the house. "A basement and two full stories, plus an attic, it looks like. It's large, and the neighborhood isn't bad. Twenty years ago I'm sure it was a very nice area, and it hasn't gone completely downhill. Well, here's the key; let's see what it's like inside."

"Is Aunt Beatrice still here?" Janie asked as they mounted the broad steps onto the veranda. "Maybe we'd better ring the bell."

"I think she's quite old, in her eighties. She may not be up to coming to the door." Muriel compromised by ringing the old-fashioned bell at the same time as she twisted the key in the lock. "This way, we'll give her warning."

The door was mostly glass, with a sheer curtain behind it that prevented their seeing inside but which would provide a view of the visitors to anyone in the entryway.

They looked around with interest, each of them lost in his own speculations. "Reminds me of my grandmother's house, when I was a little girl," Muriel mused. "Twin parlors on that side, dining room on this side."

It was rather gloomy, for the draperies and shades were drawn at most of the windows. But the rooms were spacious and, though everything looked to be seventy years old, moderately comfortable. Well, of course, Janie thought wryly; Addison Hamer would have been concerned with his own comfort, however little he'd cared about anyone else's.

"This is a bedroom," Teddy announced, peering behind one of the heavy oak doors. "I'll bet it was his. It smells funny."

Janie looked over his shoulder. "Bingo. My gosh, I didn't think anybody still had furniture like this. It must weigh a ton, every piece of it."

"Solid oak," Muriel agreed. "They liked massive furniture in those days."

"What else is back here? The kitchen. Good grief, I've seen major restaurants with less space than this." Janie stood in the middle of the black-and-white-tiled floor, disbelieving.

It was completely equipped with a modern electric stove as well as a huge black iron monstrosity that would be wood-burning. The refrigerator was old yet gave off a reassuring hum. There was oilcloth on the big round table. Muriel touched it, amused. "We always had oilcloth when I was at home. The same pattern, even—red and white checks. Is that a pantry?"

The door opened upon a walk-in closetlike room lined with well-filled shelves. Teddy reached out to take a carton down. "Hey, look! There must be twenty boxes of Fig Newtons! Are these ours, too? They belong to whoever gets the house, don't they? Can I open one package?"

"I suppose so," Janie said before she remembered. "Wait a minute. Aunt Bea lived in this house, too, and she may still be here. Maybe they're *her* cookies."

"Oh," said a sweet voice behind them, "help yourselves to the cookies, my dears. And anything else you want."

She tottered there in the doorway, a frail lady of advanced years, with wispy white hair and blue eyes behind thick glasses. In one hand she carried a newspaper, in the other a glass filled with an amber liquid that sloshed over the rim as they watched.

Aunt Beatrice, Janie assumed, and ran forward to catch her as the old lady staggered into the kitchen and collapsed on the black and white tile.

2

"What's the matter with her?" Teddy asked. "Is she dying, too?"

"I'm afraid she's had too much to drink," Muriel said, kneeling beside the old lady. Janie had managed to break her fall, with the remainder of Aunt Bea's drink dumped over her for her trouble.

Bea Stone stirred and attempted to sit up. "My goodness, what happened? I feel so strange!"

Between them, they got her into a sitting position. "Are you all right now?" Muriel asked. "What were you drinking?"

Bea had to think for a moment. "Apricot brandy. It always smelled so good when Addison drank it. It seemed the thing for shock, only I suppose I had too much? I had no idea it was so potent."

"I'm sorry if we surprised you, coming in this way," Muriel told her, crouching beside the old lady on the floor. "We only wanted to spare you from having to answer the door if you weren't up to it."

"Oh, it wasn't shock over *that* that upset me," Bea assured them. "It's so undignified, sitting on the floor this way, but I'm not sure I can stand. My head is going around and around."

They got her on her feet and walked her toward the nearest of the parlors, where she sank with a small gasp into a chintz-covered chair. "Oh my, I can't imagine how Addison drank that stuff the way he did!" She closed her eyes and rested her head against the first antimacassar Jane had ever actually seen.

"You haven't been nipping at the apricot brandy ever since your brother died, surely?" Muriel asked, and that made the faded old blue eyes open again.

"Heavens no!" She struggled to focus on their faces, then spoke frankly. "To tell the truth, I was tempted to take a tiny drink when I realized he was really dead, but I didn't. You must be Roger's wife, Muriel. And you're Jane, the girl Addison left the house to?"

Upon confirmation of this, Bea sighed. "That lawyer warned me you'd be coming. He wanted me to pack up and get myself to a rest home before you arrived, but I wouldn't do it. I may be eighty-two, but I don't belong in a rest home. All those old folks sitting around with nothing to do. Why, I wouldn't last a week in a place like that!"

In the silence they heard the ticking of a grandfather clock in the corner. Janie had an uneasy feeling that they'd inherited more from Addison than the house.

"What did you intend to do, now that your brother's gone?" Muriel probed gently.

"Well, I sort of hoped . . . I mean, I didn't know if you'd want to move in here, this old barn of a place, but I thought that if you did, you might . . . need a housekeeper."

Oh, Lord. Janie suppressed a groan. What a stinker that old man had been. No wonder his sister was glad he was dead.

"Are you? Going to move in here?" Bea asked.

"We haven't even seen the place yet, except for a few ground-floor rooms. I shouldn't think we'd want a housekeeper, though. . . ." Muriel's voice revealed her doubts about this fragile little octogenarian taking on such a task even if they'd wanted someone to wait on them.

"I did for Addison, you know, all the years I lived with him. The only time he hired any help was when I fractured my hip, ten years ago. I was in the hospital for fourteen days. Had a lovely time, lying there in bed being waited on, and the food was very good, too. Of course, that was after I got over the worst of the operation. I hated to come home. But I'm talking too much—it must be the brandy."

Janie and Muriel exchanged glances of mingled amusement and concern. Janie correctly interpreted her mother's silent message: We've inherited Aunt Bea as well as the house; what are we going to do with her?

"Mr. Nunnally told us you'd be going into a rest home," Janie said gently. "We thought it was all arranged."

"Not by me, it wasn't. Addison thought it would punish me, to put me away, but he didn't want it to happen until he had no more use for me."

"Why did he leave the house to me?" Janie asked. Her jeans reeked of brandy, and the fumes were making her feel as if she'd be smart to get some fresh air.

"Spite, of course. It's the only reason he ever did anything. He expected you to throw me out. You won't, will you?"

Janie inhaled audibly. "I don't suppose he left you any money to keep the place up?"

"He didn't leave me a penny. I have my Social Security, of course. Three hundred and forty dollars a month, after they deduct for Medicare. I could maybe keep myself, just barely, if I didn't have to pay taxes or insurance." She blinked hopefully at them.

Teddy had tired of this conversation and wandered away. He came back now, carrying the newspaper she'd dropped in the kitchen. "Are we going to look at the rest of this place? What's in the basement?"

Bea turned her attention to the boy. "You're Theodore? The one named after my father?"

"Teddy," he said. "Is there an attic?"

"An attic and a basement, both. There's a set of electric trains in the attic. They were left behind when the previous owners moved. There's nothing very interesting in the basement. The furnace, and a lot of space. Cobwebs and such." Bea seemed to be recovering from her inebriation, at least to the extent that she could talk clearly. "My newspaper, yes, I was reading it and I saw about that dreadful murder . . . I knew her, you see. She used to join us at St. Andrew's on Wednesday nights, sometimes."

She spread the paper out on her knees and indicated a short item on an inner page. "It's only a small story here, see? I don't suppose it's worth much space, since she was nobody of importance. She wasn't one of our group, and to tell the truth we didn't really like to play with her because she had such a peculiar odor, but after all, she was someone I *knew*. And she was *murdered*."

The words were mildly incoherent at first, but when Janie twisted the newspaper around so that she could read it, the matter was clear enough.

The body of Mabel Gervaise, 68, was found this morning in the alley behind the Globe Supermarket in the Shelton Mall. She had been shot in the back and apparently died instantly. She was carrying a purse which contained sixty-three cents. Police have not ruled out robbery as the motive for the murder, but local residents say that it is unlikely the woman had much cash. She had no known family. An investigation is continuing.

Bea struggled to sit up, then pressed a hand to her head. "My, how long does it last, that brandy? I wonder if I ought to lie down."

"Yes, why don't you?" Muriel agreed at once. "Would you like us to help you to your room?"

"No, no, I'll just stretch out here on the couch. You go ahead and look around. This used to be a nice neighborhood, you know. No crimes. A person didn't have to be afraid to walk on the street even after dark. Now . . ." Her voice trailed off.

They established her on the sofa and went on with their explorations.

"We can't just throw her out," Muriel said as they climbed the stairs. "Nor put her in a home, either. She's managed all this time for herself and her brother; she's probably capable of continuing alone."

"This is far too big a place for one person, I'd think," Janie mused as they reached the second floor. "And we certainly aren't in any position to pay the taxes and insurance for her. What a rotter that old man was! If he'd left Aunt Bea the house, and the money, too, instead of to some grandnephew he didn't even know, she could have managed nicely. Good grief, how many bedrooms are there in this place?"

"Two downstairs, six up," Teddy announced, popping out of one of the rooms. "Plus a neat attic! If we come here to live, can I have the attic? Hey, Janie, look at the bathtub in this place! There's three bathrooms, and they're all like this!"

They stared into the bathroom, which was larger than the bedroom Teddy had in the apartment. An old-fashioned tub on claw feet dominated the space, and there was a shower, too.

"Really weird," Teddy said. "Look, the water comes at you from all directions, on four different levels!"

"What else did you find?" asked Janie.

"Mice. In the attic, anyway. It doesn't look as if anybody's been up there in years. I'd clean it up, though, if I could live up there."

Muriel and Janie looked at each other. "It doesn't seem likely we'll be moving in," Janie told her brother. "Not unless we share the place with Aunt Bea."

Disappointment spread across his face. "Oh. Well, she probably won't live very much longer, anyway, will she?"

"Teddy, really. Uncle Addison lived to be ninety-six, so she may have quite a few years to go." Muriel opened another of the doors, peering into a large bedroom. "I wonder if they manage to heat this in the winter? The ceilings are so high, and this is a long way from the furnace."

Janie had stepped into the room across the hall, and immediately envisioned it with her own bed and desk installed. "What a great place this would be to write. Look, there's a view of that jungle of a backyard, and robins nesting in that maple. And it's so nice and light, windows on two sides."

"If I slept in the attic, and you took this room and Mom that one, there'd still be six bedrooms. Five, after Aunt Bea's," Teddy pointed out. "There's plenty of room for her and us, too."

Muriel had discovered a closet the size of a small room. "I could put everything I own in here and still have space. It doesn't look as if anyone's been on this floor in years, does it? They both slept downstairs. I wonder if she's afraid here by herself? Especially since that woman was murdered so close by. That was the Globe Supermarket we passed only a few blocks away, wasn't it, just before we got off the bus?"

"It's hard to judge when she's just had her first experience with apricot brandy, but I wouldn't think she could live on here alone indefinitely," Janie said. "Maybe if we could sell the house, there'd be enough to help her out as well as ourselves. What do you think she meant with all that business about St. Andrew's?"

When they returned to the parlor, Bea was sitting up and they asked her.

"Bingo," she said. And then, seeing incomprehension on their faces, elucidated. "Every Wednesday I play bingo at St. Andrew's. It was the only way I could get out of the house for any social life at all. Addison took it for granted it was a prayer meeting, and I didn't disabuse him of the notion. Shows you how much he knows about the Catholic Church. Of course, I'm not Catholic, but Father Byers doesn't care. Lovely man, Father Byers. I don't think even he could have saved Addison's soul. Do you believe a truly wicked person goes to hell when he dies?"

She said this rather hopefully, as if imagining her brother surrounded by flames. Fortunately, she didn't wait for a reply.

"I'm feeling rather embarrassed, to have met you in such a condition. Perhaps Addison was wise not to have ever offered me anything alcoholic to drink. I hope I didn't say anything offensive."

"No, no," Muriel soothed. "Don't worry about it, Aunt Bea."

"I never would have taken the drink if I hadn't felt upset about that poor woman's death. It makes me afraid to think of going to the supermarket anymore." She searched their faces. "And I didn't mean to put you on the spot, about the house. Addison left it to Jane, so of course you must do whatever you need to do. I was foolish to think that I could stay on in a house that belongs to someone else."

She attempted a smile, which made Janie cringe. Why hadn't Addison Hamer had the decency to leave the place to his sister, after all her years of servitude?

"We'll work something out," Muriel told her, and they took their leave, Teddy carrying along his box of Fig Newtons.

On the way home, he pressed his face against the window of the bus, craning to see into the alley near the supermarket. "That's where it happened, Mom, that's where that old woman was murdered."

"Yes. It's sad," Muriel replied. "But it's nothing to do with us, thank God."

Behind the curtains, Bea Stone watched them go. She was trembling; rage and frustration wracked her frail body. It wasn't fair. She could *kill* Addison for leaving the house to that girl he hadn't even known and the money to that young man who already had more than he knew what to do with. If *she* had had them both, she'd have been comfortable the rest of her days. Of course, she realized that she couldn't kill her brother because he was already dead. He'd made his own arrangements—no funeral. (Who would have come to it? she wondered bitterly.) And he'd already been buried. There was nothing more she could do about Addison.

What of herself, though? What was she to do? She'd been such a fool to have tried that apricot brandy when she'd known they might come at any time.

The rest home loomed, a tangible menace, in her future. This house meant nothing to the trio walking away toward the bus stop—no more than a few dollars if they sold it. While to her it meant—could have meant—security and independence.

In despair Bea walked back to her brother's study and stared at the brandy bottle, still sitting where she had left it.

No, that wasn't the answer. There wasn't any answer, Bea thought, staring around the room through the shimmer of tears. When you got old, there weren't any answers anymore. At least none that you could live with.

Maybe poor Mabel Gervaise was the lucky one after all. Like Addison, she no longer had to worry about what would happen to her.

Bea pressed her lips together and walked out of the room, wishing it were Wednesday. Only then did she see her friends, and she needed someone to talk to.

In the front entryway she stopped. A smile touched her mouth as she remembered that Addison was no longer around to ask where she was going or to monitor her infrequent telephone calls. She could do as she pleased. She could take a bus downtown or walk over to Neva Minor's (Sylvia Bonnard lived closer, but Bea liked Neva better). Of course, that would mean walking past the supermarket where Mabel had been murdered.

She wasn't ready for that, Bea decided. She'd call Neva.

"Hello, Neva? This is Bea. Do you have a few minutes?"

Briefly, temporarily, the specter of the rest home receded.

3

By unspoken consent they waited until Teddy had gone off to play basketball before they discussed the situation. They sat in the tiny living room and speculated on the various possibilities.

"We could move over there and share the house with her, but would we ever feel it was ours?" Muriel wondered. "It might be uncomfortable for all of us. I mean, it's been her house for so long."

"I wonder if she felt that it was? My impression is that Uncle Addison made it very clear to her that it was *his* home, and that even if she did all the cooking and housekeeping, she was an interloper there. I'll bet it wouldn't be any harder for her to adjust to us than to *him*. The thing I'm not sure of is how well *we'd* adjust to living with an old lady. How would we keep Teddy quiet? He wouldn't stay in the attic all the time. And he'd want other kids in."

Muriel sipped thoughtfully at her coffee. "The place is so big, we could probably allocate space for each of us, so that nobody would have to give up their privacy. I wonder how Aunt Bea would hold up under an invasion of twelve-year-olds? If we fixed them a place in the basement, say. And if the shrubs and weeds were trimmed, the back-yard would be a good place for boys, fenced in the way it is."

"I wonder if we shouldn't find out what the place would bring, if we sold it? If we could get ourselves another smaller place, even something with an apartment that Aunt Bea could use. My conscience wouldn't let me send her to an old folks home, after what she said."

"Why don't you talk to that fellow in your office building, Janie, from the real estate firm, and see what he says? What's his name?"

"Sherm Kawalski. OK. I'll drop in on my coffee break on Monday. Now I guess I'd better wash my hair. We're going to a concert at Seattle Center."

"You and Harry?" Muriel asked, yawning. "I think I'll sneak in a nap before I tackle the laundry, and then maybe if you're going to be out for dinner, Teddy and I will walk over to McDonald's."

"Me and Harry, and another couple Harry met at the beach," Janie said. She sighed, getting out shampoo and brush and towel. She liked Harry, but he wasn't . . . *exciting.*

Why couldn't she be like Molly O'Hara, who got excited about every man, at least for a while. Well, Molly wasn't finding that special man any faster than Janie was. Toweling her hair dry, Janie admitted to herself that she hoped the man would come along pretty soon. She wanted a writing career, someday, but she could do that at home and raise a family at the same time. At least she thought she could. And she wanted someone beside her, someone like her father had been— loving, supportive, fun to be with.

They all still missed him terribly. Her mother was young enough to find someone else, eventually, but Janie doubted that Muriel would even try. She certainly hadn't made any moves so far to go places where she'd have a chance to meet anybody.

While I, Janie thought wryly, go places all the time, and all I ever meet is Harry. Who is not making any noises about marriage and kids and growing old together, and who, if I'm truthful, I wouldn't want to marry anyway.

Harry was tall and good-looking, and good-natured as well. Laid back, as Molly said. He didn't mind spending money to have a good time, though most often they did things that weren't expensive, like hiking and walks on the beach and playing cards and visiting friends. They both enjoyed those things, only there was no magic in it—at least not for Janie.

Dickson Zeller was his usual obnoxious self. He managed to rest a hand on her shoulder when she was looking for a file he wanted. He bent over her desk, brushing his arm against hers as often as possible. Then he invited her out for lunch.

"Sorry," Janie told him, "I have a lunch date."

Since she almost never had a lunch date with anyone but Molly, who worked in the building across the street, Dickson drew back with an injured stare. "If you don't want to have lunch with me, Jane, just say so. You don't have to make up lies."

She gave him a cool smile. "No lie, Dick. I'm having a business consultation with Sherm Kawalski about that property I inherited from my uncle."

"Oh. Thinks it's valuable, does he?"

"I don't know. He was going over to take a look at it this morning."

"Well"—Dickson turned playful—"I only hope it isn't so valuable that you quit your job and turn to a life of leisure. We'd sure miss you around here."

Janie contented herself with another of the small smiles that so often covered the fact that she was gritting her teeth. She wouldn't miss *him* in the slightest. She kept the smile glued to her face until he'd lifted his hand from her shoulder and turned to respond to something Mrs. Kelly was saying.

There were five women in the office, and none of them except Janie were young and single. Mrs. Kelly was in her fifties and would have decked any man who dared to put a hand on her. Sally, Rose, and Candy were younger, in their late thirties and forties; and none of them was receptive to Dickson's charm, since they all had husbands whom they loved. The only other young woman on the staff was Shirley, a crisply cool blonde who had initially drawn Dickson's attention until she told him, the first time he rested a hand in a place where it was unwelcome, "My husband doesn't like it if anyone else touches me, Mr. Zeller." Once he'd met her husband, who was six foot four and had played fullback for the University of Washington, Dickson Zeller turned his attentions back to Janie.

Even aside from her boss, Janie found little of real interest in the job. She was an expert typist, but not even the purchase of a word processor to replace her old Adler could make the insurance forms interesting. If she'd had the machine at her disposal to write her book, it would be finished by now, she thought. Only there was no way she'd ever own a computer, not unless she wrote the book the old fashioned way, on the ancient typewriter she had at home, and sold it to a publisher.

She met the realtor for lunch in the little cafeteria patronized primarily by those who worked in the building. Janie usually brought her lunch in a brown bag, so today was a treat.

Sherm was there ahead of her. He was a squat, heavyset man who had to shave twice a day to keep from having five o'clock shadow from noon on. He rose in the booth to signal to her, then sank back onto his seat to wait for her to join him.

Janie carried her tray to the tiny table and unloaded it, envying Sherm's indulgence in the special of the day, spaghetti and meatballs. She had stuck with tuna fish salad and a tiny bowl of pea soup served with a microscopic square of cornbread.

"Well? Is the house worth anything? Or did my dear departed uncle leave me with a white elephant?"

Sherm speared a meatball. "Somewhere in between, I'd say. What's going to happen to that little old lady living there now?"

"I don't know. Apparently, her brother hoped she'd wind up in some rest home, but if we can prevent that, we'd like to. Trouble is, she has only a Social Security income, and we don't have anything we can share with her. What would the house bring if we sold it?"

He named a figure that sounded promising, until he followed it up with, "*If* you could sell it, that is."

Janie forgot to eat. "You mean, we can't sell it?"

"Oh, maybe you could. Nothing down, nothing a month, generally speaking, and you'd probably unload it. The way the market is right now, high interest, no funds for home loans, we have to use creative financing to sell even prime property. Which I'm afraid your place isn't."

"Creative financing? Is it legal?"

"Oh sure. Creative only means that if you can't go the old conventional route, you try different things. Like carrying your own paper—" He stopped, reading incomprehension on her face. "You don't know anything about buying and selling real estate, do you?"

"Not a thing," Janie admitted. "So give it to me in plain English, OK?"

"Carrying your own paper means you don't get financing through a bank or savings and loan; you let the buyer in for a minimal down payment, in your case, and then he pays you so much a month until it's paid for. What that translates to here is that you might supplement your income so you could afford your present apartment, but you'd never get rich. To tell you the truth, unless you set the price at less than the place is really worth, and let someone in with no more than enough cash down to pay closing costs—" He paused again. "That's the realtor's fee and the escrow charges. You gotta pay those. Anyway, I don't know if I could find a buyer for it."

"It's old-fashioned, but it seemed well built," Janie said, struggling to cover her disappointment.

"Oh hell yes! Built better than most of the stuff they're putting up these days. It'll last for years, if you put a new roof on it in a year or two. And it needs a new heating system. That furnace may get you through another year, but I wouldn't bet on any more than that. The house itself is sound. One problem is the size of it. Families are small these days. People want two, three bedrooms. They want a place that's easy to heat."

"Does that mean I'm just stuck with a house that's going to cost me more than I can ever expect to get out of it?"

"Not necessarily. I can probably sell it if you can accept a minimal down payment and carry the balance yourself over a period of years. The thing is, that neighborhood isn't a choice one for a family with young kids. Places are too big, too old, not what young couples want. Not that most young couples can finance a place anyway, but if they can, they want ranch houses or condos. It looks like a few people are fixing up their places, which may eventually make the neighborhood more desirable, but that doesn't help right now. To tell you the truth, I think you'd be better off to give up your apartment and live in the house. You could shut off the upstairs so you wouldn't have to heat the whole thing, and you could put what you're paying in rent into a fund to replace the furnace and pay for a new roof."

Janie sighed. "And keep old Aunt Bea living there, too? There are only two bedrooms on the main floor, so we couldn't completely close off the second story."

"Yeah," Sherm said, sighing too. "It's a problem. Wish I had some better news. If you want, I'll try to sell it, but I can't make any promises. That murder committed out there the other day won't help either."

Janie gazed at him with alarm. "That kind of thing doesn't happen there all the time, does it?"

"No, no. But the whole damned community is talking about nothing else right now. A prospective buyer goes out there to look around, he's going to hear how an old lady was shot in the alley. It's not exactly the kind of thing that draws in buyers. You think about it, Janie, and if you want me to find a buyer, I'll do my damnedest."

She thanked him, hoping she didn't sound as dismal as she felt. Blast Addison Hamer anyway. She wished he hadn't bothered to remember her in his will at all. Before, she hadn't even known about Aunt Bea. Now she felt a responsibility for the old woman, and she had no means to provide for her.

Janie took the elevator back to the offices of Zeller and Markham, so lost in thought that she didn't even notice when Dickson patted her on the arm. "Jane, get the Griswold file for me, will you?"

"Sure," Janie said, and wondered what in the devil they were going to do about the house and Aunt Bea.

4

Jeff Carey and Max Upton had been partners for nearly three years. Max was the older of the two by seven years, and while Jeff envied and respected the older man, he was determined that when *he* reached thirty-five he wasn't going to have that telltale sign of middle age, a roll of flesh around the middle.

Not that Max was fat. He was, as a matter of fact, considered to be tall, dark, and handsome; Jeff had noticed that he tended to suck in his gut, however, in the company of attractive young ladies.

Jeff did not yet have to suck in anything. He had broad shoulders, a trim waist, and thick fair hair that went nicely with gray-blue eyes.

Neither of them was particularly happy when the decision was made to send out officers alone instead of in teams; besides the obvious reasons for wanting to have another cop to back him up in a dangerous situation, there was the fact that Jeff enjoyed Max's company.

In a time of budget cuts and a freeze on hiring, however, having a partner was a luxury. The best they could hope for was to get together once in a while for a meal, and to know that if either radioed "officer needs assistance," his old buddy would burn rubber getting to him.

Today they'd managed hamburgers together at Tilly's Place, where Max spent as much time flirting with the waitress as he did eating. Max had been married twice already and appeared willing to take a chance for the third time if he found the right girl.

Generally speaking, Max managed to make each of them think she was the right one, at least while he was with her. He was trying to make a date with this one, a pretty redhead, and Jeff finally gave up waiting, paid his bill, and walked out to his patrol car.

"Hi, pig," a ten-year-old boy called to him.

Jeff looked down on the little twerp. "Hi, yourself. Aren't you Sadie Milos' grandson?"

The boy blinked uncertainly. "Yeah, so what?"

"So if I tell your grandma how disrespectful you are to police officers, she'll warm your butt," Jeff said genially, and read the truth of his statement on the young face.

"I didn't mean nothing," the kid said. "Hey, ain't you the one found that dead body?"

Jeff grinned. "Just make sure I don't find yours, fella." He slid behind the wheel of the patrol car and turned the key, his smile fading.

He'd found the old gal, all right. Murder wasn't common on his beat, and at first when the supermarket manager had claimed somebody'd been killed right outside his back door, Jeff hadn't believed him. He'd thought it more likely that some old wino had collapsed in the alley.

Mabel Gervaise had been dead, all right. Jeff had seen her around, scavenging for food and draining old bottles. As far as anybody in the neighborhood knew, she didn't have a real home; she slept wherever she could find a place out of the wet.

Of course, there were occasional homicides in connection with domestic disputes; all cops got used to—and hated—them. You never knew when the wife who'd called you because the old man was beating on her would hit you over the head with a frying pan if you tried to take him in. And there were the kind of killings where a couple of guys had at it in a bar, or some guy tried to hold up a liquor store or a pharmacy, and the proprietor shot him.

The old lady was different, though. She wasn't much use to anyone, but she never bothered anybody either. She didn't steal anything anybody else wanted, and she didn't beg.

Why she'd been shot remained a mystery—one that might never be solved.

Jeff swung around a corner, narrowly missing a kid on a bike who jumped the curb right in front of him. Jeff swore, glanced around, and saw that the boy had disappeared down an alley and was probably already beyond reach.

His radio crackled. "Three B fourteen," the dispatcher's familiar voice said. "Take a homicide report at 3719 Fir Street. Unknown time of occurrence."

Jeff knew the address was technically in Max's territory. But he'd left Max only seconds before, trying to line something up with that strawberry blonde.

He thumbed his mike. "Ten-four. Three B sixteen, en route from Eighty-seventh and Stanton."

The dispatcher hadn't said anything about Code 3, which probably meant the victim was dead and there was no big hurry, but he turned on his lights and watched traffic fade away ahead of him. Homicide wasn't his favorite thing to have to respond to, even though all he had to do was keep people from screwing up the evidence until the Homicide crew arrived. If it was a nasty one, he was going to regret covering for Max, he thought. There was a knot of people on the sidewalk; he didn't have to look for the house number.

Jeff left his blue lights blinking and got out of the car.

There were a dozen people, mostly housewives and teenage kids, who parted to let him through. A little bald man stood on the steps of a small house literally wringing his hands. He grasped at Jeff's sleeve the moment the young officer came within reach.

"Oh, thank God you came so fast! My wife's in hysterics, and it's—it's awful!"

"Yes, sir." Jeff kept his voice calm. "You called to report a homicide, sir?"

"A murder! A murder in my own backyard! My God, what's the world coming to?"

"May I have your name, sir?"

"Hodges. Mel Hodges."

"Can you show me where the victim is, sir? Around in the back, through that gate?"

The bald man swallowed. "Better come through the house, officer."

He'd just as soon have gone through the gate, because he could hear a female voice shrieking inside, but Hodges was already leading the way. Jeff closed the door in the face of the most curious of the neighbors, and ignored the whooping woman in the living room as they walked out into a well-kept backyard.

It seemed an unlikely spot for a murder. It was surrounded by a hedge, with a small vegetable garden, a grassy area with a couple of lawn chairs, and a redwood picnic table which contained the remains of a meal. A small dog, helping himself to the contents of a paper plate, paused from his feast to bark at the police officer.

"Shut up, Neddy!" the bald man said. "It—she's over here, officer. Against the gate. That's why I didn't think we should open it."

Jeff felt a flash of déjà vu. Only this one was not in a dirty alley but against a clean, white-painted gate. Her hands, drenched in her own blood, had slid down the boards, leaving rust-colored smears.

The woman looked much the same, though. Shapeless old clothes —a brown sweater over a brown dress—some sort of dark scarf over graying hair. One foot, in a worn shoe with a hole in the bottom of it, was twisted awkwardly under the heavy body.

"We'd come outside to picnic in our backyard, Officer," the bald man said, keeping his distance from the body. He grabbed up the dog and closed his hand around its muzzle to quiet it. "We never saw anything wrong. We sat down to eat, and Neddy wanted out, and my wife opened the screen for him. He didn't even come near the table, though, not then. He sniffed along the ground . . . there, across the terrace . . . see, there's a trail of blood. And Neddy started barking, and we couldn't make him stop, so my wife went around the corner to see what was the matter with him. . . . She's been screaming ever since. Do you think I should call a doctor?"

"Did you hear a shot, sir?"

"No, no. Nothing! Of course, the Silvettis play their radio so loud most of the time an army could move in and we'd never know it. The blood on the terrace was dry, though."

Jeff knelt cautiously beside the fallen figure, reaching for the out-stretched wrist though certain there would be no pulse. This one was beyond medical help. "By all means, call your own doctor for your wife," he said. "Will you take the dog inside, and then stand by the gate to make sure no one comes through it? And then I'd like to use your telephone."

Jeff had a strong conviction that this death was related to that earlier one. Both derelicts, elderly women, both shot in the back with what appeared to be a small-caliber firearm.

From his kneeling position, he could see the woman's face, and he wished he had not. She was cold; she'd been here for some time, he thought. She hadn't been shot here, the trail of blood proved that.

They wouldn't want him to muck anything up, but it wouldn't hurt to walk across the concrete patio area, retracing the dark stains. He stood there for a moment, looking at the place where the woman had obviously come through the hedge.

"What's over there? Beyond the hedge?" he asked.

The bald man was breathing through his mouth. "Nothing. I mean, it's an empty lot, beside the auto repair shop. Only the whole thing's closed, now. Guy went bankrupt couple of months ago."

"Do you know the victim, sir?" Jeff asked, turning back toward the house. "Ever seen her before?"

"No, never. Why'd she have to die in *our* yard? She's bled all over the patio, and the gate—who's going to clean up all that blood? My wife can't, she gets sick at the sight of blood! Why'd she have to die *here?*"

Jeff looked at him dispassionately. "I guess everybody has to die somewhere," he said.

The story wasn't important enough for the six o'clock news, but it turned up on page 4 of the following afternoon's *Seattle Times*.

Neither Muriel nor Janie saw it. Janie was bowling that evening with Harry and Molly and Molly's latest boyfriend, so she didn't have time for the newspaper. Muriel had worked late at St. Joseph's because of a crisis that tied up hospital personnel elsewhere, and they'd asked her to cover the desk a little longer. By the time she'd eaten supper with Teddy, she was too tired to look at more than the front page and the comics before she went to bed.

Bea Stone saw it. Bea read every page of the paper except the business news, the sports pages, and the classified section. At the time the paper went to press, the identity of the victim was unknown; her age was estimated at sixty-five to seventy.

The paper shook in Bea's hand. Another one. Another helpless old woman, shot and killed. What for? Robbery, of someone who probably hadn't been carrying more than a bit of loose change?

The address was only seven blocks from Addison Hamer's house on Relton Street.

Bea walked through the house, checking the locks on all the doors and windows. Somehow, though, it didn't make her feel any better.

5

The decision was made for them.

Janie knew there was something important on Muriel's mind as soon as she entered the kitchen on Wednesday evening and found her mother staring out the window instead of peeling the carrot in her hand.

"Mom? What's up?"

Muriel turned with an odd little smile. "Well, as they say, there's good news and bad news."

"What?" Janie demanded.

"The good news is that I've been offered another job. To train as an administrative assistant to Mr. Boyles."

"Hey! All right! It's the kind of thing you've always wanted to do, isn't it?"

"Yes," Muriel admitted. "Only don't forget I mentioned bad news, too."

"What can be bad about being offered a promotion?"

"Well, it isn't exactly a promotion. Not yet, anyway. The thing is, to begin with, the job is a training program. So it pays less than I'm making now."

"Oh." Janie reached for the carrot, decided it didn't need to be peeled, and bit the end off it. "How much less?"

"Fifty dollars a month. It's only for three months; then I'll get a small raise, and another one in six months, if I am handling the job well. Only . . ."

"Yeah, only . . . with the rent going up, it leaves us about seventy-five dollars a month less than we need to keep our heads above water. Maybe I could borrow on my insurance. Chances are I won't die in the next six months, and eventually you'll have a better salary than you have now, and we can repay an insurance loan."

"I thought of that, only I don't really want to do it. Maybe the wise thing would be to simply give up the apartment and move into that house of Addison's."

They looked at each other, weighing the probabilities. "With Aunt Bea still there?" Janie asked finally. "Sharing the place with her?"

"Don't you think so? Since she has nowhere else to go?"

"We'd better ask her," Janie suggested. "I doubt if she realizes what it's like living with a twelve-year-old boy."

From the living room came the sound of TV sirens, then a barrage of gunfire. They both grinned.

"I'm sure she doesn't. But it might seem preferable to a nursing home. At least if it wasn't, the choice would be her own."

Teddy poked his head around the corner. "Hey, is anybody doing anything about supper? I'm starved. How come Janie's eating the carrots?"

Janie handed him the remainder. "Supper coming right up. Shall we go over tonight and see Aunt Bea, see what she thinks? If we're going to move, it would be better to do it before we have to pay another month's rent, wouldn't it?"

They rode the bus over as soon as they'd cleared the table, for once violating Muriel's long-standing rule against leaving dishes in the sink. Though no one mentioned it, each had an uneasy feeling about being in a strange neighborhood late at night.

Nothing out of the ordinary happened. Their fellow bus passengers were mostly people returning from jobs or late shopping excursions, ordinary working people. Several older women preceded them down the street.

"Actually," Muriel observed, "the neighborhood looks friendlier now than it did in the daytime. I wonder where Teddy would have to go to school?"

"Sherman looked into that, and this is one of the luckier areas," Janie told her. "They've closed a number of schools, but the nearest one here has been consolidated with a couple of others in order to keep it open. It's about an eight-block walk."

"Eight blocks!" Teddy echoed. "That's a long way in the rain."

"It doesn't bother you to go twelve blocks to a movie," Janie pointed out. "We'll get you a good raincoat with the money we save when we stop paying rent."

Teddy snorted and kicked a beer can off the curb into the street. "If you do all the stuff you've talked about with the money we're gonna save, there won't be anywhere near enough to go around. Besides, nobody wears raincoats."

"Get wet then. And when you get pneumonia, it'll give us something else to use the money for," Janie said.

Bea opened the door for them, her face reflecting the apprehension she could not quite manage to conceal. "Warm tonight, isn't it?" she asked. "It feels a little like spring."

They followed her into the rear parlor, which Bea had sealed off with the massive dark sliding doors that separated it from its twin. In only a few days she had made the room more her own, for there were books and papers scattered around and she'd been having a cup of tea; a plate of cookies sat beside the floral teapot.

"Would you all care for a hot drink?" Bea asked nervously. "Oh, I don't suppose the little boy drinks tea, does he?"

Teddy frowned. "I'm twelve, and my name's Teddy."

"Yes, of course. How about cookies?"

He helped himself to four of them, and they all sat down.

They'd agreed that Muriel would tell her their situation, and that

Janie would watch closely for her reaction. Bea sat stiffly on the edge of her chair, not touching her own cup, until Muriel had outlined their proposal.

Incredulity spread across the old woman's face. "You mean you want to move in and we'd share the house? All of us?"

"If you think it would work. We couldn't promise to be as quiet as you're undoubtedly used to, I'm afraid. Teddy likes to have friends in and sometimes they get noisy, though we try to keep that under control. We thought it might be possible to fix up the basement for a place to play, and turn over the backyard to the kids. Unless, of course, that's your special place."

"Oh no! No, indeed. That sounds like a marvelous idea, though the basement is terribly dirty. I'm afraid I never made any attempt to straighten it up. I don't know what to say. I'd steeled myself to moving out . . . it's very exciting to think of being able to remain here."

"We thought we'd all take bedrooms upstairs, so as to disturb you as little as possible," Muriel went on. "And since there are two parlors, couldn't we each have one? It would be nice to have a place of your own, when you want it. And there are bathrooms enough, so that would leave us with the kitchen and dining room to share, which shouldn't be too much of a hardship. What do you think?"

What Bea thought was written clearly in her smile. It wasn't until after they'd looked around again, choosing rooms and figuring out what they'd need to put into storage, and what they might get rid of entirely, that Bea made her tentative little suggestion.

"You weren't planning to sleep on the ground floor, then, any of you. I wonder . . ." She inhaled deeply and took the plunge. "Would you consider renting out the bedroom, then? Addison's room?"

That hadn't occurred to them. They looked at each other, weighing the matter. The first thing each thought of, after wondering if it would add to the inconvenience to have another person in the house, was that it would bring in a little additional income.

Janie moistened her lips. "Did you have someone in particular in mind, Aunt Bea?"

"Yes, a friend of mine. Neva Minor. She's quite a bit younger than I am—sixty-four, I think. She's one of those who plays bingo at St. Andrew's. I stayed home tonight because I thought this was important, though ordinarily I never miss. It would be such a pleasure to have Neva nearby; and she's losing her apartment because the building is to be torn down. She has grandchildren the age of your Teddy, so she's used to children."

They reserved judgment on Neva Minor, thinking it wiser to meet her before they committed themselves. But they settled on the rest of it. Before the first of the month, they'd move in.

"Are there any kids my age around here?" Teddy asked as they were taking their leave. "Boys?"

"Oh, I think so. I don't know them by name, of course, except for one little boy." A slight spasm passed over her face, and Janie wondered if it was caused by the thought of this particular child. "His name's Joe, I think. Joe Milos. His grandmother, Sadie, is another of our bingo players. He's smaller than you, though, I believe."

"Where does Joe live?" Teddy wanted to know, resisting the pressure of Janie's hand as she tried to steer him out the front door.

"Sadie has the third house down on this side of the street. Her son and his family have been with her for almost a year now, since her son was hurt and can't work anymore." Bea peered out into the night. "Starting to rain, isn't it?"

They bid her good night and felt the moisture on their faces as they went down the steps.

"Well, we've done it," Muriel said, sounding pleased. "I hope it works out all right."

"If it doesn't, we'll just have to find another apartment," Janie told her. "Come on, let's hurry, so we won't miss the next bus."

Maybe, she thought, we'll be able to get a car again. At any rate, moving here would enable her mother to take the position she wanted at the hospital, and keep Aunt Bea out of the dreaded home.

Whether it would do anything for herself she didn't consider. She supposed she'd just go on working for Dickson Zeller and dodging his advances, and dating Harry, unless a miracle happened.

Bingo at St. Andrew's began at seven-thirty, and ordinarily ended about three hours later. Tonight, however, the doors had not yet opened, though it was nearly eleven.

It wouldn't have mattered so much had it not been for the rain. It was a typical Washington rain, cool and steady, and with the wind's assistance it found its way down the watcher's neck.

The watcher swore, shifting position in an unsuccessful attempt to alleviate the physical misery. How the hell long were they going to keep on? It was a weeknight; some of the players must have to get up the following morning and go to work, mustn't they?

A car swung around the corner, headlights cutting a brilliant swath through the rain, momentarily illuminating the watcher opposite the church. He blinked and moved back, although it was clearly already too late; if the driver had glanced in his direction, the watcher had been observed.

The car moved on, slowly, splashing water over the curb. It was a police car.

The car was going on. It was just a routine patrol—nothing to get alarmed about.

The double doors of St. Andrew's recreation hall swung open at last, bringing light and voices and movement. The priest stood at one side, a youngish man with a prematurely receding hairline, laughing and talking with those leaving the premises.

The watcher stepped back, deeper into the shadows of the trees that lined the street. A group of five or six reached the sidewalk, calling out good-naturedly.

"Hey, are we just going to go home and go to bed? Jacoby is the big winner tonight! Aren't you going to buy us all a beer, Jacoby?"

"No drinks tonight," a woman said. "It's too late, and the weather's too nasty. I don't want to miss the last bus and have to walk sixteen blocks."

"There comes the bus now! Flag it down, someone! Make sure he sees us!"

There was a pair of lamp standards beside the walk that led to the main doors of the church itself, but apparently the bulbs had burned out, or the priest had forgotten to turn them on. It was so dark a person couldn't identify his own mother.

Four of the first group boarded the bus; a few more hurried along the sidewalk toward it.

The bingo players scattered in various directions after the bus had gone. Some had cars parked in St. Andrew's lot, others were walking. Two women crossed the street and came within a few yards of the watcher, chattering, not noticing anyone in the shadows.

They walked on to a battered Toyota parked directly under the street-light and drove away.

The doors of the recreation hall closed, and a moment later the lights inside the building went out. The watcher stood for another few minutes, then moved away in the direction the bus had taken.

All for nothing. The evening wasted. Still, there'd be another evening, another victim.

The watcher stepped into a puddle, feeling the cold. A dry run this time. Well, hardly dry. *Momentarily amused, the watcher plodded on along the wet streets toward home.*

6

The second victim lay in the morgue, unidentified. She was on no list of missing persons; no friends or relatives claimed the body.

If a photograph had been available for publication, there were those who would have recognized her face, if not her name. Bea Stone was one of those. However, there was no photo, and probably the newspapers would not have printed it anyway. The death was only one of seven violent deaths in the county on that day, and a nameless old woman was not important enough to draw much attention.

When the third body was discovered within a period of eight days, Lieutenant Roger Zazorian began to feel uneasy. This was not a metropolitan area, and though the community had its share of derelicts, and from time to time one of them was killed over half a bottle of cheap wine, these were random killings and usually solved simply by questioning the other bums in the neighborhood.

For the most part, the usual victims were male. Still, no one in the local police department had given the deaths of two elderly female vagrants any particular attention beyond the routine investigations, which to date had turned up nothing at all. No slug had been recovered in the second body, nor in the vacant lot where traces of blood indicated the shooting had taken place, so there was nothing to match up with the one the autopsy had revealed in Mabel Gervaise's remains.

Roger Zazorian was supposed to have had the weekend off, and he'd planned to spend it with his family at a cottage on Camano Island, doing nothing more strenuous than sitting in a deck chair with a bottle of beer in his hand, looking out across Puget Sound and enjoying the sunshine while his wife herded the kids around on the beach.

On Sunday morning, however, his youngest, Tim, had managed to slip and fall among the rocks, fracturing his arm. Resignedly, the Zazorians had thrown their belongings back into their suitcases and headed for home and their own physician.

After his son's arm had been X-rayed and encased in plaster, Zazorian left his wife to cope with the disappointed children and wandered over to police headquarters to see what was going on. Whatever it was would be easier to deal with than four whining offspring.

Sergeant Koop, at the desk, looked up at him without surprise. "Hi, Lieutenant. You hear about the latest body already? They haven't even got it to the morgue yet."

"No. What is it this time?"

"Another old woman. Looked like a pile of rags, Carey said. People walked past her for a coupla hours before anybody realized it was a body."

The alarm sounded in Zazorian's mind. "Carey? Isn't he the officer on the—what was her name?—Gervaise case?"

"Yes, sir. And on the Jane Doe, too, the old woman they found on Tuesday."

Faint lines sketched themselves into Zazorian's forehead. "And this is the third body in Carey's territory in less than a week? What the hell's going on?"

Koop shrugged. "Carey thinks there could be a connection. Not too many murders in that part of town, usually. Especially not old women."

The lines became more pronounced. "Where's Carey now?"

"Back on duty. Homicide took over. Sergeant Fitz."

Zazorian looked at his watch. "Got any idea where Carey takes his meal break?"

"Yeah, Tilly's. That's where he was when he got the call on this one. Complained he didn't get to finish his hamburger, so he maybe went back there after Homicide took over. You want me to raise him on the radio, Lieutenant?"

"No. It's on my way home. I'll see if he's there. If not, I'll catch him tomorrow."

Zazorian eased his car to the curb in front of Tilly's just as two uniformed officers emerged onto the sidewalk. They came over to the car when they recognized him. "You got an ID on today's victim?" Zazorian asked, leaning out the window to address Jeff Carey.

"No, sir, not yet. She'd been shot with a small-caliber firearm at close range."

"Same as the other two."

"Yes, sir. Lady on the way home from church thought it was just a pile of trash, but some kids on bikes forced her off the sidewalk, and she literally stepped on the body. Went into hysterics when she realized what it was, and the priest at St. Andrew's heard her and called us."

"You found all three of them, Carey. You think there's a connection? They might not be random shootings?"

Carey didn't hesitate. "I thought there might be a connection between the first two, just because the victims were so similar. Nothing to prove it, so far. But we may be luckier on this one; there was no exit wound, so we ought to have something for ballistics to work with. They may get a match."

Zazorian lit a cigarette and blew smoke out the car window. "Keep your ears open. Three of them so close together, and all in this area. Not more than about two miles apart, were they?"

"No, sir. Homicide's got a squad out now, door to door."

"Well, it's your territory. You know more of the people. They may talk to you."

"Yes, sir. I hope so," Carey said. "I'll keep you posted, Lieutenant."

Zazorian flipped the half-smoked butt into the street, nodding. "We may have a psycho on our hands. Let's hope we get something before the media put things together and start scaring the crap out of this neighborhood."

"Yes, sir."

The two officers watched him drive away, then went to their separate patrol cars. Both of them fervently hoped that Zazorian was wrong about the psycho.

They spent the entire weekend, including Friday evening, preparing for the move. Dressed in jeans and an old sweatshirt, Janie shoved furniture around and cleared space for the Madisons' belongings.

Harry groaned when he saw the place. "My God, you might as well live in a mausoleum! It's so dark in here you can't find a light switch to turn it on."

"That's only because Aunt Bea keeps the shades drawn," Janie pointed out, pulling the cord that sent a shade rattling upward. "See? It's better already."

"This furniture weighs the earth. It's going to take more than *me* to get that dresser out of here."

"Who do you know you could invite to help us?" Janie asked, opening shades and draperies with a flourish. "We've given notice, Harry, we have to be out of the apartment by the first. And we can't move our stuff in until we get *this* stuff out."

For all his initial lack of enthusiasm, Harry came through. He rounded up four buddies, and Molly O'Hara brought her boyfriend Clyde, and between them they accomplished more than Muriel had thought possible. Much of the massive furniture had been hauled downstairs where the Salvation Army would pick it up on Monday. Three upstairs bedrooms had been dusted and scrubbed, along with one of the bathrooms there.

They left Addison's bedroom furniture in his room, but everything else was packed into boxes to go to the Salvation Army as well.

Janie and Molly took that room on, both of them feeling moderately uncomfortable going through the possessions of a man neither had known. It was evident that while he might have been stingy with his sister, he had not stinted himself.

He had smoked fine cigars and kept a superb liquor cabinet. "Locked," Molly commented, her red-gold curls bobbing as she turned to face Janie. "That's locked, too, that box on the dresser. Anyway, I didn't see the key for it."

"Aunt Bea must have the key for the liquor cabinet. Maybe she's found the key to the jewelry chest, too. Look at these brushes. Sterling silver backs."

"Hey, Janie?" Teddy appeared carrying a model railroad engine, holding it up for her inspection. "Isn't this neat? There's two complete sets of trains up there, and they're not cheapies, either. Look at the detail on this."

"I thought you were supposed to be cleaning out your room." Janie had discovered a key in a top dresser drawer, which she fitted into the mysterious box. "Oh, say, look here! Gold cuff links! Tie pin to match. Molly, don't these look valuable?"

Molly peered into the box. "They're so old-fashioned they probably aren't worth much as jewelry, but they're probably valuable for the gold. Look, isn't that a diamond ring? *That* ought to be worth something. You could have it reset in an engagement ring, Janie."

Janie gave her a withering look. "To whom would I be engaged? Teddy, please get out of the way. Go back upstairs and make sure that room is ready to put your things in it next weekend."

"Oh, I came in to tell you—that friend of Aunt Bea's is here. Mom says you're supposed to talk to her and see if we want her to rent Uncle Addison's room."

"Why didn't you say so? Where is she?"

"In the front parlor. She seems nice. She's been to see the *Star Wars* movies, all of 'em! I didn't think anybody that old would care about *Star Wars.*"

Janie wiped her hands on her jeans and left Molly going through Uncle Addison's valuables, hurrying to the front parlor which was half full of the stuff waiting to be hauled off by the Salvation Army.

Neva Minor was talking to Bea and turned with a smile when Janie entered the room. "I'm sorry, was this a bad time to come?"

"No, no, not at all, if you don't mind the mess. I think I'm too dirty to shake hands, Mrs. Minor. Won't you sit down?"

"I made some tea," Bea offered. "Do you think the others would like some, too?"

Janie suspected the others would prefer a cold beer. "Why don't you ask them?" she suggested, and turned her attention to their prospective renter as Bea skittered off.

Neva Minor was examining her just as openly. Janie liked her immediately. She had a warm smile and a pleasant voice. "I suppose Bea told you my apartment house is being torn down. And while I'm by no means destitute, I can't afford most of the places that are available, at least not without moving out of this neighborhood. I don't want to move. I've lived here over thirty years, and my friends are here."

Neva was a well-fed and corseted lady with carefully curled gray hair, blue eyes, and tiny hands and feet. Janie guessed at once, from the rings and the stylish shoes, that Neva was well aware of her best features.

"If there's any chance at all that you'd allow me to rent a room here, I'd be delighted. Close enough to walk to All Saints, the minimall, the theater where I go to movies. Afternoons, mostly; I'm getting leery of going out at night unless I can get a bus from door to door. If I were here, Bea and I could do things together."

Janie returned the smile. "We've never done anything like this before. It's all sort of on a trial basis, right now."

"I understand. I confess it would be an experiment for me, too; I've lived alone for many years, since my husband died. I liked it that way, really, until the last year or two; my friends, like me, are getting older, and we don't get out and around the way we used to do. It gets lonely. Both my sons live close enough so they visit, but they have their own families and their own lives. I can't expect them to be my social life. I'd be grateful for the opportunity to try living here, Miss Madison. And I assure you, if it doesn't work out for you, I'll look for something else."

"Have you thought about cooking facilities?" Janie asked. "There's only one kitchen, and you'd have to share a bath with Aunt Bea, too."

"Oh, I think we can work those things out," Neva Minor said. "I do most of my cooking in a microwave oven, and I'd bring that with me. We could all share it, as far as that goes."

"We don't even know what to charge for rent," Janie confessed.

Neva reached for the newspaper lying beside her purse on the coffee table. "I didn't know either, so I brought this along. See, here are the rooms for rent and the prices. This one here is the closest I could find to the facilities that would be available in this house, and that perhaps would be a fair rental."

"All right, Mrs. Minor, we'll give it a try. Shall we set a specific time limit, and then we'll all re-evaluate the situation? With either party free to call it quits with no hard feelings, if there are problems?"

"Why not?" the older woman said. "It would be Mr. Hamer's room, would it not?"

"Yes. Here's Aunt Bea; please have your tea, and then she can show you around. We're trying to clear out Uncle Addison's room now. Do you have furniture of your own, or would you want to use what's already here?"

Neva Minor reserved judgment until she'd inspected the room, and Janie went back to work. Molly met her, laughing.

"Look, Janie, what I found! I'll bet they're the family jewels!"

"Hey, not bad." Janie took the necklace and held it against her throat. "Rubies, do you suppose, or garnets?"

"I don't know, but this ring sure looks like a sapphire. My grandmother has one that looks almost exactly like it, and I know hers is real. You'd better have it appraised. Is it yours?"

"I don't know. The lawyer never said anything about jewelry. It would be nice if there was something that could be converted to cash. Put it back in the box, and I'll see what it's worth on Monday."

Muriel had made a pot of spaghetti, and they all ate it with salad and garlic bread around the kitchen table. Aunt Bea, rather than being out of place with the young people, laughed and seemed to enjoy their company. It looked as if it might work out very well, Janie thought. Maybe Uncle Addison had been good to her in spite of himself.

7

On her lunch hour on Monday, Janie took the "valuables" from Uncle Addison's box to a small jeweler's a block from her office and left with the promise that she could pick them up at five, along with a written appraisal.

"Pretty old-fashioned," he commented, and Janie's hopes slid down a notch or two.

She headed back for the offices of Zeller and Markham; when she saw that Dickson Zeller's car was still parked in the lot beside the building, she decided to eat her lunch sitting on the bench at the curb for bus passengers.

She was eating her tuna sandwich absent-mindedly when she heard Molly's voice.

"Janie! I tried to call you this morning." Molly sank onto the bench beside her, tight red curls gleaming in the sun. "I thought I'd catch you at noon, but you were already gone, they said."

"I left five minutes earlier than usual. You had lunch?"

"I'm too excited to eat. Janie, guess what?"

She made the obvious guess. "You've met a new man?"

Molly grimaced. "No! Idiot, I don't need a new man, I've got Clyde!"

"You have?" Janie considered that. Clyde was a nice enough fellow, though nothing special. An ordinary, industrious, average-looking guy who worked for Boeing. Half the people in King and Snohomish counties worked for Boeing. "What's up, then?"

"We're getting married! He asked me last night, after we left your place. He said any girl who looked the way I did and could work that way all weekend for a friend was somebody he wanted for a wife."

Janie swallowed the last of her sandwich and looked at her friend. Molly was clearly ecstatic, so there must be more to Clyde than Janie had supposed. It wasn't the first time someone had proposed to Molly; Molly had actually been engaged twice, for brief periods. She'd never looked quite like this, though.

"Sounds very romantic," Janie observed. "Congratulations."

Molly missed the wry note in Janie's voice; it hadn't occurred to her that being wanted for a wife because of her ability to do hard physical work was not exactly what most girls dream of. Molly was bubbling over with details, which she supplied while Janie ate a Granny Smith apple and wished she'd brought another sandwich.

"Janie, he's so sweet to me. He really is. He's been thinking about asking me for weeks, but he didn't know if we could afford to get married."

"You going to keep on working?"

"Oh yes. Until we get our furniture paid for, and everything. We want babies, though, so I'll probably quit then. Maybe I'll go back to work when the kids are older. It's hard to make ends meet on one salary these days."

"Amen," Janie agreed.

"So we're going to get married the twelfth of next month. I'm so excited I can hardly breathe. Ma says you can't get ready for a wedding that fast, but what's there to do that's going to take all that time? We can't afford anything fancy, so we'll just have Father Mc-

Cullough come over, and get married in our living room. Ma says Pa has to paint it first, but he can do that in one weekend. Clyde's apartment is pretty small, but the super has promised him the next two-bedroom one that becomes available. Janie, isn't it wonderful?"

Janie had to smile at the sheer happiness on Molly's face. "Yes," she said, reaching out to squeeze Molly's hand, "it's wonderful."

"Janie, you'll be my maid of honor, won't you? I'm taking off half an hour early today to go over to the Bridal Shop and see if I can find my dress. You could wear that pale green one of yours; you've only worn it once, haven't you? I wish you could get off early, too, and go with me."

"No chance," Janie told her. "I can't even go with you on Saturday, I'm afraid. We're moving then."

"I know. And I'm sorry I can't help, but Ma has lined up all these things for me to do before the wedding. Janie, you do wish me well, don't you?"

Janie grinned. "You know I do. If I'm looking sort of . . . lugubrious . . . it's not because I'm not happy for you. It's partly because I'm surprised—I had no idea you and Clyde were getting that serious —and partly because I'm jealous, I guess."

"Oh, Janie, your turn will come! Look at the time! I have to run. I'll call you tonight, OK?"

Janie went thoughtfully back to the office. It was the truth, she was jealous. Not that she didn't want Molly to be happily married, but that Janie herself was feeling as if it might never happen to *her*.

She had let herself slide along for a whole year now with Harry. He hadn't really, seriously, even tried to seduce her. It would have made her feel a little better to know that she was desirable enough so that a man would *try*.

The trouble was, Janie suddenly realized as she punched the button in the elevator, that as long as she was with Harry all the time, she'd never meet anybody new.

All afternoon, as she typed up forms and insurance policies on the new word processor, Janie thought about Molly getting married to Clyde, and herself *not* getting married to Harry.

How had she allowed the situation to arise, that everyone thought of her as Harry's girl so they'd stopped asking her out? It was her own fault that she'd gotten into this state; and it was undoubtedly up to her to get herself out of it.

Mrs. Kelly dropped a stack of papers on the corner of her desk. "Mr. Markham would like these done before you leave," she said, and swept away.

Janie glanced with distaste at another three hours' work. Mr. Markham, the senior partner, was seldom in the office, but when he asked one of the girls to do something for him, he wanted it done immediately.

It was already a quarter of two, Janie thought glumly. Well, most of what she was working on now could wait until tomorrow if it had to. She finished the current project, stored it in the machine, and picked up the first of Mr. Markham's papers.

It was hard to keep her mind on what she was typing; she was glad she had a machine that made it easy to correct errors, because she made more than usual.

If Harry weren't such a nice guy, it would be easy to know what to do. She'd simply say, "Harry, it's been fun, but let's call it quits. Let's each start seeing other people, OK?"

Could she do that now, though, after he'd spent all weekend shoving heavy furniture around and clearing spiders and mice out of the basement?

No, it was impossible. Not until some time had passed. She couldn't even anticipate breaking off when they had their next fight, because they'd never had one.

Now that she considered the matter, it was incredible. How could you date someone steadily for a year, and never have a disagreement? It was healthy, for heaven's sake, to express one's own thoughts and opinions.

When she glanced at the clock, it was ten to five. Well, she'd have to work a few minutes overtime. Damn, she thought suddenly. She'd told the jeweler she'd be back before he closed. Maybe she'd better call and tell him she wouldn't make it until Tuesday.

She was on the final document when Dickson Zeller came out of the glass-enclosed cubicle that was his private office. He hadn't been near her all afternoon; now he made straight for her desk.

Janie looked up at the sound of his footsteps, suddenly realizing that everyone else had left. Damn again, she thought wearily.

"Jane, could you possibly get out this policy for me yet tonight? Judge Nichols is leaving for Portland tomorrow afternoon, and we want to get his signature on it before then."

She took the sheaf of papers without comment. She was on salary, and it was unlikely that she'd be paid for working late. On the other hand, she'd be justified in asking for a few minutes tomorrow to get over to the jeweler's without sacrificing her lunch hour to do it.

By the time she had run the final material off on the printer and stored the text in case Dickson found some error she hadn't detected, it was dark outside. In fact, it was dark inside except for the light over her own desk. Janie stood, stretched, and turned to carry the completed documents into Dickson's cubicle where he'd see them first thing in the morning.

The cubicle was nearly dark, and Janie suppressed an exclamation when she found her employer sitting behind his desk. He rose and took the papers.

"Did I startle you? Sorry," Dickson said. He didn't look sorry. "I remembered a couple of calls I should make, and I didn't bother to turn the lights back on. I appreciate your getting these things out tonight, Jane."

She turned so she could see the clock. "If I run, I can catch the next bus. I'll see you in the morning," she said.

His hand closed on her arm in a proprietary way. "Oh, don't run for the bus. I'll give you a lift. I'm going that way anyhow."

"Oh?" She lived in the opposite direction from Dickson's place, and she was already feeling uneasy. Why had he sat in the dark to make his phone calls, unless he was waiting for her to finish and didn't want to call her attention to his presence there?

"Yeah," Dickson said carelessly, ushering her out of the cubicle and locking the door behind them. "I have to go on into Bellevue for a dinner meeting. Come on, I'll save you bus fare."

The building had emptied out, and there was no one else in the corridors or the elevator. He touched her arm lightly in getting in and out of the elevator and then steered her toward the outer door. She wouldn't have thought anything of it if it had been anyone else.

She saw the bus as they emerged onto the sidewalk, just pulling in at the corner. She would have made it if she'd bolted and run, but Dickson kept his hold on her arm.

"Smells like spring, doesn't it?" he asked, guiding her toward the parking lot. "Makes a young man's fancy . . . and all that, you know."

Janie didn't like that remark. Dickson was not a young man, in her estimation, being past forty. He claimed to have been married once, years ago, though it was hard to imagine what sort of woman would have wanted him.

He unlocked the door of his red Triumph and ushered her in, then went around to the driver's side. Janie wished heartily that she'd run for the bus, or made up some lie about being picked up.

Still, he wasn't likely to try anything much, was he? Once he'd put his hand on her knee, at the office Christmas party, and she'd simply moved away from him and not made a fuss about it. Of course, in the Triumph there was nowhere to move to, but it was only a fifteen-minute ride. What could happen in fifteen minutes?

It took a little more than a quarter of an hour, however. A block short of Janie's apartment house, Dickson pulled over to the curb and turned off the ignition.

"It's the next block," Janie told him. "But that's all right, I'll walk."

His hand closed around her wrist. For a small man, he had a surprisingly strong grip. "Oh, don't hurry. I wanted to talk to you, Jane."

Annoyance colored her voice. "I don't have time now. My family is expecting me for supper, and I'm already late. We can talk in the office tomorrow."

"No, no, not about business. You know I like you, Jane. I think you're a very pretty girl. I could be really nice to a pretty girl who'd return the favor."

"I'm sorry, I already have a boyfriend," Janie told him crisply. She tugged against his hand, which held fast.

"You and I could be friends without hurting your boyfriend," Dickson said. "You know, dinner once in a while after work, things like that. You've never seen my place, have you?" He knew damned well she hadn't, and she didn't intend to. "It's rather nice, I think. You'd like it. You could call your mother from there and tell her not to expect you until later."

"No, thank you. Let go of me, please."

He still held one wrist, and now he put out his other hand and closed it over her knee as he twisted toward her. "You've got great legs. Best legs in the office." The hand slid upward, and Janie stopped it by digging her fingernails into the back of it.

"That's enough. Let me go, or I'll start yelling for a cop."

"I shouldn't think there'd be any around. They're all monitoring the fender-benders in the rush-hour traffic. Jane, listen to me. I meant it when I said I could be very good to you. I mean, *very*. You'd get to like me, too, if you let yourself go."

He withdrew the scratched hand and employed all his energies in drawing her into an embrace, his mouth seeking hers with a frightening urgency.

She'd had a dream once—a nightmare, actually—about being kissed by Dickson Zeller. She had awakened in a clammy panic. She felt clammy and panicky again, only this time there was no waking up from it.

His mouth was warm and moist and unpleasant, smelling of those breath mints he sucked all day. Nausea rose in Janie's throat, and she worked her arms between them and shoved. Hard. She lifted a hand and clawed at his head, and had a moment of horror when his hair slid backward.

My God, she thought, he wore a toupee! Dickson swore and again tried to kiss her; failing that, he moved his mouth downward to the base of her throat.

Revulsion gave her strength. She was past caring if she left marks on him; his ear brushed against her own mouth and she bit, tasting blood.

Dickson swore and pulled away, and Janie jerked the door open and literally fell into the street. She felt a stinging sensation in one knee where it scraped the concrete, and then she was on her feet, stumbling, moving away from him.

"Jane, wait! Oh, God, wait!" She heard him open the other door, heard his feet coming after her, and she broke into a run.

"Jane, I'm sorry! I didn't mean to force you, it's just that you've been driving me wild, and I wanted so much to touch you."

His hand brushed her sleeve and she spun wildly, looking back at him in the glow from the corner streetlight. He'd jammed the toupee back on his head, but it was askew, and she felt an insane impulse to laugh.

"Please, I'm sorry. Look, couldn't we go somewhere and have a drink and talk about this?"

A couple coming along the sidewalk looked at them curiously. Janie's fear suddenly vanished. He wasn't going to attack her out on the street, in view of passersby. She could already see it on his face: chagrin that he'd bungled it, apprehension that she'd go into the office tomorrow morning and tell everyone about his advances, so they'd all be laughing every time they thought of it.

Going to the office tomorrow. Oh, God, Janie thought, I can't face that. I can't face *him*. Never. Never again.

"Jane, let me take you the rest of the way home," Dickson pleaded. "Look, don't hold a grudge, OK? It's a compliment when a man thinks you're so attractive that he can't keep his hands off you, don't you know?"

"I'll be in tomorrow noon, when there's nobody there," Janie said, recovering her coolness, "to clear out my desk. You can mail my last check."

"No, Jane, don't quit! You're one of the best employees we have! Listen, I won't bother you, I swear I won't. Just give me a chance to make it up to you, show you what kind of man I am . . ."

"I already know," Janie told him. "Good night, Mr. Zeller."

She strode off toward home, trying to ignore the pain in her knee, pushing his hand away when he tried, one final time, to draw her to a halt.

She didn't turn to see if he went back to his car. She didn't care what he did, as long as he left her alone.

She was halfway down the next block before it hit her. She'd quit her job.

She felt cold, colder than the evening air could account for. How could she have quit? When they needed every penny? What would she do if she couldn't find something else right away?

She could always go in in the morning and tell Dickson she'd changed her mind. It would be a lie, but he'd take her back; she knew he would. And then think maybe he still had a chance, so he'd try again some day? She choked, thinking about it. No, it was impossible. She despised him and she hated typing his boring old papers.

Janie paused in front of her own building to inspect the damage to her knee. It was bleeding and her stocking was torn.

Damn the man, she thought.

And then, remembering the way his "hair" had slid backward under her hand, she began to laugh. There was a touch of hysteria in it, but amusement, too.

Maybe she would go back to the office when the others were there, long enough to tell them about the toupee.

It would serve him right.

8

The note on the kitchen table said, "Ate early and went to the movies. See you about 9:30. Casserole in the oven, salad in refrig."

The casserole was charred beyond recognition. Another thing she could be grateful to Dickson Zeller for, Janie thought.

She got out the salad and made herself a peanut butter sandwich, added Pepsi to a tall glass of ice, and settled herself in the living room to eat. The bandage on her knee felt bulky under her jeans.

Maybe she'd be wearing jeans every day now, she thought, opening the paper to the Help Wanted ads. There were a lot of them she could skip without reading: domestic help (maybe she'd get around to those eventually), nurses, computer programmers, sales jobs. She marked all the likely ones, eliminating a few that were so poorly paid that they wouldn't be worth applying for and those too far away. She wondered if they'd want to know why she'd quit her previous job, and how they'd react if she described this evening's experience with Dickson Zeller.

The telephone rang. Hoping it wasn't Harry—she felt unable to cope with Harry at the moment—Janie reached over for the instrument and sprawled along the length of the couch to reply.

"Hello?"

"Janie? Where've you been? I've been getting no answer for the past hour."

"Oh, hi, Molly. Well, I've been having an experience, I guess." She related her little saga. Molly was always a gratifying listener: she exclaimed in wonder, disgust, and amusement.

"Are you going to tell everybody at the office about it?" Molly wanted to know.

"I thought I would. Now I don't know. He's sort of pathetic, I guess. The thought of working for him any longer is more than I can bear, though. I couldn't go through that again."

"Are you going to quit?" Molly's voice altered.

"I already did."

There was a shocked silence. "Oh, Janie! What are you going to do now?"

"Tomorrow I'll hit the employment agencies and answer some ads in the paper."

"What did your mother say? Is she upset?"

"She doesn't know yet. She and Teddy went to the movies. Thank God she's already started the new job training; at least she won't give that up on my account. You know, I wasn't sure we were being smart to rent out Uncle Addison's room, but I'm glad now we've got that money coming in."

"Janie, I wondered, after we went home last night—you've still got a bunch of empty rooms in that place. Have you thought about renting out the rest of them?"

"Yeah, there are still three rooms upstairs. There could be four, if Mom lets Teddy live in the attic. Of course, we didn't do anything about the ones we didn't expect to use."

"Well, we could get the crew back again and move the rest of that old furniture out. Or maybe if you rented to people who didn't have any furniture of their own, you could leave it all there."

"We'd have to leave it there," Janie said. "I couldn't ask Harry to do any more, and all the others, except Clyde, were friends of his."

"Why can't you ask Harry?"

"Because," Janie said, draining the last of her Pepsi, "I made a decision today. This is just between you and me, understand? But I'm going to . . . to let things fall apart, with Harry. I'm not in love with him, he's not in love with me, and it's about time I found somebody I could fall in love with. I don't want to make a big thing of it, or hurt him; I *like* Harry. But it's time for a change. It'll probably be as good for him as it will be for me."

There was another brief silence. "You're sure, Janie? I mean, you've been spending a lot of time together."

"Yes. A lot more time than it took you and Clyde to find out you wanted to get married."

"Well, that's a point," Molly conceded. "Gosh, this is a lot to take in all at once."

Janie changed the subject. "Did you find a dress?"

Molly immediately brightened. "Oh, I saw one that was beautiful! I'm going back on my lunch hour tomorrow and try it on. Janie, why don't you meet me?"

"I'd better stick with job hunting, I think."

"Maybe if you rent out the rest of the rooms, you won't need to get a job. You could stay home and finish your book."

"I don't know. I don't think it would quite make up the amount of my salary. And if the house was full of people, I suppose there'd be additional expenses. More hot water, more expense for cooking, that kind of thing."

"I suppose. Well, Clyde's here, so I'll go, but good luck with the jobs. Call tomorrow night and tell me how it went, OK?"

"OK," Janie agreed and hung up. Before she could get to her feet with her dishes, the phone rang again.

"Hi, kid." Harry had always called her *kid* and until now it hadn't bothered her.

"Hi," she said now, settling back onto the couch.

"Everything OK?" Harry asked.

Oh sure. Except that I've lost my job and my knee hurts and I ruined a new pair of panty hose, she thought. Was this the time to begin cutting loose from Harry? "Ah, Harry, about bowling on Friday —I fell and skinned up a knee, and it's feeling sort of stiff. Would you mind very much if I took a rain check?"

She thought maybe he'd suggest a movie instead, which would mean she wouldn't have to spend an entire evening trying to act normal, carry on a conversation, laugh at his jokes when she didn't feel like laughing.

He didn't though. He surprised her. "Oh, sorry, hope it's not serious. I was calling because I was going to beg off myself."

Mildly annoyed as well as relieved, Janie said, "Oh, fine, then."

"The thing is . . ." There was something strained in Harry's voice. "I've had a job offer, Janie. One I can't pass up, I think. It'll mean more money, quite a lot more. I've already agreed to take it."

"Wonderful! What is it? When do you start?"

"The first of the month. The thing is . . ." Again he didn't quite sound like Harry. "It's in Alaska, kid. I'll have to be up there for at least a year. Maybe more, if I like it and decide to stay."

"Alaska!" She felt mildly stunned. People on the East Coast considered Alaska to be part of the Northwest; what few of them realized was that it was nearly three thousand miles by road from Seattle to the Alaskan cities of Anchorage and Fairbanks.

"Yeah." Enthusiasm crept into Harry's voice. "I'll be working out of Fairbanks, but I'll be going up on the slopes part of the time. Along the pipeline, you know."

"Sounds exciting," Janie said, feeling a touch of envy.

"I think so. Listen, kid, I don't suppose you'd want to go to Alaska?"

Janie pulled the receiver away from her ear and stared at it as if it had bitten her. Go to Alaska? With Harry?

"You there, kid?"

"Yes, certainly. You . . . caught me off guard."

Well, she'd wanted some sort of declaration from him, hadn't she? She inhaled deeply.

"Is that a proposal," she asked, "or a proposition?"

It was Harry's turn to have to hunt for words. "Well, I just thought —we've had a lot of fun together. You could probably find a job in Fairbanks; they use word processors everywhere these days. I'll have to maintain living quarters there anyway, though I wouldn't be there all the time, and I thought—"

A spark of anger surged through her and then died. She was quite calm. "No, Harry, I don't think I'd be interested in going to Alaska and keeping your apartment warm while you're out on the pipeline."

"We could get married, if you wanted to, before we go."

She hoped Clyde's proposal had been more romantic than that. "Thanks, Harry. I appreciate your offer. But I think I'd better stay here and help Mom keep the family going. She'd have a tough time without me." She didn't mention that since she no longer had a job, she might not be all that essential. Harry didn't want her on a permanent basis, any more than she wanted him. She wouldn't be a lover, she'd be a convenience to Harry.

He wouldn't be even that much to her.

"Well." Harry cleared his throat. "Maybe we could get together Saturday night for a farewell dinner?"

Did he sound relieved?

"We're moving Saturday," she reminded him. "So maybe we'd better just . . . say good-bye now."

"I suppose you're right. Listen, kid, I haven't hurt your feelings, have I? Making an important decision without asking you, you know?"

"Of course not." She'd made some decisions of her own and she hadn't consulted him either. "Good luck then, Harry."

"Yeah, sure. You, too. Hey, I'll write to you, all right?"

"All right," Janie said. She knew he wouldn't.

Muriel and Teddy came in laughing, moisture glistening on their hair.

"You should have been with us," Teddy said. "It was a great picture, wasn't it, Mom? There was this creature from outer space, and he was so gross everybody in the audience screamed when he came on, and he—"

Muriel clamped a hand over his mouth. "Remember our agreement? No movies on a school night unless you go straight to bed the minute we get home. You can tell Janie about it tomorrow."

"Yes," Janie said, sounding rather hollow. "In fact, I'll probably be here when you come home from school. I quit my job today."

She hadn't meant to put it so baldly, and it hurt to see the shock, quickly masked, in her mother's eyes; it was only that when something was difficult to do, she'd found it helped to do it quickly.

"What happened?" Muriel asked, no censure in her tone.

"Old Dickson kept me working late, then offered me a ride home, and made a pass. A rather *forceful* pass."

"Is that why there's blood on your pants?" Teddy asked.

"Oh, Janie, he didn't! Did he hurt you?" Muriel dropped her coat over a chair, outrage building.

"No. I mean, I fell, getting away from him, and scraped my knee, but it's not serious. The most serious part is that he made me so furious I tore off his toupee—yes, really!—and told him what he could do with his job, before I even considered the consequences."

"You did the right thing," Muriel assured her, as Janie ought to have known she would do. "What a wretched little worm he is."

"Hey," Teddy said, "that's harassment, isn't it? Can't you get reinstated or something, if you complain to the right place? Isn't there somebody that does things about employers who try to make their employees give them sexual favors?"

They both looked at him.

"Where did you learn about sexual harassment?" Muriel wanted to know.

"I don't want to be reinstated," Janie said at the same time. "I don't want to work for that creep any longer; it makes my skin crawl to think of sitting there with him watching me all day, trying to think up excuses to touch me."

Teddy chose to answer his mother. "Gosh, Mom, I watch the news and read the paper, you know. What did he actually *do*, Janie? Did he rape you?"

"Of course not, silly. I said it wasn't serious, didn't I? Go on to bed, kid."

"I wish I didn't always have to go to bed when you're going to talk about something interesting," Teddy said, but he headed for the bathroom.

Muriel faced her daughter with concern. "You really are all right, aren't you, honey?"

"Sure. I'm just among the unemployed. I saw a few jobs listed; I'll try for them tomorrow and register with the agencies. Oh, there's one more thing. Harry's taking a job in Alaska."

Muriel tried to gauge the effect of this. "Are you upset about it?"

Janie laughed ruefully. "Do you know, I'd made up my mind that Harry and I weren't going anywhere and I was going to ease him out of my life. And then he called and said he was going to Alaska and took the wind out of my sails. He asked if I wanted to go with him, but I could tell it wasn't any really big deal to him whether I did or not." Her mouth twisted in a parody of amusement. "It sort of hurt, Mom. Stupid, isn't it? I intended to drop him, but he dropped me first, and my feelings are hurt."

Muriel hugged her. "Human nature, I'd say. I'm rather glad, I think, honey. Harry's a nice enough fellow, but I didn't think you were in love with him."

"Not the way Clyde and Molly are. Oh, they're getting married. I'm going to be maid of honor. Molly made a suggestion we can think about. She pointed out that since we'll still have a bunch of empty bedrooms, we might consider renting the rest of them. What do you think?"

"I wonder if we could find anyone to rent them?"

"Shall I pick up one of those signs from the dime store, and we'll find out? Before we try advertising in the paper?"

"Why not?" Muriel said. "Just in case it takes a while to find another job."

There was not one word to indicate that Janie ought to have thought twice before giving up her position, and nothing to reveal panic if another job was not immediately forthcoming. Instead, Muriel gave her a warm smile.

"Don't worry, honey. We'll make out all right. Let's get a good night's sleep, and be glad you're finished with Dickson Zeller. Does he really have a toupee?"

They were laughing as they said good night.

9

There were twenty-five people ahead of her for the first job, and twice that many for the second one. Janie filled out the applications anyway, though with little hope. At the third place they told her the position had been filled.

She registered at two employment agencies, besides the state one, answered endless questions, and endured the indignity of having to explain why she had left her previous job. She tried to be concise and unemotional, but when one of the agency representatives gave her a skeptical look, Janie felt herself flushing angrily.

"Are you planning to file charges against him?" one of the examiners asked.

"No. I don't want the job back, and I don't think it's worth the hassle," Janie said shortly. She'd had a friend who *had* brought suit against an employer for sexual harassment, and it had been an experience traumatic far beyond any value it had, even though she had won the case.

In midafternoon, having forgotten to eat lunch, she stopped at Tilly's, on the edge of the mini-mall. She saw no one she knew, but a uniformed police officer sitting at the counter turned around to give her an appraising glance—it was unmistakably the look a man gives an attractive woman.

He turned back to the redhead who was waiting on him, and left Janie to study him in turn. She wondered if he ate here all the time, and if he was married.

He smiled at her, and she smiled back, very faintly, when the officer finished his meal and left. The waitress, having few other customers at this time of day, smiled at her, too.

"I suppose police officers are like truck drivers," Janie said tentatively. "They eat in places where the food is good."

The waitress shrugged. "We're open twenty-four hours a day, the only place in the neighborhood that is. It's good, having cops come in here. People know it, and they don't try to rob us. Not lately anyhow."

A man entered and ordered coffee, and that was the end of the conversation, but Janie felt encouraged. This would be *her* neighborhood in a few more days, and the waitress and the officer had both seemed friendly.

She almost forgot the ROOM FOR RENT sign. She turned back to get it at a variety store on the mall, missed her bus, and decided to walk over to the house and talk to Bea about it. After all, it was her home, too.

Neva Minor had finished moving in. Janie was ushered into what had previously been Addison Hamer's bedroom and was amazed to see the changes Neva had wrought without removing any of the furniture.

She had added a platform rocker with an ottoman, a small color TV, and a bookcase filled with paperback books; most of them, Janie noted with amusement, were thrillers and science fiction epics. Teddy might well have a kindred soul here, despite more than fifty years' difference in their ages.

There was a colorful quilt on the big bed and jars, bottles, and brushes on the massive bureau. The musty odor in the room was gone, replaced by a faint, clean scent.

The two women were obviously having a grand time. They led her to the kitchen to display Neva's microwave, the largest Janie had ever seen, on one of the counters.

"My oldest son gave it to me for Christmas last year," Neva said proudly. "It'll cook a twenty-two-pound turkey. I'm sure that's why he bought it, so I'd continue to do the turkeys for the family holidays. They all like my stuffing better than anyone else's."

Bea regarded it with an expression suggesting she was a little bit afraid of the thing. "Neva says it's very easy to use, and we're all free to use it."

"We were about to celebrate my settling in with a drink, Miss Madison," Neva said. "Would you care to join us?"

"Please, call me Janie." Anticipating another of Bea's herbal teas, she was about to refuse when Neva went to the refrigerator and brought out a bottle of wine. "Well, that does look good."

They carried their glasses into the back parlor and sat down, and Janie showed them her sign. "We thought we might rent out the other rooms, too. What would you think, Aunt Bea? Would we be asking for trouble, filling the house with strangers?"

Delight crossed both elderly faces. "Why, it wouldn't even have to be all strangers," Bea said. "I know a couple of people who would be thrilled to have rooms here. So much nicer than one of those hotels where some of our friends have to stay because it's all they can afford. I'm thinking of Sylvia Bonnard, Neva."

"I thought of Charlie Silvers," Neva added. "And maybe Mr. Jacoby. I know he lives with his daughter, but he'd rather not, she bosses him around so. How many rooms were you thinking of renting, Janie?"

By the time she left, the pair were excitedly looking up phone numbers to call the people they had in mind, and since there would be a room or two to spare, Janie put the ROOM FOR RENT sign in a front window.

"I don't expect you to screen prospects, Aunt Bea," Janie assured her. "Just tell them we'll be moving in on Saturday, and they can talk to me then. If anybody asks, I mean."

"Oh, they'll ask," Neva said confidently. "Low-cost living quarters, decent ones, are in such short supply. And this is such a good location for someone who doesn't have a car. So close to the mini-mall and the bus line and everything."

Janie had already calculated what they could expect to collect in room rents, if they filled them all. It didn't equal what she'd been earning, and she had no way of estimating what the additional expense of roomers would be, but since there was no house payment to make, she thought it possible that they could hold on without too much difficulty until a new job opened up for her.

Nothing appeared to be opening up very fast. For the rest of the week she spent the mornings going to file job applications and undergoing interviews; in the afternoons, she packed their belongings into cardboard boxes and felt a very faint regret that Harry and his friends wouldn't be around to help them move.

She half expected that Harry would call before he actually left town, but he didn't. Maybe Harry had been as relieved as she was to end a relationship that had fizzled out.

On Friday afternoon Bea called to tell her that she had rented rooms, subject to Janie's approval, to Mr. Jacoby, Mrs. Bonnard, and Charlie Silvers. "I know all of them and I'm sure you'll like them," Bea said earnestly. "And there's another young man I hadn't met who's looking for an inexpensive place to live, so I told him to see you on Saturday. His name is Ernest Layton."

Janie wondered with mild amusement what Bea considered a young man.

She didn't pick up her check until late Friday. She'd already decided they were going to have to hire someone with a small truck to get them moved. It was frightening to think that there was no cash reserve, only Muriel's weekly check between the family and disaster.

To her vast relief, Dickson Zeller's red Triumph was not in the parking lot when she arrived. Dickson often managed to have "business" out of the office on Friday afternoons. None of them ever figured out exactly where he went, or what he did, or with whom. Presumably the man had friends somewhere, though it seemed odd to Janie now that he so seldom mentioned any of them by name.

She felt distinctly uncomfortable entering the office of Zeller and Markham. All eyes immediately swung in her direction, and all work stopped.

Candy left the word processor and came toward her. "Jane! We've been wondering about you!"

They converged on her in a body, even Mrs. Kelly.

"What happened?" Rose wanted to know.

"Dickson didn't say anything until we asked him," Shirley reported, "and then all he'd admit was that you'd quit. We couldn't believe it."

"And we noticed that his hands and his face were scratched," Sally said.

"Did you actually have to fight him off?" Candy asked.

She could see it in their faces, their willingness, even their desire, to believe the worst. And though the worst was true, Janie was suddenly unwilling to feed them what they wanted. She didn't think later that she would have done it even if Dickson hadn't walked in at that moment.

He stopped, stricken at the sight of her. "Oh, Jane. Your check is ready. Mrs. Kelly has it."

"Thank you. I'll clear out my desk," Janie said. She forced a smile at the women she'd worked with. "I just decided to quit, that's all. I'd been thinking about it for a long time."

They stared at her, disappointed. Dickson walked past them into the glass-walled cubicle; the back of his neck was red.

Candy leaned toward her. "He did make a pass at you, didn't he? We've all seen him practically drooling over you. And you finally had to fight him off, didn't you?"

Janie bent over the desk drawer which contained her personal belongings. "I certainly don't know how he got scratched." She dropped the items into the paper bag she'd brought. "Could I have my check right away, Mrs. Kelly? I have to get to a shop before it closes."

They didn't believe her. They didn't *want* to believe her. And though Dickson Zeller probably deserved it, she simply couldn't do it to him after all.

She made herself smile and say good-bye to them.

At the last moment she glanced around and caught Dickson's eye. He was standing behind the wall of glass, his mouth pinched and unhappy, perhaps thinking she'd told them everything.

Janie lifted a hand in farewell and closed the door behind her.

The jeweler spread the things out on the counter. "I've written down what I think the things would bring. I don't buy much of this kind of stuff, but here's the address of someone who might be interested."

Disappointed, Janie looked at the bottom figure in his neat, cramped writing. Maybe it would pay for a new furnace. She'd known that if Addison Hamer had anything of substantial value, he wouldn't have left it where the Madisons would benefit from it.

The jeweler was smiling. "Everybody's disappointed when they get an appraisal of the family jewels. They always hope they'll suddenly be rich. It doesn't often happen that way, though."

Janie accepted the small package. It occurred to her, rather disconcertingly, that if he wasn't interested in buying, there must be a charge.

"Oh, twenty dollars will cover it," he said.

Would there ever be a day when she didn't have to squeeze every penny she spent? Janie thought of Aunt Bea then and of Neva Minor, and those other old people, forced to subsist on Social Security payments of only a few hundred dollars a month; they'd consider themselves rich to have the income the Madisons had. There wasn't much comfort in the thought.

10

Neighbors of the Cottlers, on Fir Street, were used to hearing sounds of battle emanating from the tidy one-story brick house. Even during the months when no one had their windows open, Cora and Herb Cottler's angry voices could be heard.

Today, the Cottlers were outdoing themselves.

Cora was a large woman of six years more than the forty-eight she admitted to; she had a passion for brightly flowered dresses which added to her bulky appearance, and she was so nearsighted that without her glasses she could barely recognize her husband across the room.

Not that she wanted to recognize him today. She wanted to throttle him. He had retired some two months earlier, and she was in the throes of menopause; between the two, she wondered if their thirty-two-year marriage could survive until the next anniversary.

For the past year she'd read him bits out of the "Golden Years" column about preparing for retirement. Things like developing hobbies and interests to take a man out of the house for at least part of every day. Things about having reasonable expectations of the wife who didn't get to retire but must continue to perform her usual chores.

Herb had driven a bus for the past twenty-two years. He liked driving buses. (Strangely enough, he did not like driving a car and was reluctant to take her anywhere, even to the supermarket.) During his working years, he had not had time to develop much in the way of interests. He wasn't a reader, and the only things he enjoyed on television were sporting events.

He couldn't stand soap operas, and Cora watched them avidly. Their first fight today had been over whether she was going to watch "General Hospital" or he was going to watch the Mariners play the Kansas City Royals.

"For God's sake," she had finally shrieked at him, "go get yourself another TV! Don't expect me to give up all my programs for your stupid ball games!"

He hadn't bought another set, of course. They both knew that was an expenditure they couldn't make on the spur of the moment. If they hinted to their kids, the boys would see that they got a set for Christmas, but that was months away.

Instead, Herb had decided to fix the back step that she'd been nagging him about for the past six months; his hammering and pounding and swearing when he hit his thumb had sufficiently interfered with her enjoyment of the program so that she'd finally turned the set off in disgust.

At twelve-thirty Herb was hungry.

By this time Cora was doing the laundry. "Make yourself a sandwich," she suggested, trying not to sound as hostile as she felt.

Herb was a paunchy man of middle height, with thinning hair. He had a habit of many years, which had only become disgusting to her now that he was at home all the time, of scratching his chest. "I thought maybe some soup."

"Open a can, then."

"Ain't you gonna eat?"

Cora closed the washer and turned to glare at him. "How long you been retired?"

"You know how long. Two months. What's that got to do with having lunch?"

"How many times have I told you—at least once a day since you retired—that I don't eat breakfast when I first get up, I like a nice brunch about ten-thirty or eleven. And then I don't want anything else to eat until suppertime at six."

He bent over and took a Hershey bar wrapper out of the trash can. "If you didn't snack on this junk, you'd be ready to eat normal meals, same time as I want to eat."

Her color began to rise. "I fix you breakfast. I fix you supper. Why can't you fix your own lunch, for God's sake? Why do I have to wait on you? Why should I have to work harder, just because *you* retired? When the hell do *I* get to retire?"

"What's the big deal about making me a bowl of soup, for crissake?"

They stared at each other, animosity oozing from every pore.

"If it's not such a big deal, why can't you do it yourself?" Cora challenged. "Why can't you make friends down at the corner bar, like everybody else, and go talk to them once in a while and give me some peace?"

"It's my house, too," Herb stated. "I made the damn payments on it all these years. Why should I have to get out of it?"

"If we hadn't rented out the apartment, I'd move out there and let you have the whole house. See how you like it, doing everything for yourself instead of being waited on like you was the president of Greyhound instead of a worn-out driver."

"Whose idea was it to rent the apartment?" They had converted the separate garage to a rental unit several years ago; it was one of the things that made his retirement feasible, because that rent, added to his pension, made an adequate retirement income for the two of them. "And who takes the money and spends it, eh? Not me, babe. I never see any of it."

They'd said all the words before, neither of them really listening to the other, and they said them again. "If I had any place to go," Cora told him, "I'd leave you this minute."

Herb whipped out his wallet. "Here. Here's fifty bucks from my last check. Take it. Go someplace. Anyplace. Stay overnight. Then maybe by tomorrow I can stand the sight of you again."

He'd never been quite that cruel before. The bills were thrust at her, and Cora took them. Fury made her almost incoherent.

"All right. I will. Maybe I won't come back at all."

"I'll get along OK, whether you do or not."

She left the house with his final insult ringing in her ears. She was nearly blind with frustrated rage, and before she'd walked a block she wished she'd stayed. Why should he run her out of what was just as much her home as his own?

She had her pride, though. She'd show him. See how he liked coping with running a house all by himself. The damned fool couldn't even open a can of soup and heat it up—how was he going to manage anything else?

She had no destination in mind.

A movie, she thought. She'd go and sit in the darkened theater and watch a movie until she felt calmer.

The hired truck and driver arrived at nine. By noon everything had been transferred to the house on Relton Street. As Teddy started for the front steps with the final box of his own belongings, he saw the boy standing on the sidewalk, watching.

"Hi," Teddy said.

"Hi," the boy replied. He looked a year or two younger than Teddy, dark-skinned and undernourished. "You moving in here?"

"That's right. My name's Teddy Madison. What's yours?"

"Joe. Joe Milos."

"Oh yeah. Aunt Bea knows your grandma. You ever seen the trains in our attic?"

"No," Joe said.

"Come on," Teddy invited. "I'll show you."

"I never dreamed they'd all try to move in at once, the same time we were moving," Muriel said, collapsing on the chintz-covered sofa in the front parlor. "What a madhouse. How is anyone going to be able to eat with so many people needing to use the kitchen at the same time?"

"They all seem to be making out fine. Why don't I go down to the mall and get something? Hamburgers, or fried chicken?"

"Can we afford that?" Muriel grimaced. "Damn, I hate having to say things like that. We're not absolutely broke yet, and they'll all be paying rent right away, won't they?"

"I think Uncle Addison's jewelry will probably stretch to Kentucky Fried. With mashed potatoes, rolls, and cole slaw. OK?"

They were laughing when Mr. Jacoby paused in the doorway, checkbook in hand. "To whom do I make out my rent check?" he asked.

Janie had taken to Mr. Jacoby at once. He was one of the bingo players Aunt Bea had rounded up, the one who had lived with a bossy daughter. He was a dried-up little man with a few strands of dark hair combed carefully across a bald spot. Bea, who provided them with details about all the newcomers, had announced his age as seventy-three.

"To me, I guess. Jane Madison. Are you settled in already, Mr. Jacoby?"

"Enough so I can sleep. I'll worry about the rest later." He wrote slowly and handed over the check. "If my daughter comes—Rachel Civen—would you mind telling her I'm too worn out from moving to show her my room?"

"Do you think you'll still be too tired tomorrow?" Muriel asked after a quick glance at Janie.

"As far as Rachel's concerned, yes." He put the checkbook away. "Means well, Rachel does, but she treats me as if I'm her idiot child. I'm not." He gave them a grin that removed any sting from the words.

When he had gone, they made faces at each other. "This may turn out to be more interesting than I thought. If that kid is still up in the attic with Teddy, should we invite him to supper?"

"Why not? How much can such a small boy eat?" Muriel said. It was the last time she would make that mistake with Joe.

The other male renter was Charlie Silvers. Charlie was on Social Security, too, but not because of his age. Though he wasn't quite sixty yet, he was considered totally disabled because of emphysema. He was a corpulent and amiable man who wheezed and coughed a lot, especially when he laughed, which was frequently.

Teddy had won out in the discussion over where he was to sleep. He loved the attic, and if he slept there, they could rent out one more room.

Joe called home for permission to stay for supper and proceeded to eat nearly as much as the other three put together. "Thanks," he said, wiping his hands on his pants instead of on a napkin. He looked at Teddy. "I'm gonna go see a horror movie tomorrow. You wanta go?"

"Sure. I can, can't I, Mom?"

Janie left them there, settling details, too tired to do anything except go to bed. She showered, deciding that having water sprayed on you from all directions at several different levels was quite luxurious, though before she was finished, the water temperature had cooled enough to make her wonder if they'd have to install a larger heater.

Cora Cottler sat through the movie twice. It wasn't that she particularly enjoyed it, because it was science fiction and she didn't understand most of it, though the noisy kids around her seemed to find it fascinating.

She had a headache when she came out into the twilight. Probably because she'd missed her supper, she thought crossly. Damn him, anyway, why should he have deprived her of supper in her own house? Her only satisfaction was that he wouldn't have eaten either. At least not decently. The best he could manage on his own was a peanut butter sandwich. When she was home, he even expected her to make that.

Her eyes burned. She took off her glasses and rubbed at them. Did she really want to go home, obviously hungry, obviously not having enjoyed her time away at all, creeping back as if she didn't have a right to have stayed there in the first place?

She noticed that a blinking red neon announced that a small eatery called Tilly's was open twenty-four hours. Well, why not? She had the money, and this way she wouldn't have to cook it herself nor share it with Herb.

At first she thought there wouldn't be a place to sit down. There was a pair of good-looking cops joking with a pretty waitress. Cora ordered pork chops with mashed potatoes, a green salad, and pie.

It was fully dark when she left a fifty-cent tip and walked outside. The police had gone, but there were still plenty of people around, lots of lights on.

She felt better, though her eyes continued to burn. Was that little pharmacy over next to the theater still open? The way they left lights on after they'd closed, wasting all that electricity, it was hard to tell. Maybe if it was open she'd get some Murine or something. That would help.

She purchased the eye drops and decided to call a cab. It wasn't such a long walk home, but it was dark and she was tired.

The telephone was out of order. In fact, vandals had torn the receiver right off the wall.

She turned away from the useless telephone when a group of young teenagers raced toward her, laughing and shoving each other. She had just taken off her glasses to massage her eyes again, and they dangled from her hand; one of the youngsters careened into her, making her drop the glasses.

She heard them hit the concrete, heard one of the kids step on them, saw them all keep going, shouting, unconcerned.

"My glasses! My God, they've broken my glasses!"

She yelled after them; but none of them paused or looked around. Cora dropped to her knees, groping blindly. The lenses were shattered and the frames bent so that she couldn't have worn them even if there'd been any glass left.

Good grief, when she thought what a pair of glasses cost—those little brats! She wished the cops were still there, but they were gone. In fact, except for more of those horrid teenagers, it seemed that virtually everyone had gone.

Was there anywhere else she could use a phone, or prevail upon someone to call on her behalf? The pharmacy had closed.

She took a few tentative steps toward the restaurant, encountered a ridge intended to slow down speeders in the parking area, and nearly fell.

It frightened her. The surrounding parking lot, only dimly lighted, frightened her. The footsteps behind her frightened her.

Cora turned toward them, seeing only a blur of reddish light, unable to make out the figure that approached. She couldn't even tell for sure if it was a man or a woman, or another of those beastly children.

"Who is it?" she called out. "Can you help me? I've broken my glasses, and I can't see."

She took a few steps toward the figure, and the blast struck her in the chest.

"Herb," she said, and stumbled backward, arms outstretched, dying.

11

Joe was as fascinated by the trains as Teddy was. Neither of them had ever seen such a layout, not even in the big department stores at Christmas.

The attic was not finished as a room, though there was naked plasterboard secured to the studding, as if someone had intended to finish it eventually. It was a large open area with dormers on each side, so the light wasn't bad, and the entire area had been floored in planed lumber.

The miniature track formed a big figure eight, plus a few spurs to the outside, and the whole thing wound through a village of houses, stores, and depot, done to scale and in considerable detail. There were two complete trains, a freight and a passenger one, and when they were allowed to collide head-on, the engines would jump the tracks, pulling cars behind them.

Joe arrived on the doorstep while Janie and Muriel were eating breakfast, and they sent him on up to the attic.

The boys spent the morning on their hands and knees, oblivious of the dust that had escaped the perfunctory sweeping Teddy'd given the room.

Joe finally sat back on his heels and wiped his nose on the back of his hand. "Wonder what time it is. The show starts at one."

Teddy consulted the alarm clock under his bed. "We got lots of time. It's only eleven-thirty."

"I'm getting hungry," Joe said.

"I'll get us something, OK? And then we'll go. How long will it take us to walk over there to the theater?"

"Not very long. Fifteen minutes." Joe swiped at his nose again. "What you gonna get to eat?"

It took both of them to carry the food back upstairs. They had bologna sandwiches with mustard, apples, cookies, and milk. As an afterthought, Teddy added two Mounds bars. They ate upstairs and then headed for the show.

It was another beautiful day. The sun was bright and warm, and people were out walking their dogs and working in their yards. Teddy would have headed down the street in the only route he knew to the mini-mall, but Joe shook his head.

"Better to go the back way," he said. "Through the alley and across the field. Don't nobody hassle you, that way."

Teddy didn't see any reason why they should be hassled no matter which way they went, but he didn't care. He'd never seen the alley, or the field.

Joe was a snooper in trash piles and garbage bins. He kept stopping to inspect things. "Hey, they're throwing away a perfectly good box of crackers," he announced. "I'll hide 'em in the grass on the vacant lot and get 'em on the way home."

Teddy was beginning to get the idea that his new friend lived somewhat differently from himself. He'd never have dreamed of taking food out of a garbage can.

He found a mirror that had come off a car; Joe added that to his collection. "Maybe I can sell it," he offered in explanation.

The alley was an interesting experience. There were dogs in backyards, all of whom Joe knew by name. Only one of them failed to stop barking when Joe spoke to it.

"That Doberman, he's a mean dude. Don't never climb that fence to get anything," Joe warned. "He'll eat you alive."

"Do you climb fences to get things? Not just stuff people have already thrown away?"

Joe slid him a sidelong glance. "Not usually. Sometimes we play ball, and the ball goes over the fence. If that Dobie gets it, forget it."

They walked on, kicking beer cans, chattering, until they came to a high board fence where the alley dead-ended.

"Now what?" Teddy asked. "Are we supposed to climb over that?" He was concerned, because he'd never climbed a fence that high before and he didn't want the smaller boy to show him up.

"Nah," Joe said. "We go through it."

He reached out and pried at a wide board. "See? We can squeeze right through." He swung the board aside.

It was tighter for Teddy, because he was bigger, but he made it.

They were in a vacant lot behind the theater parking area. There was nothing there except overgrown grass, tall brown stuff left from last fall.

Joe led the way along a well-defined path, then suddenly stopped with a muffled exclamation. "Hey, look what's blowing around, man!"

Since Joe was blocking the path, Teddy stepped around him to look. Joe's tennis shoe rested on the edge of a twenty-dollar bill.

"Wow! I wonder who it belongs to?"

A grin spread over Joe's dark face. "It belongs to me now." He bent to pull it out from under his foot, and Teddy pounced on another bill that fluttered against a stand of weeds.

"Here's a ten. Somebody's missing this, Joe. Maybe we ought to find out who it belongs to."

"It don't belong to nobody, or it wouldn't be blowing around out here in the field," Joe said, stuffing the bill in his pants pocket. "Let's see if there's any more of it."

They discovered another five, and three singles. Joe kept the twenty, Teddy the ten, and they decided to use the rest to pay for the movies.

They went on along the path, across the parking area where a few cars were disgorging matinee patrons, and joined the short line of kids waiting to see the horror movie.

Once inside, they stared at the candy counter display. "What're we going to have?" Joe asked.

Teddy was feeling mildly uneasy, yet excited, too, about finding the money. He knew what his mother's attitude would be, that the money was someone else's property. Yet they had no way of knowing whose.

"Popcorn, I guess," he said. "And a Pepsi."

"Me, too. A big popcorn, with butter," Joe told the girl behind the counter. "And let's each have a box of Milk Duds and some of them big Hershey bars, the thick ones."

"Rich today, huh?" the girl asked.

They carried their loot on into the theater and sat down. "This is supposed to be a real scary movie," Joe said, sliding down in his seat, balancing his Pepsi between his legs. "I like scary movies, don't you?"

"Yeah," Teddy agreed.

They came out of the theater shortly after three-thirty. Teddy was feeling slightly under the weather after all the junk he'd eaten, though it didn't seem to be bothering Joe. Joe kept talking about the movie, how great the special effects had been.

A few yards off the parking area, Joe stopped and scooped up an object they'd missed before. "Hey, look! Glasses!" He knocked the few remaining shards of the lenses out of the frames and perched them on his nose. They were bent out of shape, so he twisted them, trying to make them straighter, and put them back on. "How do I look?"

Silly, Teddy thought, but he was feeling too crummy to bother saying it. At least the glasses were no good to anyone, so it didn't matter who they belonged to. Joe took them off and crammed them into the pocket of his jeans.

Halfway across the field toward the board fence, Teddy's stomach began to roil in earnest. He stopped and Joe looked at him. "What's the matter?"

"I think I'm going to throw up," Teddy said. He spun away, staggering out into the deeper grass.

And then, as he was wishing he had something to wash out his mouth, and that he was home so he could lie down, he saw something that made him stop breathing altogether.

He tried to speak three times before he could say Joe's name.

"What's the matter? You really sick? Like you can't get the rest of the way home?"

Joe took a few steps toward him, then followed the direction of Teddy's pointing finger.

Joe's expletive was the one that Muriel referred to as *the* four-letter word. He went almost as pale as Teddy was.

"It . . . it's a body," Teddy said. "Isn't it? Is she . . . dead?"

Joe took a few steps closer to the mound in the deep grass, and after a moment Teddy followed him. They stared down at a heavyset woman in a flowered dress, a woman whose mouth and eyes were open yet silent and unseeing, a woman whose breast was soaked in what, even though it was dry and brown, they recognized as blood.

Joe swore again. "It's another one, like the one in the alley. She's gotta be dead, or she wouldn't lay there and let the flies crawl in her mouth that way, would she?"

"We better call the cops," Teddy said hollowly. He felt as if he were going to throw up again, and even gagged, but there was nothing left to come up.

"Anonymously," Joe said.

"What?"

"Anonymously. Without telling them who we are. Otherwise, we'll get involved in a murder investigation, see? If the murderer reads about it, and the papers use our names, he might come after us, see?"

Teddy did manage to bring up a little more, after all. It was yellow bile, which tasted terrible, and his stomach hurt.

"There's a pay phone on the Standard station lot," Joe said. "They're always busy. They won't notice if we use it."

Teddy would have agreed with anything that would get him away from this terrible sight. It was different in the movies, you knew that was made-up, but this was *real.* He didn't want to go back by the theater, to see anybody there. He followed Joe toward the movable board in the fence and squeezed through, then cut through someone's unfenced yard toward the Standard station.

12

Janie had wakened that same day feeling tired and sore in the muscles unaccustomed to hauling heavy boxes, but good. They were in the new house, for better or worse. She didn't have a job, but everyone had paid for a month's room rent in advance, except for Mrs. Bonnard, who was coming today, and that other fellow Bea had talked to. What was his name? Layton, Ernest Layton.

She was optimistic about getting a job. And she was going to get back to writing. She had set the box containing the manuscript out on the typing table when she carried it in yesterday.

The kitchen was full of people when she went downstairs; she'd caught her mother's eye, filled two cups of coffee, and carried them toward the front parlor that would be theirs. Actually, the sliding doors between the two parlors stood open, so that it was really one very large room, somewhat narrowed in the middle. The other end of it was empty now, as Bea and her friends assembled their meals and carried them into the dining room across the hall.

Muriel listened to the amiable chatter. "Sound pleased with themselves, don't they? I don't think we need to feel guilty about Aunt Bea; I think she's quite happy to have all her friends here under her own roof. I hope they continue to get along well and we don't have to arbitrate disputes or anything like that."

The telephone rang.

Janie hesitated, cup in midair. She'd not yet answered the phone in this place, and she felt as if it belonged to Aunt Bea rather than to her, yet she was standing beside the hall table where the instrument sat.

She could see Bea through the dining-room door, waiting, so Janie picked it up. "Hello?"

"May I speak to Mr. Jacoby, please?" It was a woman's voice, pleasantly modulated, cultured.

Janie saw Mr. Jacoby's bald head with its strands of hair (held in place by what?) across the pink skin as he peered out at her. He mouthed the name: "Rachel?"

"This is his daughter, Mrs. Civen," the caller said.

"Mr. Jacoby?" Janie echoed, to make sure he understood. "Why, I'm not sure he's come down yet. I think he got very tired yesterday, moving in."

Mr. Jacoby nodded vigorously, pouring milk over his All-Bran. He grinned at Janie and began to eat.

"Oh. Well, when he does come down, will you ask him to call me?"

"Certainly, Mrs. Civen," Janie told her. She carried her coffee through the doorway beside her and sank into a chair. "This may get to be a pain if we have to do very much of it."

"Ah, well, we'll both be at work most of the time," Muriel said. "Or if you're home, writing, you'll be a long way from the telephone. Someone else will answer it."

"Yes. I've thought about that. Nobody would ever catch the phone, running from the second floor. Do you think we ought to have an extension installed up there?"

"Probably. But let's wait until we see what the usage is, and how much money it's going to take to run things. I bathed in tepid water last night."

"So did I. We're going to have to get a bigger water heater, aren't we?"

They drank their coffee in a leisurely way, heading for the kitchen and bacon and eggs only after the older people had cleared away their things. Muriel sighed. "It would probably expedite things here if we put in a dishwasher. I can see that we're going to have to spend some money to run this place as a rooming house."

"It won't be too much of a problem once I have a salary again," Janie assured her. "I think I'll take the Sunday paper and mark the ads now, so I can hit it first thing in the morning. I wonder if it would be worthwhile to canvass the businesses in the mall? I mean, it's so close to home, it would be great if I didn't have to take a bus."

"Try it," Muriel advised. "Uh-oh, there's a man coming up the front walk. Mr. Layton, maybe? Do you want to talk to him, or shall I?"

"I will." Janie drained her cup and put it on the coffee table. "Aunt Bea said he was young. Is he, really?"

Muriel peered discreetly through the semisheer curtains. "Under thirty, I'd say, though not by much."

Janie waited for him to ring the bell, so she wouldn't seem too eager, then opened the door.

The young man on the porch smiled tentatively. He was shy, she thought. "Miss Madison? I've come about a room?"

"Certainly, come on in. Are you Mr. Layton?"

"Ernie," he said. "Ernie Layton." He came into the front hallway, towering over her, a rangy, pleasant-looking fellow with nondescript features and ordinary mouse-brown hair. He looked around, nodding a little as if approving the place. From the dining room came voices and sounds of amusement.

"You aren't just renting the one room?" Ernie Layton asked hesitantly.

"No, as a matter of fact, we're renting five rooms. To elderly people, actually," Janie admitted. "I think they've just gotten up a card game or something. Would you be needing kitchen privileges?"

He hesitated again. "Well, it would help. Or I have a hot plate I could use in my room. I could get an ice chest."

"It's a madhouse, but of course this is our first day. Everybody except Aunt Bea and Neva Minor just moved in yesterday, so we haven't worked out a schedule yet. I don't know how the wiring is, whether it would be safe to have a hot plate upstairs or not. Maybe you'd better figure on kitchen privileges, at least to begin with. You want to see it, don't you, before you decide?"

"Oh, this location is good for me, and I don't see any reason why not . . . but sure, I'll look at the room."

He followed her up the stairs. Janie was conscious of her worn jeans —had she put on the pair in which she'd resewn the back seam, or the next better ones?—and the faded sweatshirt. Reasonable attire for someone just getting settled into a new house, but hardly anything to impress a young man.

He looked around the room as Janie stepped aside for him to enter. "This is the only one we have left," she told him. "You'd have to share a bath with Mr. Jacoby and Mr. Silvers. It's just across the hall."

He poked at the mattress on the heavy oak bed, nodded, and crossed to the bathroom.

"Old-fashioned," Janie said unnecessarily, and he nodded again, grinning. "Reminds me of my grandmother's place," he said. "Even has rods to hang the towels so they'll be warm when you use them."

"Is that what that rack's for? I thought it was for drying the towels after you'd used them."

He shrugged. "Either way. It is all right if I move in this afternoon, Miss Madison?"

"Sure. And you might as well call me Janie. Everybody else does. Oh, the back parlor downstairs is reserved for roomers. My mother and little brother and I will use the front one."

"I don't think I'll be using that much," Ernie Layton said. He got out his checkbook and a pen.

The house was now full.

She spent an hour going over the papers after he had gone. There were quite a few interesting-sounding jobs in Seattle, if she'd wanted to go that far. Unless she got really desperate, she wouldn't consider anything in the city, though.

Muriel had gone upstairs when the doorbell rang again. There was no cessation of conversation from the dining room, where a lively game of five hundred was in progress. As Janie passed through the hallway to answer the door, she heard Charlie Silvers say, "Listen, we'd have a lot more fun playing poker. You ladies want to learn how to play poker?"

"For money?" Bea asked, sounding uncertain.

Mr. Jacoby's tone was dry. "No fun if you don't do it for money, is it?"

Neva Minor chimed in. "I'm willing to learn, but I won't play for money to begin with. Not until I have some idea what I'm doing."

Janie opened the door. Sylvia Bonnard stood there, a bag in each hand; behind her was a rather stooped man of about fifty carrying several more pieces of luggage.

"Come on in," Janie said, smiling.

Mrs. Bonnard was the oldest of the lot, at eighty-one. She had thin white hair through which one could see pink scalp, and she appeared too frail to carry the bags. She wore very thick glasses, the kind prescribed after cataract surgery, and even with them Janie had the impression she didn't see very far. She was neatly dressed in a cotton print and sensible shoes, with a lacy white sweater around her narrow shoulders.

"Upstairs, Alfred," she said. "At the very top, just across the landing."

"All right, Mother." He smiled at Janie. "I'm Alfred."

He still had all his hair, though it was going gray; he looked as if he'd once been heavier and had lost considerable weight, so that his skin, as well as his clothes, hung on him in a baggy way.

"Mother, are you sure you want to do this? I don't feel right, having you in a rooming house with a bunch of strangers."

"I know most of them," Sylvia Bonnard said. "Why don't you bring in the rest of it?"

"I told you, I'd look for a bigger place, if you want to live with me."

"I'd rather go into a rest home," Sylvia said dampeningly. "Is everybody in there?"

"Yes. Playing cards, I think," Janie told her.

"I wonder if anyone has a coffee pot on? Or water for tea? Maybe I'll just step in and say hello."

She wandered off, and Alfred smiled at Janie. "I worry about her. She's not senile, by any means, but sometimes . . ."

He let Janie figure out what happened sometimes. "I'll unload the car, and then you can show me which room. All right?"

He carried in boxes and cartons and paper bags. "I'll have to go back for another load. She has all these hobbies, and she won't get rid of anything, even when she loses interest. Thinks she might want to do everything again someday."

It looked to Janie as if the room was filled already, before he went back for a second load, but if Mrs. Bonnard wanted to cram the room so she could hardly walk around in it, who would it bother? As long as it wasn't a fire hazard.

When Alfred had gone, Janie went down to the basement. It had been cleaned up pretty well, with the junk that the Salvation Army hadn't wanted stacked along the far wall. She stared at the furnace, a great malevolent beast in the center of the floor.

"Are you going to last another winter," she asked it aloud, "or will we have to replace you?"

Not surprisingly, the furnace said nothing.

Janie walked around it to the corner which the laundry equipment occupied along with the water heater. No wonder there wasn't enough to go around, she thought, with that little thing. She sighed and went back upstairs.

It was strange to be sitting around at home on a weekend with nothing in particular to do. If Harry hadn't been running off to Alaska, they'd probably have gone to the beach, or hiking, on a day like this.

It occurred to her that when Molly got married, she probably wouldn't be available for any excursions anymore either. Who could she call to do anything with? Practically everybody she knew had gotten married and was busy having babies, or was so immersed in a career and/or some spectacular male that she wasn't interested in going to a movie or bowling with a girl friend.

The five hundred game had been switched to poker. Bea had brought a box of kitchen matches to the table which would be used in place of money. Each match, she informed Janie, would be the equivalent of ten dollars, just to make it interesting. They had made sandwiches, which they were eating as they played. Charlie Silvers and Mr. Jacoby and Neva Minor had bottles of beer; Bea and Sylvia Bonnard had tea. Sylvia wasn't playing, only observing, because she had to wait for Alfred to return with the rest of her belongings, she said.

He came as Janie and Muriel were fixing their own lunch; they carried it to the sitting room to eat informally there, and they heard Sylvia's high-pitched voice as she let him in.

"Where's my stamp album? You've lost my stamp album, Alfred."

"No, I haven't. I remember putting it into a box."

"Well, I didn't unpack it, and it doesn't seem to be here."

Alfred sighed audibly. "I'll go look in the trunk again, but I'm sure it's here somewhere, Mother."

"And that kit for making an afghan that Louise gave me for my birthday. I don't see that either."

"I've already taken it upstairs. Mother, you said you didn't want to crochet anything more."

"Well, I don't, right now, but I might, later on. Alfred, did you remember to get that little doodad out of the electric plug in the bathroom? So I can run my hair dryer?"

"The adapter. Yes, Mother, I brought it. I put it in your jewelry box so it wouldn't get lost. I put your spare glasses in there, too. Do you want me to help you unpack now?"

"Lord, no," Sylvia told him. "You always make such a mess of things. I'll do it myself. You just get it all up there."

"Unless some of it's unpacked and put away, I don't think it will all fit in the room."

"Well, I'll get to it as soon as I've had some lunch. Did you bring in my groceries?"

"They're in the refrigerator. There's not much space there, Mother, you're going to have to watch how much you buy at one time."

The two of them moved out of hearing range.

Janie laughed. "I don't know whether to be amused or apprehensive about living with a bunch of old people. Alfred's remarkably patient with her, considering how critical she is, don't you think?"

"I'm surprised he wanted her to live with him," Muriel admitted. "Good heavens, there's the doorbell again!"

All Janie could tell through the curtains was that it was a large male figure, possibly in a uniform? She swung the door open and stared up into a face that, with no warning whatever, made her skin prickle.

He was a few years older than she was, maybe twenty-eight or twenty-nine, and he had the clearest blue eyes she'd ever seen. Thick blond hair, and a marvelously muscular body . . . in a police officer's uniform. A police officer?

"Yes, sir?" she asked, puzzled.

He consulted a small notebook he'd taken out of his shirt pocket. "Miss . . . Madison?"

"Yes. I'm Jane Madison. What can I do for you?"

"I'm looking for a little boy, about ten years old. His name's Joe Milos. His grandmother thought he might be here, maybe playing with your brother?"

"Why, he was here, earlier. He and Teddy went to the movies together, quite a while ago. They should be back pretty soon."

Muriel had come to stand behind her, now registering both concern and curiosity.

"Is your brother about twelve? So high?" He gestured with a large, well-shaped hand. "Brown hair, lots of freckles?"

Alarm began to build within her. "Yes. Has something happened to him? To both of them?"

"Not that I know of. I need to talk to them, though. Did they go to the theater on the mall?"

"Yes," Muriel spoke for the first time. "I'm sure that's where they intended to go."

"To the first show? At one o'clock?"

"Yes." Janie's mouth was dry, and a tremor ran through her.

"Do you know how much money they were carrying?"

Muriel responded to that. "Two dollars for the movie ticket, and enough extra for popcorn. Probably about three dollars in all."

"Did you hear the other boy say anything about having more than the price of the movie?"

"No. They didn't mention money at all."

"They wouldn't have had enough to buy popcorn and soda and candy bars, several of them apiece, then, as far as you know?"

Janie felt her mother's hand come to rest on her shoulder. "No, I don't think so."

"What is it? Have they stolen some money or something?" Muriel demanded.

The officer met her gaze squarely. "I think it's more likely they found it. Is there any chance they could have come back here without you knowing it?"

"I suppose it's possible," Janie said slowly. "Teddy's room is in the attic. I'll go up and see. Officer, if they found some money, they aren't in any trouble, are they?"

"If they found it," he told them, "it was at the scene of a murder. It's possible they may have seen something else as well, or picked up something that might be evidence. Do you mind if I check out that attic with you?"

Janie stared at him, unable to speak or move.

A murder? Dear God, she thought, how could Teddy be involved in a murder?

With the greatest effort, she was able to speak. "Yes, of course, officer. Follow me."

This time she wasn't thinking about what she was wearing as she led the man up the stairs.

13

At the last minute the boys had chickened out on calling the police. Teddy was convinced that they must, but Joe argued convincingly against it.

"They weren't busy enough at the Standard station, and they'd remember us. The cops would know where we phoned from, and the manager, he knows who I am."

"I don't think the cops can trace a call right away," Teddy said, though he wasn't actually sure of that. "Besides, what does it matter if the cops know we called? It's what any good citizen is supposed to do, report crimes to the police."

"I can tell you never been mixed up with the cops," Joe said scornfully. "Listen, that musta been *her* money that was blowing around the field. Like, when somebody killed her, her purse fell open and the money fell out, see? And we already spent some of the money."

"We didn't know it belonged to her. And we can give the rest of it back."

"You think they're going to believe we didn't find the purse and take it?"

"Why shouldn't they? It's the truth," Teddy said. "We never saw any purse, only the money."

Joe changed tactics. "If the cops know we found her, they'll come around asking a lot of questions, and the reporters will interview us, and it'll be on TV and in the papers. And the killer will know we were there, man. What if he thinks we saw something, some clue that will lead to him?"

"But we didn't see anything. We don't have any clues."

"How's he going to know that? He'll *think* we might be dangerous, and he'll come after us."

"No, he won't," Teddy said, but he wasn't sure. Not sure enough to risk using the pay phone. "What'll we do, then? The phone at my house is in the front hall. Nobody could use it without being seen."

"Same at my house. So we'll just let somebody else find the body and report it," Joe said.

They walked on past the service station and up Relton Street until there was a place where they could cut back to the alley.

"Where we going to go? Home?" Teddy knew perfectly well that the minute his mother saw his face she was going to be aware that something was wrong. He thought about the dead woman in the deep grass and felt like throwing up again.

"I bet the same guy did it," Joe said. "You know, the one that killed that old woman behind the supermarket. Maybe he's killed lots of people."

"Why would he do that?" Teddy asked, trying to ignore the queasiness. He passed a beer can and didn't bother to kick it down the alley.

"He's crazy, that's why. If you're crazy, you don't need any special reason to do things. That's why we got to be careful, see?"

"What are we going to do, then?" Teddy wasn't usually a follower, but he was out of his depth now.

"Let's go play with the trains some more," Joe suggested. "We can sneak in when nobody's looking, OK?"

It wasn't easy. There were so many people in the house that even though there were two sets of stairs—the ones rising from the front hallway and a narrow, steep set that went up from the hall just off the kitchen—they had to skulk around for some time. At last nobody was in the kitchen and the boys crept up the less-used stairway.

They were safe in the attic, Teddy thought, but he didn't feel safe. And sooner or later he was going to have to face his mother. He wished more and more that he'd had the courage to call the police from the Standard station lot, no matter what Joe had said.

Janie knew immediately that her little brother was guilty of something. It was written all over his open face, where the freckles stood out more starkly than usual.

Joe showed nothing, settling back on his heels, resigned, keeping his feelings well tucked away inside himself.

"This policeman wants to talk to you boys," Janie said, and heard her voice sounding odd and echoing in the big room.

She turned her head then to look at the man behind her and saw that unless he went out into the middle of the area, he couldn't quite stand up under the roof. "Wouldn't it be better to go downstairs, Officer? Where there's a place to sit down? And I think my mother should be present when you talk to Teddy."

"All right," Jeff Carey agreed. "Downstairs it is. Come on, fellas."

Janie led the way down. Nobody said anything until they reached the front parlor. That alone proved to Janie that the boys knew why the man was here, and there was a sick churning in her stomach.

"Let's have everybody sit down," the officer said, and obediently they all sank onto the chintz-covered furniture, though Janie had a strong impulse to stay on her feet, as if by being higher than the others she could maintain some measure of control.

The officer's name tag, pinned to his shirt pocket, said "Carey." He was tall enough so that even sitting down his head was well above everybody else's.

"Now," he said, in a voice that intimidated the boys so that their mouths went flat and they both gripped the edge of the sofa cushions, white knuckled, "let's have some answers." He consulted the little notebook again, more for effect, Janie was sure, than because he couldn't remember what he'd written there.

He ignored the women, and also Mr. Jacoby, who had come to stand in the doorway. "You boys went to the movies this afternoon, right? You walked across the field behind the theater, and you found something. Tell me what you found."

Teddy swallowed hard. He didn't dare look at Joe, or his mother, or Janie. He didn't dare lie either. When Joe didn't immediately speak, Teddy croaked, "At first all we found was the money."

Beside her, Janie felt her mother stiffen; she dropped a hand on

Muriel's shoulder as if to keep her seated in the chair, while Janie perched on the arm of it.

"All right." Carey's voice was deep and intense. "Tell me about the money."

Joe sat stony-faced, and again it was Teddy who replied. "It was blowing around the field. Joe—Joe found a twenty, and I found a ten, and then there was a five-dollar bill and three ones. That's all. We just found it and—picked it up."

Muriel made a small movement as if to speak, and Janie's fingers tightened on her shoulder, holding her silent.

"And you took the money and went to the movies? And bought popcorn, soda, and candy. Right?"

In a courtroom it would have been called leading a witness. Now it was intended to prove to the boys that the officer already knew the truth and wanted to see if they were willing to admit to it, Janie surmised.

She saw Teddy's wild, pleading glance at Joe and his own acceptance of the fact that the policeman was only verifying what he knew to be the facts. There was no point in lying, and Teddy knew it, though Joe's face remained stubbornly impassive.

This time Carey didn't let Teddy continue to carry the entire burden. He addressed Joe directly. "The girl at the candy counter in the theater knows who you are, Joe. She knows you had more money today than usual. Your mother and your grandmother both say you didn't have more than the price of the ticket. Do you still have any of the money, or did you spend it all?"

Slowly, with obvious reluctance on Joe's part, and relief on Teddy's, the boys brought out the remaining cash and put it on the coffee table.

The officer's words were low and firm. "What else did you see in the field, boys?"

"Nothing, before the movie," Teddy said. "Afterward—" His face crumpled, and so did his voice; the brimming tears spilled over. "I got sick, because I'd had too much junk to eat, and I went off the path . . ."

"And what did you find, off the path?"

"Her," Teddy blurted. "A fat woman. There was a fly crawling in and out of her mouth, and we knew she was dead."

Janie's heart constricted, and she felt her mother lurch forward, restrained only by her gripping hand. Janie couldn't hold back Muriel's cry, however.

"Teddy, why didn't you tell us? So we could call the police?"

Officer Carey didn't remonstrate over her outburst, though his glance was eloquent. *Be quiet, or I'll take them away and question them somewhere else, in private.* Janie slid her arm around her mother's shoulders, holding her, trying to draw comfort as well as give it.

"Did you touch her?" Carey asked, now very gently.

Teddy's breath came in a painful gasp. "No! No, no, we didn't touch her!"

"Did you touch anything around her? Pick up anything off the ground near her?"

"No!"

Joe spoke at last, in a raspy small voice. "The glasses. The glasses coulda been hers, I guess."

"What glasses, Joe? What did you do with them?"

The boy had to stand up to remove the frames from his pocket. He handed them over, wordless again. Janie stared at them, beside the money on the table, seeing how they were twisted, the lenses smashed out except for a few remaining traces of glass around the edges.

"Did you see a purse? Anything like that?"

Both boys shook their heads. Teddy was cracking under the strain, tears running freely, silently. He swiped at his nose and Muriel passed him a tissue, into which he blew loudly.

Joe's voice was louder. "We didn't have nothing to do with killing her."

Carey's mouth twitched and Janie felt something indescribable twist within her. "I never thought you did. But you should have called the police, you know."

The words tumbled out of Joe then: his defense, his fear of the killer, his justification for concealing his knowledge. "Are they going to put my name in the paper? So he'll know where I live?"

"No. I'll have to have a statement from you, though, for our records. From each of you. I'm going to ask your mother"—he lifted his head and looked straight at Janie then—"or your sister, to bring you into headquarters, where you can tell a stenographer exactly what happened, and when it's been typed up, you can sign it. OK?"

There was a barely perceptible tremor in Joe's question. "You ain't gonna arrest us?"

"No. We don't arrest witnesses, Joe. Only if they tamper with the evidence. You picked up the money before you knew there'd been a murder committed, but I don't think you meant to conceal evidence, did you?"

The boys both shook their heads vigorously.

Carey looked at Janie again. "I wonder if I could trouble you for an envelope, Miss Madison? To put the evidence into?"

His gaze held hers, and something sparked between them. Or was it only within herself?

Janie stood up, murmuring compliance. Mr. Jacoby swiveled to follow her into the dining room, watching as she sorted through the odds and ends for the envelopes.

"If you need a lawyer," he said, "my son-in-law's one. An ass in every other way, but a good lawyer."

Janie thanked him with a smile. "I don't think we'll need one, but I'll remember."

"Myron Civen," he said. "He's in the book. Civen, Schuster, and Civen."

Sylvia and Alfred Bonnard had just come down the stairs and were staring through the doorway at the police officer.

"Is something wrong?" Sylvia's words were shrill.

Janie passed them without comment, correctly guessing that Mr. Jacoby, behind her, would be happy to explain. She handed over the envelope and watched Carey seal the items in it, then label it and put it into his shirt pocket.

"Can you have Teddy at headquarters first thing in the morning, Miss Madison?"

He was going to leave. Teddy was in no immediate peril, except possibly from Muriel when she got him alone. Janie instinctively sought some way to keep this man here a little longer, and came up with nothing that wouldn't have sounded inane and contrived. She said only, "Thank you, officer. I'll have him there."

News had already traveled through the house. They were all there, the renters, except for Ernie Layton. Bea's query was undoubtedly in every mind.

"Is it true? Has there been another murder? In our neighborhood?"

For a moment it seemed he would not answer. Then he told her quietly, "I'm afraid so, ma'am."

"Who?" Neva Minor asked. "It isn't someone we know, is it?"

Again Carey hesitated. The police did not, as a rule, give out such information. Janie didn't know that she herself was the catalyst, his reason for delaying. Hell, he thought, the information would be on the evening news, and again in tomorrow's paper. What difference did it make if they knew it now?

And it had happened in their neighborhood, where they had to go on living. They had reason to want to protect themselves.

"She's been identified. Her husband called in to report her missing this morning, when she hadn't come home all night, so we had a description. A man walking his dog found the body, probably only minutes after Joe and Teddy saw it, and called in. No official ID had been made when I left the scene, but there isn't much doubt about it." He didn't have to consult the notebook this time. "She's a Mrs. Cora Cottler, lived on Fir Street."

Nobody, least of all Jeff Carey, expected the reaction he got to the name. Sylvia Bonnard gasped and pressed a hand to her narrow chest. "Why, that's . . . that's . . ." She turned to stare wildly at her son.

Alfred, too, appeared in a state of shock. "Mrs. Cottler? My God, it can't be!"

Jeff, poised to go, waited. "You know her, sir?"

"God, yes! She's my landlady! I talked to her day before yesterday when she came out to collect the rent! I live in a garage apartment behind their house. Oh my God, I don't believe it."

Jeff took the notebook out again. "May I have your name, sir?"

"Bonnard. Alfred Bonnard. My address is the same as hers, only I put a half on the end of the street number. Herb, does he know yet?"

"Her husband has been called to identify the body, yes, sir. How long have you known the Cottlers, sir?"

Alfred was dazed, stunned. "I don't know. How long have I lived there, Mother? Two years? Something like that. How was she killed? Are you allowed to tell us that?"

That, too, would be public knowledge in a matter of hours. "She was shot," Jeff said. "Did you know the Cottlers well, sir?"

"Well, I didn't socialize with them or anything like that. I visited with Herb sometimes when he was working around the backyard or fixing something in my apartment. We didn't have much in common, really. I don't know anything about driving a bus, and he doesn't know anything about accounting. I'm an accountant. He's a nice enough guy, though."

"And Mrs. Cottler? Did you see any more of her?"

"Yes, certainly, she was there all the time. Until he retired recently Herb was gone a lot." Alfred produced a handkerchief and wiped his face with it. "God, I can't believe it. She wasn't a woman I *liked,* exactly. I mean, she and Herb argued a lot, when he was around, and I didn't care to be drawn into any of *that,* but she was pleasant enough to me except when I complained about something. The wiring isn't as good as it ought to be—I think Herb did it himself, and he's no electrician—and if I tried to use my coffee pot and my toaster at the same time, it would blow fuses. Well, no, that circuit breaker thing, so somebody'd have to go out and reset it, and I told her it was quite inconvenient not to be able to make coffee and toast at the same time."

He was distraught, and when Bea appeared at his elbow with a glass of what Janie recognized as Uncle Addison's apricot brandy, he accepted it and drank it without seeming to realize what it was.

Jeff Carey still had his notebook in hand. "How did Mrs. Cottler react to your complaints, sir?"

He wiped his face again and put the crumpled handkerchief back into his pocket. "She made it plain that if I wasn't satisfied, I could move. Plenty of people looking for an inexpensive place, she said. Which is true. It's the reason I stayed there, though I'd been looking at two-bedroom places recently, in case Mother wanted to move in with me. Before she decided to come here, that was."

"What would you say the Cottlers' relationship was, sir? Would you say they didn't get along well? Argued a lot, you said?"

Alfred gave the others a stricken look. "Good God, I didn't mean to suggest that he did her in, or anything like that! Oh, Lord, no! Herb would never—I mean, they squabbled, like so many couples do, but I'm sure they were actually devoted to each other! There's no reason to suspect *Herb,* is there?"

Jeff Carey wrote something in the notebook and closed it. "No, sir, not that I know of. Someone from the Homicide Division may be in touch with you, sir, since you did know the victim."

Alfred swallowed. "Yes, of course." He blinked and turned to Bea, who stood with hands clenched together at her breast. "Mrs. Stone, do you by any chance have any more of that brandy?"

"I'll be going now," Carey said, and Janie opened the door for him, then stepped out onto the porch and pulled the door closed behind them.

"Officer—Carey, is it?"

His smile, his full smile, was blinding. "That's right. Jeff Carey."

"Ah—" For a moment she had forgotten what she intended to say. Surely Molly hadn't felt like this when she'd met Clyde. She couldn't possibly have kept quiet about it if that had been the case. Janie touched the porch rail for support. "Teddy and Joe aren't in any real trouble, are they?"

"No, I wouldn't think so. But it doesn't hurt to impress on them that when they discover a crime, they notify the proper authorities."

"Yes, of course. I don't suppose you'll be there, when I take Teddy in to make his official statement?"

"No. I don't spend much time in the office except doing paper work. As a matter of fact, I'm off duty tomorrow, except for making a court appearance in the morning. Should be free by noon. Would you by any chance be interested in taking a ride with me? I have some papers to file on Whidbey Island, so it'll mean taking the ferry."

"Why, that would be very nice. Thank you."

The grin widened. "Good. I'll be here by twelve-thirty, one at the latest. We can picnic on the ferry, OK?"

"OK," Janie agreed. "I'll see you tomorrow."

He started down the walk, then paused to look back. "Are you running a rest home here, or what?"

"No. My aunt lived here, and my uncle left the house to me, and it's so big, we decided to rent out the extra rooms. Most of the people who've moved in are friends of Aunt Bea's."

"Oh. I wondered. Sounds interesting." He was gone then, and Janie returned to the house, bemused.

Unless she was badly mistaken, she'd said good-bye to Harry just in time.

14

Whatever words were exchanged between Muriel and Teddy were said in private. Janie was just as glad; a glance at Teddy's face before he went up to the attic evoked her sympathy, though she knew her mother would not have been unfair or unduly harsh.

Imagine Teddy finding a murder victim. That alone was extremely unsettling. And then to have him keep money he'd guessed must have belonged to the dead woman, and *told no one about it*—it was incomprehensible.

For the first time Janie gave some serious thought to what it was going to be like for Teddy, growing up without a father, without a strong male figure in his life. There weren't even any uncles or adult cousins who might have stepped in to fill his father's shoes.

For some reason, that led to thoughts of Jeff Carey. Janie settled down again, for the tenth time, it seemed, to perusal of the Help Wanted ads in the Sunday paper; Jeff's smile swam in front of her eyes instead of the fine print.

She had just circled an ad—*Secretary wanted, small office, heavy typing, salary based on experience*—when it dawned on her that she had to take Teddy to the police station in the morning, and that she'd promised to go off with Jeff Carey in the afternoon. When was she going to go job hunting?

She didn't know how to get hold of him to cancel the date. When she'd thought about it for a few seconds, she knew she had no intention of doing it. No, the job hunting would have to wait. Maybe if it didn't take long at the police station, she'd have time to talk to some of the people on the mall and see if there were any employment possibilities there.

As she thought about the mall, though, Janie frowned. The first body had been discovered in the alley behind a supermarket there;

now there had been another one, behind the theater. Both places where boys might legitimately have walked or played. What if they'd happened on the scene when the murderer was there?

She'd never before lived in a neighborhood where murders were committed. Aunt Bea had actually known the first woman, at least by sight, and now this one was someone Alfred Bonnard knew. It gave her a most uncomfortable feeling.

Janie gave up on the want ads and flipped to the news section. On the third page she stopped, and a peculiar sensation crept through her, something close to horror.

There were two sketches by a police artist, with the caption below: *DO YOU KNOW THESE WOMEN? Two victims of recent violence remain unidentified, and authorities seek the assistance of the public. Anyone knowing either of these women should contact Lt. Zazorian at the local police department.*

There followed a brief summary of the circumstances under which the victims had been found, and where.

Janie read the item several times, her mind riveted on those addresses. Unless she was mistaken, both bodies had been discovered within a few miles of this house.

Feeling considerably disturbed, she rose and carried the paper into the dining room. The old people were gathered around the big table, enjoying Aunt Bea's latest treat: chocolate cake with chocolate frosting.

"Would you like a piece of cake, dear?" Bea asked, looking up with a smile. Not even her preoccupation with the newspaper article kept Janie from realizing that Bea seemed younger, brighter, and more vivacious since her home had been turned into what almost amounted to a three-ring circus.

"It looks good. Aunt Bea, did you see this in today's paper? Aren't these areas close to here?"

"Goodness, I never got around to the paper, so much going on," Bea said, craning to see the story as Janie laid the paper beside her on the table. "Oh my stars! Neva, look at this! Isn't this the woman who came to bingo a couple of times? Remember, she won a box of groceries? She sat all by herself and didn't talk to anybody."

Neva rose from her chair to bend over Bea's shoulder, and Charlie Silvers asked from across the table, "What's she in the paper for?"

"It looks like the same one. I don't recognize the other one," Neva said.

Bea answered Charlie. "She was murdered. Two pictures, both of them women who were shot and killed."

"Near here?" Janie persisted.

"Yes. Yes, both of them quite near here," Bea confirmed. "Why do you suppose they have drawings instead of photos of them? It's hard to be sure if it's the same person, in a drawing."

Charlie lumbered, wheezing, around to where he could see the paper. "Probably because they didn't look so nice after they were shot, and the artist could try to make them look the way they did when they were alive. Sure, that one's only about seven, eight blocks away. The other's a couple of miles, maybe."

Janie hardly recognized her own voice. "That makes four, then. Four murders, in a little over a week, all within a few miles of this house."

She saw the uneasiness, the beginning of fear, creep over all their faces, and guessed it mirrored her own. "Old women," Mr. Jacoby said. "All of them old women."

Sylvia Bonnard's voice was squeaky. "Cora Cottler wasn't so old. Sixtyish, maybe, though she claimed to be younger. There must be a madman loose!"

Neva sat back down and cut off a piece of cake with her fork. "I wonder if we should call the police?" she asked thoughtfully.

"What for?" Charlie wanted to know. "Anybody know her name? The one you said came to bingo?" He studied the sketch, then shook his head. "I don't remember anybody looked like either one of 'em."

"Well, we *saw* that one," Bea said.

"They want somebody to identify her. Tell them who she is. Was. Where she lived. Who her family is, that kind of thing. We don't any of us know that, do we?"

Nobody did. The paper was passed along so that the others could study it. Only Bea and Neva recalled the first victim; none of them recognized the second one.

Only they weren't the first and second, Janie thought. They were the second and third, and Alfred's landlady today was the fourth.

What had they done, bringing their family here?

The fact that all four victims had been elderly was not reassuring.

Anyone who would kill old women would kill anyone else, if it suited his purpose.

What *was* his purpose? Janie wondered. Except for Mrs. Cottler, none of them had had any money, from the sound of it, although she knew plenty of people had been robbed for no more than small change.

Sylvia Bonnard shivered. "I'm glad I moved in here," she said. "I was afraid, after my sister Maude went to the rest home. Somebody tried to break in one night last week, did I tell you that?"

Apparently, she hadn't. "No, of course not—I didn't get to bingo last week, that's why. It was Tuesday night I woke up and heard someone prying off a screen. Terrified me, I can tell you. I tried to call Alfred, but his line was busy, so I called the police. They sent a car around right away, shined a spotlight on the house. Whoever it was went away, of course. The officer came to the door, and I made him show me his identification before I opened it. He walked around the house and didn't see anything. Told me to go back to bed. As if a person could sleep, after that!"

"What did you do, then?" Neva asked, scraping the last of the frosting off her plate.

"I sat up in my chair, praying he wouldn't come back, whoever he was. When I finally got hold of Alfred, he was most annoyed with me, waking him up. Said to go back to sleep, just like the police officer. It was losing my rest that made me susceptible to the cold, I know. I had the worst cold the next day, and I wasn't up to going to bingo. So I didn't tell any of you."

"Take extra vitamin C," Neva suggested, "when you're overtired or under stress. It'll keep you from getting colds and flu."

"Anyway," Sylvia said, "I knew I couldn't stay alone there. I'd never sleep again, waiting to hear that sound at the window. Alfred said I could move in with him, if I wanted him to find a bigger place, but I told him no." She sighed deeply and took a bite of cake. "Alfred means well, but he's such a . . . a *klutz*. He breaks things, loses things. Heaven knows what he'll be like by the time he's *my* age."

Bea was still thinking about the murder victim. "Maybe we ought to tell the police where we saw that woman. Someone else there might know who she is."

Charlie had returned to his chair and was finishing his cake, too.

"You said she didn't seem to know anybody. So why do you think anybody would know who she was?"

"Well, maybe they wouldn't," Bea admitted. "But it might be a clue, that she was there. Maybe the police could get something out of it. What do you think, dear?" She looked at Janie.

"I'm seeing Officer Carey tomorrow afternoon," she said without thinking. "I'll tell him and see what he says."

"Oh, are you?" Bea beamed at her. "How nice. Such a good-looking young man, isn't he?"

Unexpectedly, Mr. Jacoby winked at Janie. "Has good taste, too."

That made her smile a little, and she accepted the generous slice of cake Bea cut for her and carried it back to the parlor. Nothing could take that feeling away, however. The fear that in moving here they had somehow exposed themselves to danger, a danger that might touch their lives in a far more concrete way than Teddy's finding one of the murder victims.

Janie came down early the next morning, having allowed for extra time in order to deal with the anticipated chaos in the kitchen. It didn't develop.

Aunt Bea was there before her, stirring something in a big bowl, which she then put into the microwave. She wore an apron over her dress, and she was smiling. "Good morning, dear. The rest of us are having oatmeal and toast. Would you like some?"

"Sounds good. Only how are we going to keep track of who pays for what? Whose oatmeal is it?"

"Addison's," Bea said cheerfully. "We talked last night, after you'd gone, about the meal situation here. All of us stepping on each other, trying to cook something different, having to wash out pans so the next person can cook, and how to keep everybody's groceries in the refrigerator at one time. We decided to chip in to pay for things. If you and your mother want to join us, you're welcome. Or we'll understand if you'd rather not." Bea brought out a big pitcher of orange juice and began to take down glasses. "I'm rather a good cook, you know. I'm getting forgetful, but I haven't forgotten how to cook. I suppose that's the main reason Addison kept me here, because he liked my cooking. And the free housekeeping that went with it. He liked things nice, but he didn't want to do any of the work himself, nor pay anybody to do it either."

"What's in the microwave?" Janie asked, peering through the door into the lighted interior, where the bowl was covered with a sheet of waxed paper.

"That's the oatmeal. Isn't that a nifty way to cook it? Never burns, Neva says. When the bell rings, stir it again, and then in another few minutes it should be done. Oh, we thought a sensible way to handle the coffee would be if everybody put a dime in that can when he has a cup, and then we'll use the money to buy more coffee. Otherwise, everybody'll have to make his own, or use instant. What do you think?"

"Very sensible," Janie said. She poured coffee and was carrying it to the table when Muriel appeared, looking sleepy.

"Here, take this and I'll get myself another one," Janie said, handing over the cup. "Is Teddy up yet? I wanted to get that business over with as soon as possible so I can check out a few places for jobs."

"He's brushing his teeth. I was so upset with him yesterday, Janie. I hope I got through to him how wrong he was not to report both the money and the body immediately. He'll have to have a note for school, I suppose, since he's going to be late. Or maybe we should just wait and let him start tomorrow; in a new school, that probably won't make much difference."

It hadn't occurred to Janie that Teddy might be home the rest of the day, after he'd signed his statement. "Will he be OK here, do you think? I feel sort of funny, expecting our renters to be sitters, but I . . . I've made other plans."

"I doubt that he'll get into any more trouble for a while. I'll tell him he's to stay in the house today, if Aunt Bea doesn't mind."

They all ate together—microwaved oatmeal, toast with jam—and Bea brought out some watermelon-rind preserves which everybody exclaimed over. "The secret is lots of lemon rind along with the melon," she said, pleased.

Charlie Silvers leaned forward to examine the tray in front of Neva's plate. It held a multitude of small glass containers, each filled with pills or capsules.

"What's that? The pharmaceutical department?" he asked.

"Vitamins and minerals. Been taking them for years," Neva said. She began to count them out, one or two from each container.

"I'm surprised you need to eat," Charlie said. "Expensive, aren't they? So many of them?"

"Not as expensive as doctor bills," Neva told him complacently. "I've only been to a doctor once since I started taking them, almost ten years ago. And that was for gallbladder trouble, which I'd had for years until they took it out."

"Regular geriatrics ward we got here," Mr. Jacoby said, putting sugar on his oatmeal. "I hope it doesn't get to be too much for you young people, broken down old hulks that we are, limping around with our arthritis and our weak kidneys."

"You have arthritis?" Neva asked sharply. "You ever tried zinc for it?"

"Zinc?" Mr. Jacoby gazed at her with raised eyebrows. "What's zinc got to do with arthritis? I take some pills the doctor gave me for it."

"Does it stop the pain? Relieve the stiffness?"

"Not very well," Mr. Jacoby admitted.

"Then try zinc." Neva opened one of the jars and passed him two tablets. "They did a study at the University of Washington several years ago. Showed that in many cases, eighty to a hundred milligrams of zinc a day would stop arthritis. Doesn't cure it, mind, if you stop taking the zinc it comes back, but you'll feel a hundred percent better with this. Get some next time you're at the drugstore."

Mr. Jacoby shrugged, and swallowed the tablets with his juice. "What have I got to lose?" he said.

"I'll clear away the table," Bea offered when Muriel and Janie rose with their dishes. "I don't mind, really. Go on to work and don't worry about it."

On their way out a few minutes later, Muriel was thoughtful. "This may work out well for all of us, if too many problems don't develop. If it makes Aunt Bea feel she's earning her way in our house to cook and do dishes, let's let her do it. I only hope"—and she broke into laughter—"that it doesn't really turn into a geriatrics unit. So that we end up running a rest home instead of a rooming house."

"If Mrs. Minor fills everybody up on vitamins and minerals," Janie predicted, "we shouldn't have any trouble at all."

She didn't know why she hadn't mentioned to her mother that she had made a date with Jeff Carey. She didn't mention it to Teddy either. To her relief his statement was taken in routine fashion, and Teddy signed it; they were free to go by the time school started. She left him there in the principal's office, to be introduced to his new teacher. Though she sympathized with him in hating to change schools, she didn't voice this; let him stew for a day or two in the realization that he'd transgressed, and the impression would be a more lasting one, she decided. If feeling alone right now deepened the impression, so much the better.

There were about twenty-five businesses on the mini-mall, excluding the theater and Tilly's. Methodically, Janie began to make the rounds, speaking to the owner/manager in each. Most were small establishments, one-girl-office places, and she was met with head shakes at once. Not hiring, sorry.

In a tiny insurance office tucked away at the far end of the mall, she finally struck pay dirt. The door stood open, allowing the occupant to take advantage of the fine warm day. Inside, a sweating, red-faced man rose from his seat before a word processor screen to greet her across the counter. "Yes, ma'am, what can I do for you?"

He sounded harassed and irritable, but Janie decided to try anyway. "I'm looking for work," she said frankly. "I've worked for an insurance company, I'm an excellent typist, and I know about—"

He interrupted her. "You know anything about those damned things? Computers?"

Janie craned around him to see it. "Well, the one I used wasn't that brand, but it was similar, I think. Yes, I can operate a word processor."

The color flamed deeper in his face, then subsided. "Come around here and show me," he invited.

Twenty minutes later, feeling stunned, she had a job.

15

His name was Harold Weinberger. He ran a one-man insurance business, and he'd only recently moved into this new office. He had hired a secretary who suited him so admirably that when she introduced him to the wonders of word processing, he had made what he considered a stupendous investment to buy "one of the damned things."

It had only become a "damned thing" when something happened to the young lady trained to operate it.

"Run over by a bus, can you imagine, when she was crossing the street. She says the light was green; the bus driver says *he* had the green, and the passengers were apparently all blind. At any rate, my secretary is in the hospital with a fractured pelvis. So here I am, with a twelve-thousand-dollar machine I can put things into but can't get them back out of. A typewriter I could manage, but this confounded thing . . ." He glared at it. "Diane said she'd never use the typewriter, so I got rid of that, fool that I was."

"It's a very good machine," Janie told him. "In the other office where I worked, it nearly doubled production."

He had thick, shaggy eyebrows jutting over blue eyes. "It would be only a temporary position, you understand. Until Diane is out of the hospital and able to return to work. Several months, they think."

"I understand. Would you allow me to continue to look for permanent work? With the assurance, of course, that I wouldn't leave here until Diane comes back?"

He considered that. "I guess so. When can you start?"

Janie thought of Jeff Carey and the promised ferry-ride picnic. "Tomorrow?"

From his expression she judged that he'd have preferred her to say "Now" and sit down before the computer screen at once.

"I have some other business to take care of this afternoon," she said. "I could be here at eight in the morning, though."

"Don't open until nine," he said. "Same salary as I give Diane, all right?"

He didn't say what it was, and Janie didn't quibble. A job was a job, and since it was temporary, why make a fuss? It was within walking distance of home, and it would give her a breather to find something permanent.

She walked home feeling elated. Now she could fully enjoy the time with Jeff Carey without guilt.

Ernie Layton was about to ring the bell for admittance when she climbed the front steps. He turned and smiled in his shy way.

"Oh, I got more keys made. Here"—she thrust one at him—"you can have that one, and I'll pass out the rest to everyone else."

"Thank you." He unlocked the door and stood aside for her to enter first.

"Home for lunch?" she asked, making conversation. "Do you work in the neighborhood?"

She thought he hesitated. "Uh, yes. Excuse me, I want to get rid of this jacket. It was cool when I left this morning."

He was gone, running lightly up the stairs.

She followed him at a slower pace, trying to decide what would be appropriate for a ferry ride. She'd looked terrible yesterday when she met Jeff Carey, in those worn-out jeans and sweatshirt. Yet it would be going too far the other way to dress up for a ride out to Whidbey Island.

She took a quick shower, noting wryly that late morning was a good time; the water was gratifyingly hot. Jeans again, she decided, inspecting her choices, only relatively new ones this time. And a white terry pullover with pale blue trim. Muriel had a light blue zip-front sweatshirt, too, that was almost new; Janie borrowed that and inspected herself in the full-length mirror they'd attached to the back of her bedroom door.

It would be a beautiful day on the water. She stood for a moment looking out the window into the tangled jungle of the backyard, wondering if Teddy was mature enough to be put to work taking a little of the wildness out of it. Maybe if she paid him to do it, he wouldn't mind. He could perhaps get Joe to help him, only she wasn't sure she wanted to encourage *that* relationship after the way things had turned out yesterday.

No, she amended, that wasn't fair. She couldn't blame Joe for the fact that Teddy hadn't used his own judgment. It sounded as if Joe had had an unfortunate experience with the police at some time; he looked underfed and not too well dressed, so maybe the child had stolen something he wanted badly. She could see the boy's logic, to some extent. The money *had* been blowing around loose in the field, and though they'd realized it must belong to the murdered woman, it was clear *she* couldn't use it.

No, instead of keeping Teddy away from a boy who might be a bad influence, it might be better to try to use Teddy as a positive influence on Joe. Influencing could work both ways, after all.

Her gaze rested on the manuscript box beside her typewriter. It would have to wait just a little longer, she thought. If only she could use a computer to write it, how much faster and easier it would be!

She turned and went down the stairs in time to answer Jeff Carey's ring.

It hadn't been a mirage. The magic was there, for Janie anyway, and she thought with soaring spirits that it was there for Jeff, too.

They were comfortable together. They didn't have any trouble finding things to talk about. Yet they didn't feel the need to talk all the time. Silence was comfortable, too.

He wasn't in uniform, of course. Like Janie, he wore jeans and a plaid shirt with a red nylon Windbreaker and blue and white Adidas.

He looked at her shoes. "You run?"

"A little. I haven't, since we moved, at all. I'm not sure it's safe in that neighborhood." She shivered a little, sinking into the deep wine-red upholstery of his two-year-old Granada. It was a beautiful car, white with a wine-red top, and he'd taken loving care of it. "There have been four murders within a few miles of us in only about a week! I've just gotten a job on the mall, and now I'm wondering if it's safe to walk back and forth to work, let alone go running alone."

"I'll run with you," Jeff offered, "when I can. OK?"

Warmth pushed back the fear she'd allowed herself to feel. "Sure. You work days mostly?"

"Well, I have been. Will be for another week, and then I'll go to swing shift for a month. I'm supposed to have two days off a week, but they usually turn out like this one. A court appearance this morning, and papers to deliver to the courthouse in Island County in the afternoon." He drove easily, glancing at her with a grin.

"I don't often luck out and have a pretty girl for company."

She grinned back, acknowledging the compliment. "That's not much of a day off. You don't get paid for going to court?"

"Not on my day off." He surveyed the heavy traffic as he swung onto the freeway. "Times like this I miss my patrol car. The siren and the blue lights cut right through this congestion."

Janie twisted in the seat so that she could watch him. She liked his profile, strong nose and chin, wide, expressive mouth. She liked his hands, too, so competent on the wheel. Something about his hands set up that sensation within her again, and she let it grow, enjoying the anticipation. Good-bye, Harry! she thought. Enjoy Alaska! Find a nice girl up there who'll send shivers through you.

As if reading her mind, he asked, "You don't have a steady boyfriend?"

"He left for Alaska this past weekend. I mean, it was about to become nonsteady anyway."

Jeff nodded, flipped the turn signal, and pulled around a logging truck probably heading for one of the mills in Everett. "Good."

He glanced at her then, and they both laughed.

There was nothing special about the day, except that they spent it together. They boarded the ferry *Cathlamet* in Mukilteo and spent the quarter-hour ride across the sound standing on the bow with the wind in their faces, eating hamburgers and drinking hot cider. It was glorious on the water, sparkling blue and dotted with sailboats and occasional fishing vessels. To the east Mt. Pilchuck and Three Fingers reared snowcapped peaks; to the west, on the peninsula, the Olympics provided a spectacular backdrop to their passage.

Janie wouldn't have minded if they'd spent hours on the water, though the wind was cold enough to cut through her sweatshirt. She felt more alive than she had in a long time. Since her father's death, she suddenly realized. She sneaked a sidelong glance at her companion, now coping with a leaky hamburger, and wondered what sort of influence Jeff would be on Teddy.

Good, was the immediate reaction. Very good.

Inevitably, the subject of the murders came up. "Do you think they're connected?" Janie asked. "I mean, were they all done by the same person?"

His hesitation was imperceptible. "Yes. Ballistics report says three of them were killed by the same weapon. A .25 caliber Italian gun, a Beretta. The fourth victim didn't die where she was shot, and the bullet passed through her body; it wasn't recovered. Lieutenant Zazorian, in the Homicide Division, is assuming all four murders were committed by the same assailant."

"Do you think . . . will you get him? Before he kills again?"

Jeff tossed a bit of hamburger bun over the side, where it was caught by an enterprising gull before it hit the water. "We'll get him. God only knows when, though. It's the most difficult kind of killer to catch, one who kills at random. So far, we don't find anything the women all had in common; the first three were derelicts, no real homes, scavenging for food. The last one had a decent home, was respectable."

She remembered then. "Aunt Bea had seen one of the women whose pictures were in yesterday's paper. Mrs. Minor remembered seeing her, too, at a bingo game. They play every Wednesday at St. Andrew's. The others didn't remember the woman, and Aunt Bea said she didn't talk to anybody. She won a box of groceries, though, so maybe the priest would remember something about her. They talked about calling the police but decided against it, since none of them really knew her. I guess she only came to bingo once or twice."

"That right? I'll pass that along to Homicide. God knows they don't have many clues so far, from what I've heard. If there's any kind of common thread, it gives them something to go on, somewhere to look. Right now it sounds like some psycho who gets his kicks shooting old women."

Janie was subdued. "But who knows when he'll decide to shoot somebody else. Nobody's really safe until he's caught, are they." It wasn't a question; she knew the answer.

"One thing about psychos," Jeff offered, draining the cider that had cooled to lukewarm, "a lot of them really want to be caught. To be stopped. So sometimes they start leaving clues so somebody will catch up to them. Anonymous calls to the police or to newspapers, things like that. Or notes left at the scene of the crime. Something to tantalize the cops, dangle a little bait in front of them, daring them to figure out who he is."

"Only until that happens, he may keep on killing," Janie speculated.

"Yeah," Jeff agreed softly. "He may. I'm still hungry. You want one of those big chocolate-frosted doughnuts? I'll go get a couple."

They disembarked in Clinton and climbed the hill on the road going up-island. Whidbey was the largest island in the sound, being sixty miles long and up to fifteen miles wide; Janie wouldn't have cared if it had taken them the rest of the day to carry out Jeff's task. She enjoyed driving between stands of dark evergreens, watching for glimpses of bright blue water.

Most of all, of course, she enjoyed Jeff's company. She was sorry when it was time to go home.

16

At the promise of fifty cents an hour (after Joe's initial protest that it was well below the minimum wage), Teddy and Joe agreed to tackle the backyard. Janie and Muriel worked with them the first evening, pointing out what needed to be done. They decided that pruning a hedge was beyond the capabilities of boys their age, although they could hack at the incredible growth to some extent before the final shaping was done.

There was a lawnmower in the basement, an ancient contrivance without a motor on it; the grass proved too tough for it until they'd gone over it once with a scythe (also from the basement, obviously before Addison Hamer's time) to bring it down to manageable height.

Luckily, there was only one scythe, or the boys would have been doing battle; Janie allowed Teddy to use it only when he was alone, and then felt she had to supervise to keep him from getting carried away with it. At first, the blade was rather dull, but Charlie Silvers sharpened it for them, then sat on the back steps to give good-natured advice.

It was Joe who discovered the real treasure, which made both of them work harder on the promise that when they'd finished the job, they could take it over as a clubhouse.

"A tree house, Janie! You ought to see it! It's big enough for both of us to sleep in at once, and it's got a roof and windows, and there's boards for a ladder, going up that big maple tree!"

The tree house must have been there for years, undiscovered by the occupants of the house as the brush and foliage grew around it in a concealing curtain. When sufficient trimming had been done to make it feasible, Janie climbed the ladder behind the boys, smiling at their excited chatter, to see it for herself.

"Isn't this neat?" Teddy demanded. "It's practically hidden from everybody, but it's easy to get to now. Can we sleep out here?"

Janie withheld a commitment on that until she'd examined the structure more closely. As far as she could tell, it was well made and secure. Having tested her own weight on the ladder, she tested the floor of the house, finding it to be solid.

"I don't see why not," she agreed finally, "if it's all right with Mom. After you get the yard in shape, naturally."

It spurred them on. Joe came over after school (which meant that it took twice as much in the way of fruit and sandwiches to enable the work to continue until mealtime) to help, and they worked until suppertime, and then for another hour or so afterward. "On the weekend, we'll work all day," Teddy promised, "and then maybe by Saturday night we can sleep out here."

While the boys struggled with the yard, Janie and Muriel undertook essential changes inside the house. In relief that Janie had hardly missed a paycheck, they sold Uncle Addison's old-fashioned jewelry, and with the proceeds they replaced the water heater with one of commercial size.

They got three estimates for the installation of a new furnace. The prices were a shock, but all the estimators assured them that they'd be lucky if the present heating system held up through the summer, let alone another winter. (Puget Sound summers have been known to be so chilly that morning and evening heat are welcome.)

They told the lowest bidder to go ahead and install a new furnace; Janie winced as she wrote out the deposit check. And then, since there was a little money left over, they bought a dishwasher.

"It's funny," Muriel said, "the first time we came into this place I thought it was gloomy and sort of depressing. It's amazing how much it's changed. It feels . . . spacious and comfortable to me now."

"We've opened it up and let in sunshine and fresh air," Janie pointed out. "We have books and papers around, and people. It may be the people, more than anything else. Listen to them in there."

As if on cue, there was a burst of hilarity from the dining room.

"I think they're getting the hang of poker," Muriel observed dryly. "Teddy asked if he could learn, too."

Janie laughed. "What did you tell him?"

"I had to think about it. I don't want him to gamble, but your father used to play poker sometimes. So I said he could play, as long as they're using matches for money."

Her tone changed so that Janie looked at her sharply. There were tears in Muriel's eyes. "I miss him so, Janie. It's nearly a year, and I still miss him terribly."

Janie reached out to cover her mother's hand with her own. "I know."

Muriel swallowed. "I worry about Teddy, growing up without a father. Isn't it odd? A man can raise a girl pretty well by himself, but a woman can't raise a boy alone. A boy needs to learn a man's attitudes, a man's way of looking at things, that he just can't get from a household of females. Teddy's coming to the age right now where he needs a man the most, and there isn't one."

"I thought about that, too. When I went out to Whidbey with Jeff Carey the other day. He'd be a good influence on Teddy."

Muriel had been told about the excursion, though Janie hadn't placed any undue emphasis on it. Now Muriel scrutinized her more carefully.

"He's nice, isn't he?"

"Very nice," Janie agreed, and felt a hint of warmth in her face which she knew Muriel would correctly interpret. "We're going jogging together tomorrow morning."

"Before you go to work?" Muriel asked, eyebrows rising. "He *must* be nice! I've never known you to get up early for anything short of a fire."

Janie's mouth twisted into a grin. "He is sort of kindling a fire, at that."

It made her feel good, that she could talk to her mother this way, could find understanding and support, as if Muriel were another girl friend, not her mother.

She wished she knew some way to make her mother get out and have some kind of social life, or that one of the renters was of the right age to be of interest to Muriel. Nobody would ever take her father's place, Janie thought, but there might be someone who could ease the loneliness.

Look at all those old people over there, she thought. All of them had been married at one time, except maybe Charlie Silvers, who'd never mentioned a wife. All of them had lost their mates through death. They were far older than Muriel, and none had remarried, and they'd been lonesome, too. They assuaged that emptiness with welcome companionship, and Janie hoped that her mother would find contentment again, somewhere, somehow.

They ran for half an hour on Wednesday morning; Jeff was due in court at nine, and he had to allow time to go home for a shower first, or they'd have made it an hour.

Janie luxuriated in a long shower of her own, as hot as she could stand it, then cooling to tepid before she turned the water off. The new water heater was worth the exorbitant price.

She'd had one day on the job and had only seen Mr. Weinberger for ten minutes in the morning and five minutes more at quitting time. There was plenty of work to do, most of it scribbled in his cramped hand that would have been difficult to decipher if she hadn't already known much of the information needed to fill in the blanks on the forms; he did take pains to print names and addresses.

It didn't take long to familiarize herself with the computer; it was only slightly different from the one at Zeller and Markham and in some ways simpler to operate.

At the end of the first day, Mr. Weinberger handed her a key to the front door, resting an elbow on the stack of forms she'd completed during his absence. "I'll be working awhile tonight. I'll leave stuff on my desk for you to do in the morning," he said. "I have a meeting, may not be in before eleven or so."

Janie stared at the key in her hand. "Are you sure you want to hand over a key to a stranger?" she asked.

He made a snorting sound. "You think I would, without checking on you? I may be a fool, but I'm not a *damned* fool. I talked to your former boss, Mr. Zeller."

Janie felt the heat in her face. "Oh. What did he say?"

Mr. Weinberger's blue eyes were discerning. "He said you were one of the best workers he'd ever had. Honest, trustworthy, dependable, and capable. In fact, I never heard such a glowing recommendation."

"Oh." What had she expected, that Dickson Zeller would blackball her because she'd rejected his advances? No, to be fair, she didn't think he'd do that. Maybe he realized by now that she hadn't tattled to the other women about him either.

"I asked him why he let you go if you were so good," her new boss added, watching her with a hint of amusement. "He said the same

thing you did. Personal reasons, not connected with your work perfor-
mance."

"Oh," Janie said again.

"So I make my own guesses, right? I been around long enough to
know why a pretty girl leaves a job she's good at. Well, don't worry
about that in this office. I never chased a secretary around a desk yet,
and I won't. I been married to Mrs. Weinberger for thirty-six years,
and if she ever caught me doing more than looking, she'd kill me."
He grinned, and Janie suddenly found herself grinning back.

Now she came downstairs for her second day on the job just as
Ernie Layton came out of his room. They went out the door together,
and as they reached the sidewalk, Ernie hesitated so that she nearly
ran into him.

"Oh," he said awkwardly. "Forgot my wallet."

He turned and went back into the house. Janie shrugged and
headed for the mall, walking briskly. The early morning run had given
her a good supply of oxygen, and she felt good. Maybe it would be
worth it to get up early every morning and run, even when Jeff
couldn't make it.

She laughed, knowing she'd never do it. She liked that last ten
minutes of sleep too much. Anytime Jeff asked her, though, she'd give
it up to run with him.

She and Harry had run together from time to time. Harry had to
show off, though, he'd always had to beat her. She knew perfectly well
that Jeff could outrun her easily, too, yet he hadn't. He'd matched his
stride to hers, and he hadn't been the least bit winded when they
wound up back at her front door. From the way his chest and shoulders were developed, she suspected he lifted weights or worked out in
a gym on a regular basis.

She wasn't afraid to walk along the street during daylight, though
she wasn't sure why, exactly. There was no reason to think the killer
only shot people at night. Still, with others walking and driving along,
too, it didn't seem dangerous.

She thought about Harry. She'd gone with him for such a long
time, and now she wondered why. Was it because she, as well as
Teddy, had simply needed a male figure in her life? And after her
father died, Harry was the first one who came along? She wondered
what it would have been like if it had been Jeff who'd come into her
sphere at that time instead of Harry.

Mr. Weinberger didn't come that morning at all; he called to say he had a luncheon date with a client, and he'd be in around two. Janie had decided to take a conventional noon-to-one lunch hour; she changed her mind when she saw a police car across the mall at Tilly's at a little after eleven. She'd only had coffee and a hot cinnamon roll for breakfast (Aunt Bea's baking was going to be a problem if she didn't watch herself), so she could eat early.

She didn't *know* the patrol car was Jeff's, of course, but she knew that when he could, he ate at Tilly's. They'd exchanged that sort of information, knowing why they were doing it. If you knew where a person was likely to be, you might arrange to be there at the same time.

She locked the office and walked across the parking area. It was warm and sunny, and she thought longingly of sand and water. It was too bad Jeff's hours wouldn't coincide with her own; they'd be lucky (if he wanted to get together as much as she did) if they managed it once a week.

She knew the moment she walked through the doorway that it wasn't Jeff. Her disappointment was more keen than it had any right to be. Well, since she was here, she might as well eat. Janie walked past the dark, good-looking officer at the counter and sat in a booth just beyond him.

"Be right with you," the redheaded waitress called out.

She served up tacos and chili to the officer, then came around the end of the counter, smiling. "What'll you have?"

"The taco salad, and a Pepsi," Janie decided.

While she waited for her food, Janie listened to the banter between the waitress and the police officer. The girl brought Janie's salad, then went back behind the counter.

"When you going to catch the creep that's shooting everybody? I'm afraid to go home when I get off duty," the girl said. "Two people murdered, right here in the mall, and the cops don't do anything."

"I'm not Homicide, so don't blame me. Everybody's trying, though, I'll tell you that. Some slob knocks off his wife, it's usually easy to bring him in. But some guy goes berserk and starts killing strangers, it's hard to get a handle on it." The officer shoved his cup toward her for a refill. "This guy didn't leave much in the way of clues, except the bodies and some slugs from an Italian gun."

"That's what's so scary. He could shoot at anybody next. She was in here for supper, you know, that last one. She wasn't an old wino like the others, she was just an ordinary housewife who came to the show and had something to eat before she went home, and look what happened to her. The theater manager was in last night, and he said that business is way off. Who wants to have to park right next to the field where it happened?"

"All I can tell you is that they're working on it. They'll get him sooner or later."

The girl gave an exaggerated shudder. "Yeah, but when? How many more will he get before you guys get *him?*"

They turned their attention to the door when it opened, and Janie felt exultation swell in her chest. She had picked the right time and place after all.

Jeff came through the doorway, lifted a hand and said, "Hi, kids," to the pair at the counter, then came straight to her booth. "Feed me over here today, OK, Rosie? Bacon, tomato, and lettuce on rye, and a piece of pie. Rhubarb, if you've got any left."

The girl brought coffee without being asked. "Well, I didn't know you were meeting a friend here, Jeff."

He grinned. "I didn't know I was either, but I had hopes. How's the new job going, Janie?"

"Fine. I've hardly seen my boss, and it's a nice, quiet office. And best of all, there'll be a regular paycheck. What more could a girl ask for?"

"An interesting guy, maybe? This is my last day on days for a month. Which translates to this is one of my few evenings off for some time to come, probably. Could I talk you into having dinner with me? Maybe taking in a show later?"

"I'd love to." She said it quickly, then wondered aloud, "Does that make me sound overeager?"

"Not to me," Jeff assured her. "Hey, Max, come over and meet Janie. Janie Madison, Max Upton."

Max had swiveled around on his stool. When he stood up he was very tall, and as attractive as she'd thought. He had an easy smile, a nice voice. "Hi, Janie. I knew something was up with this guy. He turned me down to go bowling tonight, said he thought he could line up something more interesting. Obviously, he did."

"Somebody's radio's squawking," the waitress warned, and Max waggled a hand at them and moved toward the door.

"Hope it's yours, Jeff," he said, but when he reached the patrol car he slid in, thumbed the mike, and reached up to turn on the blue light as he roared out onto the street.

"I hope to God it isn't another murder," the waitress said, rubbing her upper arms as if the thought made her cold.

"I hope so, too," Jeff agreed. "If he keeps it up, though, he's bound to leave some evidence, so we'll get him eventually."

"If that's supposed to be comforting," the waitress told him, "you're missing the mark somewhere. The whole neighborhood is scared stiff."

Janie made a mental note to tell Mr. Weinberger that she wasn't willing to work overtime, not late enough so that she'd have to walk home in the dark, not until the killer was captured.

17

Lieutenant Zazorian went to the rectory at St. Andrew's. He spread the pictures out on the battered old desk in the study with an apology. "I'm sorry to take up your time, Father, but we understand you may have seen some of these women. There are two of them we haven't yet identified. I'd appreciate any help you can give us."

The young priest stared down at the pictures, both the sketches by the police artist and the photographs, which showed too much of what the victim's last moments had been like. He had strong, well-shaped hands; with a forefinger he pushed aside the top photo, that of Cora Cottler.

"I don't recall ever seeing this woman," he said. Father Byers had a reputation for a sense of humor and considerable warmth and compassion; the latter now showed on his face. "This one . . ." It was the sketch of Mabel Gervaise. "I believe she came to bingo a time or two. Won a box of groceries a month or so ago, if my memory serves me correctly. I had a complaint from a woman who sat next to her,

Mrs. Oakes. Said she smelled." His grin was wry. "She did, actually. I doubt that the poor woman had a place to bathe, from the look of her."

He picked up the sketch and studied it. "I doubt that Mrs. Oakes could tell you anything about her, since I don't think they spoke. I'll give you her address, though, if you want to check with her. The poor woman may have said something to give you a clue as to who she was."

"We have that one's name, Father. Mabel Gervaise. She was a street woman. No family we've been able to find. It's the last two there that we haven't identified."

"Oh." He picked up the next picture. "They look different after they're dead, don't they? Especially when they've died violently. No, I don't remember ever seeing this one."

He held the final picture, turning so that the light fell more fully upon it.

"Some of your bingo players thought they might have seen that one," Zazorian said. He sounded tense, and he was. The citizens were beginning to be aroused about these killings, and he wanted them solved before any more pressure was brought to bear upon his department.

Father Byers' head began to nod ever so slightly. "Yes, maybe. Not more than once, I think. I really don't remember anything about this one. She didn't win anything, I'm sure. I usually remember the winners. This is our bingo night, Lieutenant. Would you like me to post these pictures? Ask anyone if they remember anything about them?"

"That would be good of you, Father."

The young priest sighed. "Such a waste, isn't it? Four lives. And it's frightening everybody so badly. They're afraid to go to work or to the store, let alone to come out at night to play bingo. I hope you stop the man soon, whoever he is."

"So do I," Zazorian said grimly. "So do I, Father."

Janie was chilled walking home through the growing twilight. Soon the days would stretch out into summer, she thought, and it would be broad daylight far past the time she had to be on the street. And long before the days began to shorten again, the police would have arrested the madman who stalked the streets and the alleys, preying on helpless women. She sincerely hoped so anyway.

She could hear the voices and see the lights before she let herself into the front hall, and she welcomed the company in the house. The aroma of cooking food drifted to meet her as she took off her jacket and hung it in the front closet.

"That you, Janie?" Muriel came out of the parlor carrying the evening paper. "It's finally made the front page. They've decided all four of those women were murdered by the same man, and they're calling him The Sniper. It makes it worse, somehow, to give him a name. It makes him more real."

Janie told her what the officers had said about catching a killer who murdered at random, victims who were nothing to him personally so that there were no individual motives; unless he left something of his own behind at the scene of the crime, there was no way to trace him.

Teddy dashed by, and Muriel grabbed him before he got more than one foot on the stairs.

"What's the hurry?"

"I'm going to get Mr. Jacoby's watch. He left it in the bathroom."

Muriel released him, and he thundered up the stairs while she shook her head. "Boys are different from girls. You never raced through the house like that."

Janie grinned. *"Vive la différence!* Gee, whatever that is smells delicious. I'm almost sorry I'm going out to dinner with Jeff."

"But not quite," Muriel said, and Janie laughed aloud.

"No, not quite. What's Aunt Bea cooking this time?"

"I believe the menu is homemade lasagne with garlic bread and a green salad. And Neva contributed cherry tarts."

"Wow! I'm going to have to learn to check with the cook before I make dinner dates. Teddy, slow down!"

The last was too late, as Teddy had already leaped down the last four steps and nearly collided with the pair in his way. "Yuck," he exclaimed. "There's somebody's teeth in a glass in that bathroom!"

Unappreciative of their amusement, he ran on with Mr. Jacoby's watch. "Well, it looks as if everyone's assembled down here," Janie observed, "so I should have the bathroom and the hot water to myself. Jeff's never seen me in anything classy, so tonight I'm going to bowl him over."

She had been considering all day what to wear. Nothing flashy, nothing low-cut, just something with *class.* Simplicity, that was the key. And color. One of her best colors was green. Her eyes would pick up and reflect the tint, and even Harry had said she had beautiful eyes when she wore green.

The evening was cool enough so that she could wear the dress she wanted, a soft, sheer wool with a cowl neckline. No jewelry except gold earrings. She was reaching for her short white coat when the doorbell rang.

Jeff was early, she thought happily, and headed for the stairs.

It wasn't Jeff Muriel had admitted, however, but a strikingly pretty and smartly dressed woman of about thirty. The door had not yet been closed, and through the opening, at the curb in front, Janie glimpsed a new beige Cadillac.

Janie recognized the voice; she'd heard it on the telephone. "I hope that this time my father is not too tired to speak to me?" Rachel Civen said rather crisply.

Muriel was not to be intimidated. "I'll certainly ask him, Mrs. Civen."

Janie came down the stairs slowly, not wanting to barge into a family conflict, if there was going to be one. A moment after Muriel went into the dining room, Mr. Jacoby emerged, napkin in hand.

"Oh, Rachel. I'm in the middle of dinner. Bingo tonight, so we're eating a little early."

"You don't look worn-out," Rachel said. She had jet black hair and dark eyes, and was beautiful enough to be a model or a movie star. "How are you, Father?"

"I'm fine. Very comfortable. How are the kids?"

"They're fine. They miss you. We all miss you, Father."

"How's Myron?"

Exasperation made her mouth twitch. "Myron is the same as he always is. Father, when are you coming home?"

Mr. Jacoby was the same height that she was in her three-inch heels. Not wanting to interrupt them, Janie simply stopped on the stairs and waited.

"This is home," Mr. Jacoby said. From above, his head looked shiny and pink under the hall light. "I'm very happy here. We're teaching the ladies to play poker."

One toe tapped the entry-hall floor. Rachel Civen looked around, saw Janie on the stairs with no change of expression, and then stared at the old man.

"Tell me why you prefer this to our home," she requested, and Janie had a vision of luxury and opulence.

"I have my independence here," Mr. Jacoby said. His tone was gentle, but the words were not. "You're the spitting image of your mother, Rachel, and a more beautiful woman never lived. But inside you're nothing like her at all, I'm afraid. I'm not a slightly retarded child who has to be told what to eat, and when to go to bed, and what's good for me. I've survived seventy-three years by using my own judgment; I can pick out the right tie to go with whatever suit I'm going to wear, and I know enough to get the amount of sleep I need. What's it matter if sometimes I don't get enough green vegetables? It's hard for me to chew the damned things these days, so I take an extra multivitamin tablet. Even if I didn't, what's the difference? If it shortens my life by an hour or two, why, that's no worry to me. Here I can sit around in my shirt-sleeves without being concerned that I'm an embarrassment to anyone, and I can be me, Aaron Jacoby, retired tailor, not rich but with enough income to live out my days in peace. If there's anything left when I'm gone, I've willed it to the kids."

The color had washed out of Rachel Civen's face. Her voice was little more than a whisper. "You never said anything like this to me before."

"Hard to say it, in your house," Mr. Jacoby pointed out softly. "Myron's home, too, and he has to work too hard at being a good son-in-law when I'm underfoot all the time. While I'm talking, I might as well say it all. Those two kids of yours are bright enough to think for themselves. They don't need to be bossed around all the time any more than I do, Rachel. Untie the apron strings a little."

Rachel's breast heaved with her inhalation. "Is that how you see me, Father? Bossy? Domineering? *Strangling* my family?"

He smiled faintly, perhaps sadly. "You'll have to excuse me, Rachel. We'll be leaving for bingo in twenty minutes, and I haven't finished my dinner."

Rachel's lips trembled, but she spoke evenly. "Will you come over for dinner on Sunday, Father? At two?"

"I'd be happy to," Mr. Jacoby said. "Good night now, Rachel."

He left her there in the entryway. Janie came down the remaining steps and at close range saw that moisture glistened on her lashes. Rachel gave her an odd, crooked smile, then turned and walked out of the house to her Cadillac.

Jeff's Granada was parked directly behind it. He spoke to Rachel as they passed, then bounded up the steps to the front door. "Something wrong?" he asked, seeing Janie's face.

She shook her head. "No, I don't think so. I think I just heard a wise old man give some very good advice to a daughter who is probably going to consider it quite seriously." She linked her arm with his. "I've been smelling Aunt Bea's cooking for the past hour. Where are we going to eat?"

Alfred had offered to chauffeur the bingo players to the church. "I know it isn't a long walk, but it makes me nervous to think of you being on the street after dark," he said. "I suppose I'll have to make two trips, to take everybody."

"Very kind of you, Mr. Bonnard," Charlie Silvers wheezed. "We were talking about calling a couple of taxis."

"Well, I was going to suggest that for coming home. I'm going to be out this evening, and I'm not sure I'll be back in time to pick you up then. Playing cards with some friends," Alfred explained. "You'll call a cab, won't you, Mother?"

Sylvia looked at him impatiently. "Yes, of course. I'm not an idiot, you know. Just because a person gets old doesn't mean she's lost her mind. Where's my purse? I had it only a minute ago."

Neva was peering out at Alfred's car at the curb. "It's a big car. Don't you think we could all squeeze into it at once? For such a short ride?"

"Be a tight fit," Mr. Jacoby said, "but someone could sit on my lap. You're not averse to sitting on a gentleman's lap, are you, Mrs. Minor?"

She giggled. "Not at all. Let's all go together and save Mr. Bonnard the trouble of a second trip."

Alfred smiled at Muriel. "How about you, Mrs. Madison? Why don't you join the bingo players?"

"Oh no thank you. I'm much too tired to go out on a working night. And Teddy's here, too; I couldn't leave him alone. I think I'll just go to bed early and read until I'm ready to fall asleep. Thank you anyway."

Muriel watched them go, keeping her amusement under control until they'd packed themselves in and managed to get the doors shut. She hoped Alfred didn't take a corner too fast and spill them out.

"Looks like a small crowd tonight," Charlie said, gasping, as they went up the walk to the recreation hall. He'd been crushed between Sylvia and the door in the front seat, so it had been even harder than usual to breathe. "Because of those murders, I suppose. People are afraid to come out at night."

"I certainly would be if we didn't come in a group," Bea said. "It's too bad if attendance is down, but maybe that will give us a better chance to win. Though I suppose if it stays this way, the games won't pay. I'd hate to see them close down."

"We'll play our own bingo at home if they do," Mr. Jacoby contributed, only to be countered by Neva Minor.

"Yes, but what'll we use for prizes? What's the matter, Sylvia?"

The other woman stood staring in the direction where her son's car had disappeared. "My purse. I must have left it in the car, and Alfred's gone with it. Now what'll I do?"

"I'll loan you enough for your cards," Neva told her. "Come on, it'll be safe. Alfred will lock the car, even if he doesn't notice your purse."

"I didn't see it on the seat," Charlie puffed. "Must have fallen on the floor. Chances are nobody else will see it."

They entered the hall and took their places. Father Byers' assistant came around with the cards, and they paid for them. They each played four cards at one time.

Before they began, Father Byers pointed to some pictures on the bulletin board. "If you know anything about any of these women, please talk to me before the evening is over," he said.

He didn't mention murder, yet everyone in the room knew that the women in the pictures were the victims of the madman the papers had nicknamed The Sniper.

18

Several of the bingo players, including Bea and Neva, admitted to Father Byers that they had seen two of the women at the church recreation hall in earlier sessions. None of them had had much conversation with the strangers; most of them came regularly and sat with their special friends, and while they would eventually warm up to newcomers, no one had with these particular ones.

A man in a wheelchair recalled that the winner of the box of groceries had seemed very pleased, but she had not given anyone her name nor said anything about herself.

Nothing of possible interest to the police had been learned. Between games, and at the refreshment break at eight-thirty, there was considerable speculation about the murders and when the cases would be solved, the killer apprehended. Virtually no one had come alone tonight.

As usual, though, everybody had a good time. Charlie was the first one to cry "Bingo!" in his raspy voice. His prize, to everyone's amusement, was a child's Easter basket filled with candy eggs and a small fuzzy yellow chick.

He accepted it with good humor. "Guess I won't be buying any round of drinks on that win," he said as he sat back down, making the chair creak beneath his weight.

Neva Minor had seated herself beside Mr. Jacoby. She put herself out to be pleasant and helpful, getting down on her hands and knees to assist in retrieving the pieces he knocked off the table with his elbow, bringing him a glass of punch when she got one for herself.

Mr. Jacoby looked at her through his spectacles. Neva met his gaze with a provocative smile, and he quickly returned his attention to his cards.

Right after the midevening break, Sylvia Bonnard rose to her feet.

"I won, I won!" she crowed, and her friends clapped when Father Byers handed her a twenty-dollar voucher from Bennie's Delicatessen.

On the last game of the evening, when the prize was thirty-five dollars, it was Neva Minor who called out the winning card. Her hand came down on Mr. Jacoby's in a hearty squeeze.

"We can have a party," she announced to the table at large. "Sylvia, if you'll use your winnings from the deli, I'll get the wine and whatever else anyone wants. We can have a real celebration! What do you say?"

They were jubilant. Neva generously offered to pay for the taxis home, too. It would take two cabs, they decided, since it was unlikely a cab driver would allow them to pack in so many passengers in one. Neva went to call the cabs, and was assured that they would arrive within a few minutes, then returned to her friends.

It wasn't raining, and there were cars coming and going, picking up other players. Father Byers stood in the open doorway, allowing the light to stream out for the benefit of those finding their way to transportation. The lamps at the foot of the sidewalk leading to the main doors of the church were lighted again. It did not look dangerous.

"Let's wait outside," Charlie suggested. "In the fresh air."

Tobacco smoke irritated Charlie's emphysema, and the hall was full of smoke, as usual.

About the only place a man could go where there was no smoking allowed at all was church (the church itself, not the rec hall) and Charlie hadn't been to so much as Sunday School since he was ten years old.

His friends, all nonsmokers, insulated him as best they could against this invasion of his damaged lungs. If anyone else tried to light up a smoke at their table, they were politely but firmly asked (by one of the others, never by Charlie) to do it in some other location.

Tonight a man with a cigar, one table over, had enveloped Charlie in a cloud; Charlie's wheezing breath was so labored that they were all concerned for him.

"Yes," Sylvia said, "let's wait outside. It's rather warm, it smells like spring."

They walked out of the lighted recreation hall into the night.

Muriel and Teddy watched television until nine; then Teddy was sent up to bed with the promise that he and Joe could sleep Saturday night in the tree house. Muriel went upstairs shortly thereafter; she made the rounds of the lower floor to make sure all doors and windows were secured.

While it was true that she already felt at home in the big old house, she was strongly aware of its size tonight, its emptiness. She liked it better when it was full of people.

It was not only large, it was badly lighted. And it was full of shadows. She left the porch light on, hesitated over the tiny lamp on the hall table and left that on as well, and climbed to the second floor. She turned off the light at the head of the stairs once she'd switched on a lamp in her bedroom and left the door open, light streaming into the hallway, while she had her bath two doors down.

The old Victorian bathtub on its clawed feet took a horrendous amount of hot water to fill it to a reasonable level, but since there was no one else at home, and the new heater did not seem strained to produce sufficient quantities for the household, Muriel indulged in a deep tub and bubble bath, where she soaked and almost fell asleep.

She had intended to read, but she was too drowsy for that. She turned off the lamp and slid down under the covers. She wondered how Janie was enjoying her evening with that young police officer. How lovely it would be if they really hit it off.

She woke abruptly and sat upright in bed. What had she heard? A sound seemed almost to echo in her mind—the tinkle of breaking glass?

What had she been dreaming? It was gone, but she didn't think it had had anything to do with breaking glass. Could she possibly have really heard something that had awakened her?

Muriel sat for long moments, listening. The old house creaked and groaned around her, but that was normal for old houses. They expanded—or was it contracted?—as the temperature changed.

It was several minutes before she realized that when she had gone to sleep, her bedroom door open so that she might hear Janie when she came in, that doorway had been faintly visible because of the night-light left burning in the lower hallway.

There was no illumination now; it was pitch black.

If anyone had come in and accidentally knocked over the lamp and broken it, wouldn't they have turned on another light by now? There was a switch for the overhead entryway light just inside the front door, and another at the bottom of the stairs for that fixture.

To her relief, the bed lamp came on at the touch of her fingers, and Muriel slid out of bed and reached for her robe. "Janie?" she called out.

There was no response. She looked at the clock and saw that only a few minutes had elapsed since she'd gone to bed. No wonder she felt so groggy.

She padded barefoot across the room and peered into the hall. There was no light anywhere.

"Janie? Is that you?"

At nine-thirty? Unlikely. Muriel leaned out into the hallway now and called more loudly. "Who's there?"

The house was silent except for a creaking board when she took a few tentative steps toward the head of the stairs and the wall switch there.

Had she made the sound herself, or had it come from below?

Her heart was beating audibly; she heard the blood pounding in her ears, and she was glad Teddy was asleep in the attic.

Good lord, what was she thinking of? That someone had broken into the house? Impossible. All the doors and windows had been securely locked. Still, there had been that echo of breaking glass when she awoke.

They hadn't done anything about getting a telephone extension installed upstairs. She would tomorrow, Muriel thought. It was absurd not to have one up there for an emergency.

She was distinctly uneasy, but she was not yet considering this an emergency. She groped for the switch at the top of the stairs, and the whole entry hall sprang into light below.

The night-light on the table was out, though the light was not broken or overturned. The doorways into the dining room and the parlors were black holes, revealing nothing.

Muriel suddenly did not want to go down those stairs. She stood for a moment, hearing her own unsteady breathing, and told herself she was a fool. She'd dreamed something that had awakened her and left her frightened, and she was letting her imagination create terrors where there was no basis for them.

The stairs *did* creak under her weight, especially the fourth step from the bottom. It sounded exactly like what she'd heard when she came out of her bedroom.

The house felt cold. She'd left the thermostat at sixty degrees, cool enough for comfortable sleeping, yet not leaving the place icy for elderly people who had to get up at night.

It felt icy now, under her bare feet. Muriel made herself walk all the way down the stairs and pick up the phone. There was a reassuring hum on the line, but there was nothing yet to make her feel compelled to call the police. She'd feel like a fool, calling them for nothing.

Automatically, she checked the lamp. It came on at her touch.

Alarm prickled at the back of her neck. Muriel whirled around, staring into the darkness of the parlor across the hall, seeing nothing, hearing nothing. Yet she *felt* something.

Fear. She felt it in the cold perspiration that suddenly oozed out of her pores.

Beyond the curtains at the front door there was no light. She flicked the wall switch, which clicked but made no difference to the blackness on the front porch.

The bulb could have burned out, of course. Yet how had the inside lamp gone out unless someone had turned it off?

Nothing in the world could have induced her to open the door and see what was out there. Yet she couldn't simply go back up to bed either. The rest of the household would be home soon, and then what? Would they be in any danger, if there was someone here?

There was a flashlight on the shelf in the front closet. Swiftly, Muriel threw open the door and reached for the red plastic handle and thumbed the switch. Then, by pulling a section of the curtains aside, she aimed the light through the front door.

She *had* heard breaking glass. Bits of it caught the beam from the flashlight, scattered there before the door. The beam also outlined a rock, perhaps as big as a golf ball, amid the shards of glass from the porch light.

Children? Mischievous boys throwing rocks for the fun of it? Or something more sinister?

The police, Muriel decided. Something *had* happened, and she'd let the police deal with it, checking to see if there were any signs of attempted forced entry.

She picked up the receiver and had her finger in the hole to dial 9 when the pain exploded in the back of her head. She was vaguely aware of striking her forehead on the lamp table (although, oddly enough, it caused no additional pain) and then . . . nothing.

19

Tonight, the watcher thought. Tonight, and then it would all be over. Frustration and rage were subsiding, and, yes, the fear. There had been fear tonight, for the first time. Every other avenue had been explored, for nothing, and now it came back to this, to the original plan.

The final phase of the plan would be executed tonight, within the next few minutes. Executed, yes, that was the right word. Amusement surfaced briefly, then was gone.

The doors of the recreation hall at St. Andrew's were opening. Noise, voices, light. The same as before, only this time it wasn't raining.

The watcher stood unseen in the deep shadow of the massive cedars. Ready. Ready to kill again.

Car engines revved up. The bus came around the corner and stopped to take on its customary load. A small knot of lively elderly people paused near the priest, their good-nights carrying across the street, then came down the sidewalk.

A woman's voice asked clearly, "You all right, Charlie?"

The reply was not audible. The group paused on the curb, directly in front of the lamps flanking the main walk.

"Oh, I dropped it!" another woman said, and bent to retrieve a white envelope just as the watcher fired.

There was a grunt, screams, an oath. It was impossible to tell which one had been shot, for they all went down, falling, crying out, huddling around the victim.

The watcher melted away into the shadows before the pair of taxis arrived seconds later. By the time the police came, there was no sign that anyone had ever stood beneath the cedar trees across the street.

It had been a heavenly evening. They had eaten at El Torito in Everett, savory Mexican food, leaning over their plates to manage tacos without landing lettuce and cheese in their laps, laughing over tall glasses of Sangria, eating slowly to make the meal last as long as possible, and ending with flan, which both of them were really too full to finish.

Janie felt as if she'd known Jeff forever. She'd learned that he had two brothers and a sister, that he'd had two years of police science at College of the Redwoods south of Eureka, California, before he attended the Police Academy at Chico.

"My folks were a little bit alarmed, I think, that I was given a badge and a gun before I was legally old enough to buy ammunition for the gun. I spent a year on a small-town force there before I came here. I didn't want to be on a big P.D. like Seattle, so this was a compromise between village and city."

"You like being a cop," Janie said.

"I love it. Oh sure, there are times when I don't like it very much. It's sort of like . . . oh, long periods of relative boredom, routine matters, interspersed by moments of extreme excitement and exhilaration."

"My mom finds the same thing working in the hospital. Mostly the work is routine, but when there's a major emergency, she's run off her feet, and she feels she's doing something worthwhile. She deals a lot with the families of those who are sick or injured, and she's good with them. After Dad died, I guess she has a good idea how they feel; anyway, she seems to know what to do and say to make them feel better."

They talked even after their half-eaten flans were carried away, until they began to feel self-conscious about taking up a booth any longer.

Jeff consulted his watch when they went out onto the street. "It's pretty late for a movie, unless you don't mind missing your sleep before you go to work tomorrow."

"Why don't we take a ride?"

"There's time to take a ferry over to Whidbey and ride it back. Just leave the car in Mukilteo and go on as foot passengers; then we wouldn't even have to get off the boat on the other side."

"Let's," Janie said, laughing.

There weren't very many people on the ferry at that time of night on a Wednesday evening. They walked around inside at first, but the lights were too bright, so they went out onto the bow again.

There were lights at Everett, and a few on the southern end of Camano, and ahead in scattered homes that lined the eastern shore of Whidbey. Out on the bow it was not really dark except for the water itself, but no one else was there.

"The wind is colder than it was during the day," Janie said, and Jeff immediately wrapped an arm around her.

"That any better?"

"Much better," she said.

Jeff bent his head to kiss her. Her hair was flying in the wind, strands blowing across her eyes; he brushed them away and cupped her face in both hands, then kissed her again, sliding his arms inside her coat, pulling her close.

She was sorry when the ferry had unloaded at Clinton and headed back out, leaving them on what was now the stern. It was a little warmer that way, for the boat wasn't creating its own wind, but it hardly mattered. By that time Janie had her arms around him, too, inside his jacket, warming them both.

They almost forgot to get off the boat when it docked at Mukilteo. An employee called out to them in the dimness. "Last boat tonight, folks," and they disengaged themselves at last, laughing.

"I hate to take you home," Jeff said as he unlocked the Granada. "Especially when I'm going on nights and I don't know when I'll get to see you again."

"My life will be well ordered and uneventful," Janie told him, "and therefore predictable. Let me know when you have time off."

It struck her later as a peculiarly inappropriate description of what her life was to be like for the next few weeks.

It was Jeff's muffled exclamation that brought Janie upright, peering ahead, when they turned onto Relton Street. She had been leaning her head against his shoulder, eyes closed, listening to the radio, liking the strength and the gentleness of him.

Suddenly, Jeff swore and accelerated.

"What . . . ?" Janie started to say, and then she saw the blinking red lights and a gathering of people on the sidewalk, some of them in nightclothes.

"Our house? Oh my God!"

She was out of the car before Jeff had set the brake; he came around the front end of the Granada in time to grab her hand before they went up the steps.

The front door stood wide open. There was an ambulance, not police; that registered, though Janie was frantic to see who the attendants were lifting onto their gurney.

Teddy huddled at the bottom of the stairs in red and white print pajamas, hair standing on end, looking upset and bewildered. The bingo players were scattered, some inside, some outside the house. Mr. Jacoby turned as Janie and Jeff came up behind him, putting out a hand to keep them to one side.

"What's happened?" Janie cried. "Is it my mother? Oh, God, what happened to her?"

"Looks like she fell down the stairs, knocked herself out," Mr. Jacoby said. The porch light was out; Janie suddenly became aware of broken glass gritting under her feet. "We found her when we came home, but we were so late because Charlie was shot and we all went along to the hospital with him—" He looked at Jeff then and recognized him. "You're the police officer, aren't you? We called the police from the church, because of Charlie. This looked like an accident, so we didn't call them again. The front door was locked, no windows broken into or anything like that. It looked as if somebody threw a rock and broke the porch light, and maybe Mrs. Madison came down to investigate and fell on the stairs."

The ambulance attendants had put a sheet over the still figure on the gurney and were strapping her in. Janie pushed past the men and stood at Muriel's side. There was a gash on her forehead, not a deep one, though it had bled profusely. Janie couldn't see anything else wrong, except that Muriel was unconscious.

"How badly is she hurt?" Janie asked, her voice wavering.

An attendant with the EMT insignia on his sleeve gave her a reassuring glance. "She knocked herself out, but as far as we can tell she isn't hurt too badly, though she's still unconscious. Fell down the stairs, it looks like. She may have a hairline fracture, but there's no spongy area, the way there often is with a massive skull fracture. The

X rays will tell the story. Any particular hospital you want us to take her to?"

"She works at St. Joseph's, and that's the closest. Jeff, will you take me over, behind the ambulance?"

"Yes, sure. Let me look around, make sure there wasn't a break-in. With all that's been going on around here—wait a minute. Where's the old gentleman who said someone had been shot?"

Sylvia's hands fluttered in agitation. "Oh, it was terrible! Terrible! They shot Charlie. He wasn't feeling well, because of all the smoke, and we went outside where he could breathe the fresh air. I had won a twenty-dollar gift certificate from the deli, and I dropped the envelope it was in. When I bent over to pick it up, there was this shot, and Charlie cried out behind me, and everybody was screaming. Charlie fell on the ground, bleeding, and Father Byers came running. He told Neva to go back inside and call the police and an ambulance."

Janie's eyes met Jeff's and he put out a hand to her. She was shaking.

"They're taking Mother away," Janie said, tugging against him.

"That's all right, we won't be far behind." Jeff spoke to the nearest attendant as they began to move the stretcher out toward the steps. "Tell them we'll be right there. Who's her doctor, Janie?"

"Morrison. Alan Morrison."

"Tell them to call Dr. Alan Morrison, and her name is Muriel Madison."

Teddy moved toward her, so that she could wrap one arm around him. "Honey, what happened? Did you see it?"

"No. I was asleep until I heard the siren when the ambulance came." Teddy hugged her. "She's gonna be all right, isn't she, Janie? She isn't going to die like Dad?"

She fought against an incapacitating ache in her throat. "I'm sure she'll be all right. I'm going to the hospital, and I'll tell you how she is when I get back. You stay here with the others, OK?"

Jeff had let go of her hand and was speaking to Mr. Jacoby in the doorway to the dining room. "You're positive the door was locked when you got here, sir?"

"Oh yes, no mistake about that. My hand was shaking so I could hardly get the key into the lock. Shocking thing, to see a man, your friend, shot down right in front of your eyes."

"He wasn't killed?" Jeff asked quietly, but the words carried to Janie's ears.

"No, at least he was alive when they got him to St. Joe's. He has emphysema very badly, though; they had to give him oxygen, and he still sounded terrible. Do you think it was him, that sniper?"

"It's possible. Well, make sure everything's locked up tight here, sir. Then, just to be on the safe side, I think I'd better call in and let my sergeant know about this. Just in case there's any connection. That way the guy on patrol will keep an eye on the house, at least for the rest of the night."

He couldn't use the phone at once, however. Sylvia was on it, speaking to Alfred. "What took you so long to answer?"

Janie saw the ambulance pull out and heard the wail of its siren as it disappeared. The neighbors began to drift back toward their own homes.

Aunt Bea touched her arm. "We'll see to Teddy. Don't worry about him, even if you don't come home until morning. What a dreadful night this has been! Poor Charlie . . . there was blood all over everything. I suppose we shouldn't have gone to bingo, but everybody can't stay behind locked doors forever until that madman is caught, can they?"

"I don't know," Janie said, and she was replying to more than Bea's words.

"I left my purse in your car," Sylvia was saying into the phone. "Did you find it? Oh, you did. Good. Would you bring it over, please?"

Apparently, Alfred was not immediately agreeable.

"Well, yes, I thought tonight, if it wasn't too much trouble. I don't have any money or my keys or anything. Why do I have to wait until . . . ? Oh. Oh, you've already gone to bed. Well, I suppose so. All right. Listen, Alfred, while you're at it, see if you can find my cribbage board, will you? Well, I haven't found it. Maybe it slid off the top of a box, down behind a seat in your car, or something."

Janie thought she would scream if Sylvia didn't get off the phone. "Mrs. Bonnard, Officer Carey needs to call . . ."

"Oh. Oh yes, certainly. Alfred, you wouldn't believe what's happened tonight. First Charlie Silvers was shot and wounded, coming out of St. Andrew's, and then Mrs. Madison fell down the stairs and was knocked unconscious, and they've taken her away to the hospital, too, in an ambulance. . . . Oh, you will? Well, if you don't mind getting dressed and coming over, dear. Yes, the policeman wants to use the phone. I'll see you in a few minutes, Alfred."

Jeff gave Janie a pat on the shoulder. "It'll only take me a minute. Why don't you wait in the car?" he suggested.

She had turned to comply when Ernie Layton appeared on the doorstep. "Is something wrong?" he asked uncertainly. "I heard a siren, saw an ambulance . . . and now all the lights and . . . did it come from here? The ambulance?"

She told him, succinctly, about her mother and Charlie. He didn't quite seem to take it in, she thought, though he said, "My goodness. How awful."

"You weren't here all evening?" she asked. "You didn't see anything?"

"No, I had a . . ." He left her in doubt as to what he had had. "I wasn't here. I'm sorry, Miss . . . Janie. I hope your mother will be all right."

"Yes, I hope so, too," Janie agreed. Behind her, as soon as Jeff hung up, the phone began to ring.

It couldn't be anything about her mother, because the ambulance couldn't have reached St. Joseph's yet. Janie ran down the steps, allowing someone else to answer it.

20

Janie sat in the small, green-walled waiting room for hours. The emergency-room nurse knew Muriel, and she also knew Jeff, which meant that they were given more information than might normally have been the case, though it wasn't much.

"She does have a hairline fracture in the occipital region," the nurse reported. "As far as we can determine, there's no severe pressure on the brain, so we won't attempt any surgical procedure at this time. For the moment, we'll simply keep her under observation."

It was terrifying. Observe her until Muriel did what?

Jeff held her hand after the nurse had gone. "Chances are she'll come out of it before too long, wake up and tell us what happened. Listen, if you're OK alone for a few minutes, I'll see what I can find out about Charlie Silvers."

She'd almost forgotten Charlie. "Yes, of course," Janie said. "Poor Charlie."

She waited for nearly half an hour before Jeff returned; the priest from St. Andrew's was with him. She liked Father Byers at once.

"Shocking thing. Shocking. I don't know if anyone will dare come to my bingo nights again until this sniper is captured. And no clues at all to his identity, apparently. Officer Carey has told me about your mother, Miss Madison. I'm terribly sorry."

Janie sounded choked. "What did you find out about Charlie?"

It was Jeff who replied. "They moved him from the emergency room to intensive care just before we got here. It looks like another small-caliber weapon was used, quite possibly the same .25 as on the women. The slug is still in him, and they can't take it out, so we may not ever know. Unless he dies, and the coroner finds it on autopsy."

The words were common ones to Jeff; to Janie, they were assault and battery. "Why can't they take it out? Where is it?"

"The entry wound is about here." Jeff touched his own rib cage on the left side. "They think it entered at an angle like so." He gestured. "Apparently it didn't hit anything vital or he wouldn't still be here. But he has severe emphysema. Which means," he added, seeing incomprehension on her face, if not on the priest's, "that they can't give him a general anesthetic in order to go after the slug. If they did, it would kill him."

"Oh, poor Charlie," Janie said.

"I feel rather responsible," Father Byers said, "since it happened at St. Andrew's. It seems odd, does it not, that two of the women who were killed had attended our games, and now Charlie. Does this sniper have something against St. Andrew's?"

Jeff regarded him thoughtfully. "So far as I know, it's the only thread of evidence that links any of them. Three indigent women, a middle-class housewife, and a disabled, middle-aged man. And three of them played bingo at your church. Yes, it does seem odd. But what about the ones that you *didn't* remember?"

Father Byers sighed. "It's possible that both the others had been there at one time or another. I honestly think I'd have remembered their faces, though I cannot swear to that, of course."

They were left with the quandary unresolved. The priest took his leave of them with an apology. "I have a mass to say at seven, which allows me about three hours' sleep if I go directly home. I'll pray for your mother as well as for Charlie, Miss Madison."

"Thank you, Father," Janie said, and blinked against the sudden moisture in her eyes.

Jeff took her into his arms after the priest had gone. "I'd better take you home, too. You're worn-out."

She leaned into him, grateful that he was with her, that she was not facing this ordeal alone. "Can't I see her first? Just for a minute?"

"Sure, probably they won't mind. They've taken her upstairs by now, I think."

Muriel, too, was in intensive care. Janie had never been in this part of a hospital before, and it was awe-inspiring and frightening. The patients were all clearly visible in their glass-enclosed cubicles, most of them attached by electrodes to monitoring devices that read out information on TV screens at the nurses' station. Blinking lights, EKG printouts, oxygen masks, all the paraphernalia modern medicine brought into play to deal with severe trauma and life-threatening illness were there. To the uninitiated, there was little in the ward that was reassuring, except the quiet, efficient, white-uniformed young nurses.

Janie had a glimpse of Charlie, looking very pale and still as two of the nurses did something, bending over him, and then the nurse stepped aside so they could enter the tiny room where Muriel lay in her deep sleep.

The gash on her forehead had been sutured and was not covered by any sort of dressing; the black stitches stood out starkly in the dim light. Janie knew they had shaved the back of Muriel's head, though that didn't show. She did not look as if she'd been injured, except for the wound on her forehead and a bruise on her chin; she appeared only to be asleep.

Tears filled Janie's eyes. She grasped the unresponsive hand and squeezed it, then turned quickly away, unable to bear it.

The smiling, sympathetic nurse bid them good night in a low voice, and they walked out into the main corridor, Janie struggling to control herself. "What if she doesn't regain consciousness?"

"Don't borrow trouble," Jeff advised, putting an arm around her shoulders. "By morning the entire picture may have changed. Are you going to go to work tomorrow?"

"I don't know," Janie said miserably. "There's a lot to do at the office, and poor Mr. Weinberger already has one secretary out of commission. . . . I suppose I'd better go in, at least for part of the day."

"Good girl. You're better off keeping busy than sitting around thinking about things, and you can check with the hospital anytime to see how things are going."

She gave him a wan smile. "I'm glad you were with me, Jeff."

He grinned back. "So am I. And don't worry, I'll stick around. Come on, I'll take you home."

She couldn't help worrying, though, about what she'd do, if by some terrible mischance Muriel didn't completely recover.

The following day was a wretched one. Janie dragged herself from bed a little before eight; not even a shower and black coffee and toast, solicitously served by Aunt Bea, could pull her into any normal semblance of herself.

"I've already called the hospital," Bea said. "There's no change. In either of them."

By the time she was ready to leave the house, the others were all down. Teddy wanted to stay home—he didn't like the school, didn't like his new teacher, and he was worried about his mother—but Janie decided that he wouldn't benefit from sitting home brooding. "I'll call you at school when there's any news," she promised, and sent her little brother reluctantly on his way.

Ernie Layton, also looking as if he hadn't slept well, or long enough, came down the stairs as they were leaving, greeted them with a nod, and muttered something about having forgotten a handkerchief. He disappeared back up the stairs, and Janie went on outside and down the front steps. Teddy was still there, tying his shoe, so they walked together for the first two blocks until Teddy had to turn off.

"That Ernie Layton is certainly a quiet one," Janie observed, looking for a safe topic of conversation. "And awfully forgetful. The other day it was his wallet, today it's a handkerchief."

"I think he just doesn't want to walk with you," Teddy said unexpectedly.

"What? Why do you say that?" Janie looked down at him, puzzled.

"Because you started out the same time before, and he came back inside and just waited until you were out of sight before he followed you. And he had a handkerchief today, I saw the top of it in his pocket."

Janie pondered that briefly. "He didn't go back upstairs to get his wallet?"

"No. He stood just inside the front door and peeked out through the curtains. He's kind of spooky, isn't he?"

"Spooky? In what way?" Janie asked uneasily. She was suddenly aware that though Aunt Bea could vouch for all the others, nobody had known Ernie Layton. They had simply rented him a room, asking for no references, and handed over a key to the front door. Outside of his name, she knew nothing about him whatever.

If it hadn't been for all the shootings, and Muriel's unexplained fall, she probably wouldn't have given it another thought. As it was, she decided she'd better find out something. Such as where he worked—she didn't even know that. He didn't have a car, and he didn't seem to hurry to catch a bus, which suggested that he might be employed in the neighborhood. On the mall, too?

She wasn't sure what knowing where he worked would prove. A man could work anywhere and still be involved in something sinister after hours, couldn't he?

Janie was appalled at what she was thinking. She waved good-bye to Teddy as he cut over toward the school, and was unable to put the idea out of her mind.

She wasn't thinking that Ernie Layton had anything to do with the snipings, was she?

Mr. Weinberger was in ahead of her. He had a briefcase of papers he dumped on her desk as she explained what had happened the previous night.

"Good grief! You want to take the day off?" he asked, looking worriedly at his papers.

"No. At least not right now. I'll check with the hospital around noon and then figure out what to do next. If Mother wakes up, I think I should go over and see her. And if I can get caught up on the work here, I wouldn't mind leaving early this afternoon. I didn't get much sleep last night."

"Sure. You do whatever you need to do. I'd appreciate it if you could get these out before you leave, though."

Janie nodded and turned on the computer so that it could warm up. Then she turned and asked, "Mr. Weinberger, you've been here several months, haven't you?"

"Yes, why?"

"I wondered if you'd met a young man named Ernie Layton. I think he may work on the mall; I'm not sure where."

He shook his head, reloading his briefcase for the next foray into the world of commerce. "Don't know the name, but then I probably wouldn't. Know most of the regulars by sight, but never met them formally."

"He's about twenty-eight to thirty. Six feet tall, rather slim, brown hair—" Janie stopped. There was nothing notable about Ernie Layton, nothing especially distinguishable. He was so ordinary.

Mr. Weinberger recognized her dilemma. "Just a regular-looking guy, huh? Tell you what. Most of the people work on the mall eat over at Tilly's, if they don't carry their lunches. Somebody over there might know him, if it's important."

"I think maybe it is," Janie said slowly. "Thanks for the suggestion."

She had trouble concentrating on what she was typing. At eleven-thirty, unable to bear the suspense any longer, she called the hospital and asked to speak to ICU. The charge nurse there was pleasant without helping much.

"Mrs. Madison's condition remains unchanged. Her vital signs are good. Dr. Trent examined her this morning and was pleased about that."

"Dr. Trent?"

"He's a neurosurgeon. Dr. Morrison called him in on consultation, because of the head injuries, you know."

"I see. And what about Charlie Silvers?"

"Mr. Silvers remains in stable but critical condition."

"Is he conscious?"

"He is somewhat responsive at times," the nurse said.

"Would you tell him, if he does understand, that Janie and all the others from home asked about him? That we're all concerned and want him to get well?"

"Yes, of course."

Janie hung up feeling dissatisfied and unhappy. She had no sooner hung up than the phone rang, and it was the administrator from St. Joseph's.

There was no question of the man's genuine concern for Muriel. Janie was grateful, yet even more discouraged about the long-term possibilities. What if Muriel didn't come out of the coma? What if she did, but only after weeks of care?

Muriel was well insured for medical emergencies, through the hospital. Few insurance policies paid 100 per cent of any bill, however, and intensive care was extraordinarily expensive. And there was the matter of the lack of a paycheck while she was unable to perform her job.

She had caught up with the work left for her by two o'clock. Janie stacked the papers neatly on Mr. Weinberger's desk and was about to write him a note saying she'd finished and gone home early when she spotted a yellow card posted on the wall beside the telephone there.

It was a list of businesses on the mini-mall.

Janie slid into Mr. Weinberger's chair and read through the list. Did Ernie Layton work for any of them? Was he, as Teddy had said, "spooky" enough to be investigated?

He'd said he was not around last night when Muriel was hurt, but he could have been. He had a key and could easily have been in the house.

What was she thinking? Why should she suspect that Ernie, or anyone, had done something to make Muriel fall? Why would he have done that? He had a right to be in the house, and she couldn't think of any reason why he'd have been doing anything Muriel would have objected to.

It was only that Muriel was not clumsy, and if she'd been coming downstairs to investigate the sound of breaking glass, she would have been moving slowly and cautiously, Janie was certain. She was wearing a robe, but it wasn't long enough to trip on.

No doubt Janie would have taken it for granted that the mishap was an accident if it hadn't been for the other things that had been happening. Four women shot and killed, and then Charlie. Poor

Charlie, whose injury probably would not have been life-threatening if it hadn't been for his lungs.

Everybody assumed that Charlie had been shot by The Sniper, though the police had taken no official position yet according to the latest radio reports. Another random shooting. Perhaps The Sniper had not even cared which person was hit when he fired into the group.

A psycho, Jeff said. Could a psycho masquerade behind a facade of normalcy, an ordinary person living an ordinary life, going to work, speaking to people in a rational way about everyday things?

Yes, of course.

She felt moderately foolish, considering the faint chance that Ernie Layton could fall into such a class, but not foolish enough to ignore any clue, no matter how small or how unlikely it seemed.

Janie sat at the desk and called each number on the yellow card, checking with every business on the mall, asking if they had an employee by the name of Ernest Layton.

Halfway through the procedure, she realized that if she found Ernie and he was called to the phone, she had no idea what she would say. Hang up, she supposed, and let him wonder what it had all been about. But she felt compelled to learn something about the man, and where he worked would be a starting point.

It was a waste of time. No one on the mall knew Ernie Layton.

Janie pushed back the chair and stood up, ready to lock up for the day. How did you ask someone for references after you'd already rented them a room and handed over a key?

She walked slowly home in a warm green-and-golden afternoon. Probably she was only letting her imagination run wild anyway. Ernie might simply not have wanted to walk with her, and made up flimsy excuses to return to the house until she'd gone on so that he didn't have to talk to her. He was shy—she'd already guessed that. He would probably be astonished and horrified to know that she suspected him of any part in the crimes that were taking place in the neighborhood.

She let herself into the house and immediately smiled. Aunt Bea was baking again. Bread, by the fragrance. Homemade bread. Bless Aunt Bea. What a waste it had been for her, living for years with that grouchy, disagreeable old man. Janie wondered if Bea had made bread for *him* and guessed not.

She hadn't forgotten about Ernie, though. She'd have to remember to ask Jeff about him. Jeff would have ways to learn something about him.

Beside her the telephone rang, and she picked it up with mingled hope and foreboding.

"Yes? Jane Madison speaking."

"Miss Madison," an unfamiliar voice said. "This is Mrs. Helmer at St. Joseph's."

Janie felt her heart stop. "Yes? Is it my mother?"

"We wanted you to know right away. Mrs. Madison seems to be regaining consciousness."

Janie's spirits soared. "Oh, thank God! I'll be right there!"

She forgot Ernie Layton.

21

Muriel was still in ICU, and they were allowed to go in one at a time. Janie went in first, and was disappointed to find that her mother was not totally conscious.

"She's moving a little now," the nurse explained, smiling. "She's begun to moan occasionally, which is a good sign, too. And she's regaining her responsiveness to stimuli as well." She put her hand firmly over Muriel's and said in a clear voice, "Mrs. Madison. Your daughter is here. Can you speak to her?"

Muriel groaned.

Janie thought it a dreadful sound; the nurse was plainly gratified. "See? She heard me, she reacted to me. That's very good. You try talking to her. Touch her at the same time, and see if you can get her to answer."

Janie put a tentative hand on her mother's arm. "Mom? Can you hear me? It's Janie."

Nothing.

Janie bent over her, holding back tears. "Mother? Can you speak to me? It's Janie. Teddy's waiting outside, he wants to see you, too. Please, let him know you know he's here. He's been so upset about you. We all have. Mom? Can you hear me?"

Deep in her throat, Muriel made a sound. And then her mouth worked as if she were trying to form words.

Janie slid her hand down to Muriel's, clasping it as Muriel had done with hers, years ago when Janie was a little girl.

"Mother, if you hear me, squeeze my hand."

Faint yet definite, it came, a tightening of Muriel's hand around her own. Why that should have made the tears brim over, Janie didn't know, but she left some of them on Muriel's cheek as she bent to kiss her.

The nurse standing by handed her a tissue and Janie wiped at her eyes. "She *is* going to get better, isn't she?"

"I'd say there's a very good chance. I had orders to call Dr. Trent when she gave signs of coming around. He's on his way over now. We'll let your little brother see her for a few minutes before he gets here, shall we?"

Janie waited in the corridor while Teddy visited, hoping it wouldn't be too distressing for him. Though she'd tried to prepare him for what he would find, he was, after all, only twelve years old.

He emerged grinning, not the least depressed. "She squeezed my hand, too, Janie. I'll bet she'll be talking to us by tomorrow. I saw this TV show where a guy was in a coma like that, and once he started to move around he came right out of it and he was fine."

It showed that television was good for something, Janie thought as they rode the elevator down.

Jeff called shortly after she arrived home, so she was able to give him the good news. "Wonderful. Look, I'll try to stop by during the evening and give you a lift over to the hospital to see her again during visiting hours, if you like. Though patients in ICU aren't subject to regular visiting hours anyway. OK?"

"Are you allowed to do that?" Janie wondered. "While you're on duty?"

"I'll clear it with my sergeant. In San Francisco the cops regularly escort senior citizens to the bank on the day they cash their Social Security checks; it's the only way it's safe for them to handle their money. I don't see where this is any different from that. I don't want you on the street, either walking or taking a bus. I can probably wait for you for a few minutes, if nothing comes over the radio that demands action; they won't let you visit more than five minutes anyway."

"Thank you. I'll be ready anytime you can come," Janie assured him.

The doorbell rang as she hung up, and she turned to open the door.

Two youngsters stood there, a boy of about ten and a girl of twelve. They were dark-haired, handsome children, very well dressed. Even if she hadn't seen the Cadillac at the curb, Janie would have guessed who they were.

"Could we see Mr. Jacoby, please?" the girl said.

Janie invited them in and left them in the back parlor while she sent Teddy upstairs for Mr. Jacoby. The old man came down beaming, to gather them one at a time into his embrace.

"Linda! Morrie! It's good to see you! I swear, Morrie, you've grown another inch just since I left! Miss Janie, meet my grandchildren!"

Janie left them there to visit with him, hearing the boy say as she closed the door, "What did you say to Mother, Grandpa, when she came over to see you? She was crying when she came home."

"Was she now?" Mr. Jacoby asked, and the girl contributed, "She's been funny ever since, Grandpa. You know what? She said I could stop the ballet and take piano instead if I wanted to!"

Janie smiled. Mr. Jacoby was as wise as she'd thought him to be.

Aunt Bea had put together a meal that would have cheered them all immensely had they not been so concerned for the two household members in the hospital. The news about Muriel was encouraging, of course, yet Charlie remained in critical condition. X rays had revealed the location of the slug, and the doctors did not think it posed any further danger, but he'd lost considerable blood and his general condition had been poor to begin with.

Upon hearing that Jeff would be taking her over to the hospital later on, Mr. Jacoby fixed her with a glance.

"You suppose he could bend the rules far enough to take me, too? I'd like to run in and see Charlie. He might know I'm there. Might make a difference to him."

"I'll ask him. I don't see why not," Janie replied.

She had helped clear the table when Molly called. "Janie, isn't that man who was shot last night living at your place? What's going on?"

That led to a conversation that lasted for nearly half an hour. They'd have to have a long cord put on the extension when they installed it upstairs, Janie decided. Standing up to talk in the front hallway left a bit to be desired when conversing with Molly.

She hung up as Teddy bounded down the stairs and handed a sweater to Sylvia Bonnard, then frowned when she saw the old lady press a coin into his hand.

"Teddy? What's going on?"

"I brought down her sweater so she didn't have to run upstairs." Teddy looked mildly guilty.

"And you're taking money for that? Shame on you!"

He stared at her defensively. "Well, they ask me to run and get something every few minutes. I'm not a slave or anything, am I?"

"No, but they're all on pensions, except Mr. Jacoby. They can't afford to pay you to run errands, and you're much younger than they are. It wouldn't hurt you to donate a little exercise on their behalf, would it?"

"It's only a dime. And I don't get something *every* time I go," Teddy said. His mouth had a stubborn set.

Neva came out of her bedroom and heard the conversation. "Oh, don't worry about it, Janie. Nobody will pay him more than they can afford, and it is a tremendous convenience to have young legs to do those stairs. Here, here's another errand for you, Teddy, this one with no pay attached. Give these to Sylvia, too, will you?"

Teddy accepted the envelope proffered and ran off in the direction Sylvia had gone. Neva laughed.

"See? It isn't just for money. He's a good boy, and it's entertaining to all of us to have him around. That was stamps from Australia. My nephew there writes to me. I don't save stamps, but Sylvia likes the pretty ones. Oh, Mr. Jacoby, if they let you see Charlie, tell him I'm thinking about him, will you?"

Mr. Jacoby had come across the hall carrying the evening paper. He nodded. "Certainly."

"They won't let us send flowers while he's in intensive care. I suppose we could send cards, though. Maybe we could each send one in turn, so he gets something every day. He has no family at all except a sister he hasn't heard from in ten years. I think she lives in Nebraska or somewhere like that. We're the closest thing to a family Charlie has."

Sylvia and Teddy reappeared from the back of the house. "I'm not getting paid for this one either," Teddy said to Janie, and pounded up the stairs.

Sylvia waved the stamps. "Beautiful! Thank you. I've sent Teddy up to the attic to get the album to put them in; I lent it to him a few days ago because he was intrigued by all the strange animals on the foreign stamps. I found my cribbage board, by the way. Can I challenge you to a game, Neva?"

"Sure." Neva sighed. "We were going to have a party on our bingo winnings. It wouldn't seem right now to have it without Charlie, would it?"

"Wait until he comes home," Mr. Jacoby proposed. "He's a tough old bird; he'll make it. Then we can party. Mrs. Madison will probably be home by then, too." He gave Janie a smile that made her want to hug him. "There's a blue light blinking out front; I can see it through the curtains. Could that be our police chauffeur?"

"Give my love to Charlie," Sylvia cried after them as they went out the door.

Friday was a better day.

It was raining when they got up, which didn't bother anyone; in their part of the world they were used to plenty of rain. It was what kept Washington State so beautifully green year-round.

Janie's early morning check with the Intensive Care Unit produced the information that Muriel had been moved into a semiprivate room because she was improving rapidly. She had opened her eyes and spoken a few words.

Janie's impulse was to delay going to work and rush over there; she was discouraged from this by the charge nurse. "It would be better to wait until regular visiting hours, Miss Madison. Dr. Trent has scheduled several procedures for her this morning, so she may not even be in her room."

"What procedures?" Janie wanted to know.

"More X rays, an EEG, and some routine lab work. We have your office number; we'll call you at once if we need you."

Dampened, though not very much, Janie thanked her. Out of ICU. Soon, maybe, she'd be able to come home. "Has she said how she came to fall?" she asked before the nurse could hang up.

"I don't know about that, I'm sorry," the nurse said. "Good-bye, Miss Madison."

As Janie was leaving, the workers arrived in a panel truck to begin installing the furnace. She dodged around a man carrying a huge carton and found Ernie Layton doing the same thing, so that they nearly collided.

"You walk to work the same way I do, don't you?" Janie asked deliberately.

"Uh . . ." He stopped, and she wondered if he were going, again, to pretend to have forgotten something he had to go back for. Looking at his face, it was impossible to believe that he had any ulterior motive for avoiding her. He was simply too bashful to make the attempt to carry on a conversation, she decided. She had made the opening, however, and was determined to find out one thing, anyway. "Where is it you work?" she asked point-blank.

He stepped back from her, straight into the path of one of the men from the panel truck; Ernie went sprawling, the worker apologized for what was clearly Ernie's fault, and the two of them scrambled around picking up the contents of a spilled tool chest.

It would be awkward to repeat the question after all that, Janie thought. Was the man really that badly coordinated? Or had he created a diversion to keep from saying where he worked? Why on earth should he do that, though? It didn't matter where he worked; and whether he worked or not couldn't have any bearing on his reliability as a roomer—could it?—as long as he paid his rent.

Janie made one more try. "You don't have to catch a bus, do you?"

Ernie Layton shook his head, still looking flustered, and said, "I forgot, I have to make a phone call. It's all right if I use the telephone, isn't it?"

She stared after him in complete bewilderment. It would almost be worth it to go back inside after him and see if he actually called someone, she thought. Only it was time she left if she were going to open the office on time.

She'd forgotten to mention him to Jeff, and by this time she'd decided he was simply one of those people who were terrified by social contacts, especially with the opposite sex. Maybe she'd sic Mr. Jacoby on him, she thought, amused, as she walked away toward the mall. Though he'd accepted kitchen privileges, he'd done virtually no cooking.

She buttoned her coat at her throat against the rain and walked on briskly, wondering if Jeff would be able to give her a ride to the hospital again tonight.

Muriel turned her head on the pillow as Janie entered the room. "Janie."

"Mom! You're awake! How are you feeling?"

Muriel's expression revealed the answer to that before she spoke. "I've got a terrible headache, and they don't want to give me anything for it that would mask symptoms, I guess." A reassuringly mischievous smile touched her lips. "I've got a terrific new doctor, though. Wait'll you see him."

"Dr. Trent? Is he cute?"

Janie settled into a chair beside the bed, reaching for her mother's hand.

"Darling. All the student nurses think he's adorable. I'd seen him before a few times, and now I've been exposed to his bedside manner as well." She turned her head to see Janie better, winced, and sighed. "Slow and easy does it, I guess. Anyway, he's twenty years younger than Dr. Morrison, very distinguished, with touches of silver in his sideburns—premature, I think. Mrs. Helmer says he's only fifty-two."

"Oh, very young to have silver sideburns," Janie said quickly, and they laughed, though Muriel broke off sooner.

"Damn, everything I do hurts."

"I'm glad you can laugh, anyway. Mom, what happened? How did you fall down the stairs?"

Muriel grew reflective. "Isn't that strange? I can't remember. I remember being awakened out of a sound sleep, thinking I heard glass breaking. And that's all."

"You don't remember going downstairs?"

"Not even getting out of bed. Dr. Trent says it'll probably come back to me soon, though it seems odd I'd forget something that happened *before* I got hurt, doesn't it? I guess some kids threw a rock at the porch light and broke it, and I just got clumsy trying to go down and see what had happened."

"You've never been a clumsy person."

"No. But I don't think I'd been asleep very long, and I was undoubtedly groggy. Anyway, I guess I'm lucky it wasn't worse."

"How did you fracture your skull in the back and get that gash in your forehead at the same time?" Janie wondered aloud.

"Nobody's figured that out yet. Maybe pitched forward and hit my head and then fell the rest of the way down the stairs and hit it back there at the bottom. I don't suppose it matters, as long as it's going to be all right now. How are you getting along with that young police officer?"

"Pretty well, I think. Only he's been switched to night duty for a month. He brought me over last night and tonight. Mr. Jacoby came with us this time; he's visiting Charlie."

That was a mistake. Muriel hadn't known about Charlie. There was no way out of telling her now.

"How dreadful!" Shock made Muriel's weakened condition more apparent. "Janie, listen, I want you to come and visit me, so if Jeff can't bring you, come in a cab. Don't go out at night by yourself."

Being with other people, a lot of other people, hadn't helped Charlie, Janie thought. But she had no trouble reassuring her mother about visiting. There was no way she'd go out alone at night. Ever.

22

Janie and the boys spent Saturday morning working in the backyard. The rain had passed, leaving the air sweet and clean; the sun was warm on their bare arms and faces and Janie welcomed the physical activity.

"Getting it into nice shape," Mr. Jacoby said from the back steps, and Janie flashed him a smile that quickly faded as she remembered how Charlie Silvers had sat on those same steps, giving advice.

By midday, most of the household had been out to see how they were doing; Bea and Neva and Sylvia brought chairs to sit where they could enjoy the activity and the fresh air, and Mr. Jacoby climbed to inspect the tree house.

"Always wanted something like this myself," he admitted when he came down. "Never had one. My Morrie would like it, though I don't suppose Rachel would ever allow him to climb that high into a tree." He sank down on a chair Janie had brought out to use in lieu of a stepladder. "Or maybe she would, now. Seems she's having second thoughts about how things are run in that household, though I suppose I can't expect miracles. She's made Linda take ballet for nearly eight years, although the child has hated it for most of that time, and finally Rachel said she could drop the classes and study piano instead." He sighed. "It's a great responsibility, bringing children into the world, and it's so easy to make mistakes. Don't know exactly what we did wrong, raising Rachel. Made her think she was the only one who had any sense, who could make decisions."

He didn't seem to need any response, and Janie was content to pull weeds, listening to him. The women chatted in the background. Sylvia was hooking a rug, Bea was knitting a sweater, and Neva was halfheartedly writing letters to various relatives scattered in far places.

It was a peaceful, domestic scene. Janie was almost sorry when it was time to clean up and go to the hospital to see her mother. She left the others taking a cookies-and-milk break.

Ernie Layton was in the kitchen when she passed through it, putting a carton of milk into the refrigerator. His grocery bag also contained a package of Oreos, a box of cornflakes, and a jar of grape jelly.

He glanced at her warily, as if anticipating another verbal attack. Janie merely smiled and said "Hi," to which he responded with a murmur.

What was the big secret anyway? He spent scarcely any time with the others, which wasn't too surprising since they were all old enough to be his grandparents, except for the Madisons. When he was home, he was usually closeted in his room upstairs, where he kept the radio playing.

She showered and put on a dress and sandals. It felt like summer today, and she felt changed, too, as much as the season. She felt young and optimistic and happy. Her mother was getting better, they seemed to be retaining some semblance of control over their finances, and Jeff was coming to run with her this afternoon before he went to work.

When she came out to let the others know she was leaving, there was no sign of the boys, though after a moment she heard them. On the roof of the porch.

"Teddy? What are you doing?" She went down the steps and looked up at them, striding about on the slanting shingles.

"It's easy to get here from the tree house," Teddy informed her. "See, we just walked out that big limb and stepped off on the roof."

"Well, get down. Sherm said we'd probably need a new roof, but we can't afford one yet, so I don't want you falling through that one. I mean it, Teddy, get off from it before you break your neck."

"It isn't dangerous, Janie. It has hardly any slant, not like the main part of the roof. We could walk right up to the second-story windows and it wouldn't be dangerous at all."

"Get down anyway." She returned to the shaded porch where only crumbs remained on the cookie plate. "Is Mr. Jacoby going over to the hospital, too?"

"I think so," Aunt Bea said. "Tomorrow he has to have dinner with his daughter's family, so we thought we'd all go visit Charlie. He said they'd probably let us in, one at a time, even though we're not actually related, since there *is* no family. I think your mother pulled some strings so we could visit. We'll look in on her, too, of course. Give her our love."

Love, Janie thought, walking back through the house. Odd, how quickly they'd knitted themselves into a family group, those old people and the younger ones. There was genuine affection and concern between them. She remembered ruefully how they'd wondered if it would turn into an old folks' home, with herself and Muriel tending half a dozen geriatric patients. And instead, it was Muriel who was in the hospital, the oldsters who were providing moral support.

They liked Teddy, that was obvious. They talked to him and listened to him; Janie had come upon her little brother in various conversations with them. It was good for him to have these pseudograndparents in place of his own, who were so far away he seldom saw them.

Muriel's color was somewhat better today, though the headache was severe and she could not lift her head from the pillow. Dr. Ken Trent came while Janie was there, and she was immediately intrigued.

He was one of the most attractive men she'd ever seen, though it wasn't a classic movie-star handsomeness. The silver sideburns were only part of it. He had a thick head of dark hair, dark eyes that seemed constantly amused, and a wide mouth that smiled easily and often. He acknowledged Muriel's introduction to her daughter with a broadening of the smile.

He sat on the edge of the bed to take Muriel's pulse. Then, talking in a disarming manner about a TV program in which the doctor was a complete idiot, he examined Muriel's eyes and queried her on how many fingers she saw and asked a few other questions. "Still hurt, does it?" he asked finally, turning her head to the side so that he could probe the area at the base of her skull.

"Like fury," Muriel admitted.

Dr. Trent rested his hand briefly against her cheek. "Well, you're doing fine. No sign of any additional problems. The headache will go away in its own good time, if you're a good girl and follow orders."

"When am I going to be able to go home?"

He laughed and looked at Janie. "You'd think she didn't like my attentions, wouldn't you? It's too early to say about that, Muriel. I certainly won't release you until it's safe to send you home. Don't get overeager to get out of our nice hospital when we're doing our best to entertain you."

"Some entertainment," Muriel muttered, but she was smiling.

Dr. Trent slid off the edge of the high bed. "That's right, keep your sense of humor. It's a good medication. I'll drop by again this evening. Glad to have met you, Janie."

They listened to his heels receding along the corridor, and Muriel produced another smile, one wan enough to be a clue to how she really felt. "See? What did I tell you?"

"Is he married?"

"No," Muriel said, and Janie leaned forward to kiss her.

"Good. I'm going to go now, too. I don't suppose you've remembered any more about what happened?"

"Not a thing. It'll come to me eventually. Give Teddy my love."

"Yes," Janie said. She saw Dr. Trent at the nurses' station, writing in a chart, and wondered if it had *all* been bedside manner or if there might be a spark of something between him and her mother. How lovely that would be, though it probably was too much to hope for.

She met Mr. Jacoby coming from the direction of the ICU wing. "How's Charlie?" she asked.

"Holding his own. He knows when we come," Mr. Jacoby said. "It's frightening, the way his breathing sounds."

"And there's nothing more they can do for him about that."

"No. He hasn't lost his humor, though. Told me he was going to get up his own bingo game on Wednesday nights, and enforce the NO SMOKING signs. He wanted to know if we'd had the party yet, with the bingo winnings; I told him we were waiting for him to come home."

"Mother's new doctor says a sense of humor is good medicine. I hope he's right," Janie told him. "Are you going home now?"

"No. I promised my grandson, Morrie, that I'd watch him play ball this afternoon. Little League."

To her delight, Jeff Carey was waiting for her when she came down the hospital steps. She slid into the white Granada with a grin. "This is a bonus I didn't expect."

"Your Aunt Bea told me you were here. I didn't want to take unfair advantage of you, running after you'd already walked home from the hospital. How's your mother?"

She told him, and about Charlie. "Haven't the police discovered anything yet about The Sniper? How long will we have to live with this thing hanging over us?"

"Well, I'm not on Homicide. I know they're working on it. I hear that they don't have much to go on, though. It's the hardest type of killer to catch, because there's no logic to what he does. Most murders are committed by acquaintances or relatives of the victims; there's nothing to link this guy to the crimes."

"You said once that sometimes a psychopath actually wants to be caught. That he starts deliberately leaving clues."

Jeff guided the Granada through the Saturday afternoon traffic. "It happens sometimes, but it hasn't happened in this case. Oh, I think they've had a few crank calls—they often do—but none of them have panned out. When they question the caller, he can't tell them details that only the killer would know, things that weren't revealed to the media people, and they release him."

"Why would anybody confess to crimes they hadn't committed?" Janie wondered, smoothing her skirt over her knees with nervous fingers.

"To get attention, usually. To be in the limelight for a while. You've seen the protesters on TV. A lot of them are doing the same thing, on a lesser scale. They protest atomic energy, Trident submarines, anything that will bring out the media to take their pictures so they can have the pleasure of knowing their friends are watching them on the six o'clock news. I don't say all protesters are kooks and publicity seekers, but see how long most of them will march and chant and chain themselves to things if nobody is taking their picture. Here we are. I suppose you want to change shoes before we run?"

He grinned, looking at her sandals and nylon-clad legs.

"Give me ten minutes," Janie said.

Teddy and Joe had stocked the tree house with cookies, sandwiches, fruit, and bottles of pop in a small ice chest. They each had a sleeping bag: Teddy's was nearly new, having been bought for the last camping trip he'd taken with his father, Joe's borrowed from an older brother and showing considerable wear.

Joe brought several comic books. Teddy added a magazine he'd found in the trash can in the alley behind the house. He expected to see Joe's eyes bulge when the magazine was opened to the centerfold picture of a striking brunette with no clothes on.

He was carrying his portable radio and an extra blanket when Janie came downstairs after her run with Jeff. "Where you going with all that stuff?" she wanted to know.

"Taking it to the tree house. We're going to sleep out there tonight, remember?"

Alarm flared at once in her face. "Oh no you're not!"

Teddy stopped, feet planted far apart in a belligerent stance. "We are, too. Mom said we could."

"That was before everything happened. Before Mom fell down the stairs and Charlie got shot."

"What's that got to do with anything? Charlie wasn't shot *here*, he was over at that church. And nobody pushed Mom, did they? She just had an accident. So why can't I sleep in the tree house?"

Janie hesitated. She didn't want to frighten him unduly, yet common sense dictated keeping him locked safely inside at night as long as The Sniper remained on the loose.

"Teddy, there's a murderer out there somewhere. Nobody knows where he is. And Mom isn't here to make decisions, so I have to make them. If she *were* here, I'm sure she'd say the same thing I'm saying. You sleep in the house until that sniper is behind bars."

Teddy scowled. "That could be years. Maybe they'll never catch him. Come on, Janie, it's right in the backyard and the tree house is practically hidden. Nobody'd even know it was there. We're probably safer there than in the house."

"No," Janie said firmly. "Tell Joe you're sorry. You can play there in the daylight, but not at night. Not until The Sniper is caught, or Mom comes home and says you can do it."

Teddy's scowl deepened. "You're a real spoilsport, Janie."

"I'm sorry. It's not that I don't want you to have fun. I only want you to be *safe.*"

He didn't answer. He dumped the radio and the blanket on the bottom step of the stairs and stomped off toward the back door.

Joe had been in the kitchen, surreptitiously putting a few more of Aunt Bea's chocolate chip cookies into a plastic bag. Teddy could see by his face that he'd overheard the conversation.

"She won't let you do it?" Joe, too, registered disappointment.

"She's not my boss just because Mom's in the hospital," Teddy said gruffly. He glanced around to make sure no one could overhear. "We'll do it, only we'll have to wait until later. Tell you what, your mom already thinks you're staying overnight, so we'll just let Janie think we're going to bed in the attic. OK? And then after everybody's gone to sleep, we'll sneak out there."

Joe's dark face cracked in one of his rare smiles.

"Sure," he agreed. He put a few more cookies into the bag and stuffed it inside his shirtfront, and then they each ate one cookie before they went out across the back porch in front of the old ladies.

23

Muriel awoke to intense pain, disorientation, and terror.

She stared up at the ceiling and realized almost at once where she was: the hospital. Dr. Ken Trent had been in to see her this evening, and though she had been uncomfortable, she had been grateful for his company. He'd spent half an hour with her, simply talking: about his grown family, his dead wife, his job.

No terror there. Why did she feel it, this suffocation, this fear? She remembered.

The chill swept over her, actually making her teeth chatter. "Janie. I've got to tell Janie." She knew the phone was there, on the table between her bed and the empty one in the other half of the room. She tried to reach out for it, awkwardly raising herself from the pillow; her head hurt so badly when she tried to move. She fell back, gasping.

She had been trying to use the telephone to call the police, and someone had struck her from behind.

She gave up on the phone and reached instead for the button that would call the nurse. A red light went on over her door in the outer corridor. Muriel waited.

Talking with Molly was exhausting. For a small home wedding, there were plenty of plans, and Janie was to be included in everything. She had dragged a chair into the entryway so that she could at least sit down while she listened; she made notes as to date, time, and so on.

"Do you want to bring him, this Jeff Carey?"

"I doubt if he'll be free. He's working evenings this month. I'll ask, though. I want you to meet him."

"And your mother? Do you think she'll be out of the hospital by then? Shall I send her an invitation?"

"Yes. I mean, send the invitation. I don't know if she'll be able to come, but she'll be pleased if you invite her."

Molly had a great deal to tell her. About the apartment they were furnishing, the gifts they'd already received, the honeymoon plans.

Once Janie paused when Ernie Layton went out, another time as Alfred Bonnard came in. She put her hand over the receiver to say to Alfred, "Your mother's in the dining room with the others."

"I just thought I'd check, see how she's doing and if she needs anything," Alfred told her in a genial way.

Janie nodded and spoke into the phone. "I'm back, Molly. Yes, I'll handle the guest book for you. There won't be many guests, will there? Fifty? Well, that's quite a few, but all I have to do is be maid of honor and then I can do the guest book. Are you going to open your gifts then, or wait until after the honeymoon?"

Joe and Teddy came down the stairs, laughing and poking each other. "We're hungry," Teddy said, seeing her there.

"Ask Aunt Bea what you can have to eat. Don't forget that other people have things in the refrigerator, so don't just help yourselves. Yes, Molly, I'm back. This place is like Grand Central Station."

"You sound as if it's agreeing with you, though."

Janie laughed. "It is, I think. I like them all, and they've been marvelous since Mom got hurt."

It was another ten minutes before she managed to hang up and put the chair back where it belonged. The boys came through with a loaded tray and frosty bottles of Dr. Pepper. "It's nearly time to go to bed," Janie told them. "Don't stay up talking too late, OK?"

"OK. Not past eleven," Teddy said, and carefully made his way up the stairs without spilling anything.

Eleven hadn't been quite what she had in mind, but what difference did it make? They weren't going to have to get up early tomorrow. If her mother had been home, they might have gone to church. As it was, Janie was not interested in going alone. They could all sleep in.

Snacks were being served in the dining room when she walked through it. Neva had been working out a menu for the party they would have eventually and made herself hungry while doing it, so she'd made sandwiches, and they were sipping cups of steaming cocoa. "With marshmallows," Neva said, grinning, "just like the kids. There's some left; help yourself." She turned to the others.

"You'll like piña coladas," she assured them. "They're delicious."

"You know I never drink alcohol," Sylvia protested.

"You don't have to put alcohol in these if you don't want to. They're made from pineapple and coconut, run through a blender with ice. Maybe I'll make some before the party, so you can see."

"What is this party you're having?" Alfred wanted to know. He'd been served a cup of cocoa, too. "Somebody's birthday?"

"No, it was going to be simply to celebrate our winning," Sylvia told him, "Neva and I, on the same evening. Then after poor Charlie . . . we decided to have it when he comes out of the hospital."

"He's going to be all right, then?"

"Well, he's still in critical condition," Neva said. "Only they say every day that passes, his chances are better. So we're certainly hoping he'll be out before too long."

"And Mrs. Madison? She's getting better, too?" Alfred paused to help himself to a chunk of cheese from the plate in the middle of the table. "Has she remembered how she came to fall?"

"No. Tripped on her hem, more than likely," Sylvia said. "I've done it a number of times. Alfred, do you remember seeing my dark brown sweater? The very heavy one? I can't seem to find it anywhere."

"I'm sure you packed it, Mother. Maybe in the box with the other sweaters?"

Sylvia gave him an exasperated glance as Janie joined them at the table. "Don't you think I had sense enough to look there? It isn't in the box. And I can't find those brown shoes either, the ones I always wore to church with my brown suit. Would you see if they could have fallen out in the trunk of your car?"

"Mother, I've already looked in the trunk for various other things that were missing. If your shoes were there, I'd have found them. You haven't unpacked everything, have you?" He pushed back his chair. "Let me go finish unpacking, and I'll probably find everything, only in different boxes from where you thought you put them."

"No, no, sit down," Sylvia said in a cross voice. "I *hate* it, Alfred, when you act as if I'm retarded."

"Mother, I never act as if you're retarded." Alfred's own tone was heavy with exaggerated patience. "It's only that you have so much stuff in that room, and there isn't the space for it. Nobody could find anything in such a mess. Why don't you decide what you need to have with you right now, and I'll store the rest of it at my place until you need it? After all, you can call me any time to get whatever you want out of it."

"I like having my belongings here with me. Are you going to be staying on at that place, after that woman was murdered?"

Alfred drained his cup and used his tongue to remove the rim of marshmallow from his upper lip. "She wasn't murdered *there*. Yes, I suppose I'll stay on. I didn't find anything in the paper for the price, and it's comfortable enough, except for not being able to make toast and coffee at the same time. Besides, poor Herb needs the rent money, and strangers might be wary of moving in after what happened to his wife."

"How's he taking it?" Neva asked. "It must be very hard on him, losing his wife that way."

"Oh, it is. He's so distraught he doesn't know what he's doing half the time. I went with him to make the funeral arrangements, and it was a good thing. He was feeling so guilty, because he'd had a fight with her and that's why she left the house the night she was killed, that he'd have bought the most expensive casket in the place. You wouldn't believe what they want for those things."

"Yes, I would," Neva said unexpectedly. "I ordered my own recently."

They stared at her. "You expecting to die soon?" Mr. Jacoby asked, eyebrows raised.

"No, of course not. I only thought I'd save my kids the trauma of making funeral arrangements when the time comes, for just the reason Alfred's talking about. At a moment like that, nobody has good judgment, and while my kids have no reason to feel guilty about the way they've treated me, they would probably spend more than they ought to. Nobody likes to feel cheap, especially when it's the last act they can perform for somebody they loved. It seemed to me a nice present to give my family, to save them that chore."

"Not a bad idea," Mr. Jacoby mused. "I may look into it myself. Though Rachel is so competent it probably wouldn't faze her to pick out my coffin." For some reason, he chuckled.

Bea's hands fluttered around her empty cup. "It would be a kindness to make one's own arrangements, wouldn't it? Where did you go, Neva?"

"That funeral home on Cedar and Hamilton. Just beyond the mall, right on the corner." Neva was nibbling cheese. "Chalmers, Halvorsen, and Montgomery. Why do they always have such dreadful names to remember? Anyway, they were very pleasant. And it wasn't morbid at all, arranging my own funeral."

Her face split in a grin. "As long as it doesn't take place right away, you know."

Bea glanced at Janie. "Maybe I should do the same thing. It would be a kindness, wouldn't it, not to leave the matter to someone else? Not that I minded making the arrangements for Addison, of course. Perhaps I will talk to those people, too. What was their name again?"

"Chalmers, Halvorsen, and Montgomery. It was Mr. Chalmers I spoke to. A very pleasant man. Oh, I wondered about Mr. Layton. He was there, speaking to Mr. Montgomery. He pretended he didn't see me, the same as he does with everyone around here, and I didn't make an issue of it, naturally. I never saw anyone so reserved, or shy. I wondered if that was why."

"Why what?" Sylvia wanted to know. "Sometimes you don't talk sense, Neva."

This didn't seem to bother Neva much. "Well, you know, he was there at the funeral home, and I thought maybe he'd lost someone recently, and he's preoccupied with grief. Too much so to be able to carry on everyday conversations. I was a bit that way when my husband died. I was all right as long as nobody mentioned George, and then I started to cry. So, at least among strangers, I hoped nobody would ask about him."

"Curiouser and curiouser," Janie murmured. And then, when they all looked at her: "I've been wondering about Ernie Layton. It occurred to me, somewhat after the fact, that we might have been smart to ask a few questions about him before we gave him the run of the place. In the light of that sniper running around loose."

There were several exclamations around the table. Neva's jaw had dropped. "You don't think *he* could have anything to do with that, do you?"

"No, not really. Only he's been here as long as any of us, except for Aunt Bea, and the rest of us have become friends, almost family, while nobody knows anything about *him*. Do they?"

A glance around the circle confirmed it. They were shaking their heads.

"He goes to such lengths to keep from talking to any of us," Janie concluded. "I've tried to ask him, several times, where he works. He doesn't refuse to answer, he just falls over something or bolts back into the house to get something he says he forgot—that kind of thing."

Mr. Jacoby tapped his fingers on the polished tabletop. "Interesting puzzle. I'll make it my business to learn something about the mysterious Mr. Layton. Janie's right, it would be a good thing to know more about someone who has a key to the house."

Sylvia shivered and pulled her sweater tighter around her shoulders. "Imagine what it would be like to live in the same house with a murderer. It makes me ill to think of it."

Alfred shot back his cuff to consult his watch, then stood up. "Well, it's most unlikely that you're in such a predicament, Mother. If you change your mind about letting me unpack the rest of your belongings and storing part of them for you, give me a call. I'll be shopping for groceries on Monday evening, so if there's anything you want, write it down."

"Cough drops," Sylvia said. "You know, those ones that clear your sinuses. Oh, and if they have any new crossword books, bring them to me, will you?"

The group broke up shortly after Alfred had gone. Mr. Jacoby reminded Bea that he would be having dinner with his daughter's family on Sunday. Neva intended to spend the day with a friend who would be picking her up before noon.

"I'd go to church," Sylvia said, "if Alfred would take me. It's the one thing he refuses to do, go to church with me."

Bea was gathering cups and plates to carry to the dishwasher. "You're lucky, though, Sylvia, to have a son who cares about you and sees to whatever you need. So many old people don't have anyone." She looked at Janie and smiled. "Like me, before I found Muriel and Janie and Teddy."

Teddy, Janie thought. I'd better go check on him, make sure they're going to sleep and not running trains over Mr. Jacoby's head all night.

They scattered to their various rooms and baths. Janie climbed the stairs to the attic and eased open the door.

The light was still on, and the boys were sprawled across the bed in their pajamas, looking at a magazine, giggling.

"Lights out, kids," Janie called.

Teddy lifted his head. "OK. As soon as we finish this."

She closed the door and went back to the second floor. Bea had left the night-light glowing on the telephone table downstairs; there were no other lights on the ground floor.

She was heading for the bathroom, wishing that Jeff had found time to call her on his break, when the telephone rang downstairs.

Maybe that was him now. She hurried down, though being careful not to get in such a rush that she fell. "Yes, hello?"

"Janie?" The voice was not Jeff's, but Muriel's.

"Mom? What is it? Is something wrong?"

"Janie, I've remembered what happened." Muriel's words were tight with strain. "Janie, I didn't fall down the stairs. I heard the breaking glass, and I went out into the hallway, and I heard something else. Like a board creaking, when someone steps on it. I went down the stairs—the night-light was out, as well as the porch light, though I'd left them both on—and when I had nearly reached the bottom, I heard the sound again, when I stepped on the fourth stair from the bottom. I turned the night-light back on—it hadn't burned out or anything like that—and had picked up the telephone to call the police. And something hit me on the back of the head."

Janie felt her scalp crawl. She swiveled, glancing around at the doorways into darkened rooms. Her hand was damp around the receiver.

"Janie," Muriel said, "there was someone in the house."

24

The constriction in her chest was so great that Janie pushed against it as if massaging out a muscle cramp.

What should she do?

Call the police? And tell them what? That her mother, who had been thought to have fallen downstairs on Wednesday night, had instead been hit over the head by a person or persons unknown? That except for the breaking of the porch light and possibly a footstep on the stairs, she had heard nothing? Seen nothing?

What could the police do with that?

If there were a tie-in with The Sniper, they'd probably act quickly enough. At least they'd send someone out to look around, make sure the house was secure. What else could they do? Whoever had been here Wednesday night certainly wasn't here any longer.

Or was he?

She heard her own breathing, sounding nearly as bad as Charlie's. Someone had turned off the night-light, had hidden in one of the darkened rooms—probably the front parlor, since he'd managed to reach Muriel without making any noise—and had done . . . what? . . . after that.

It had happened the same night that Charlie was shot. That was no reason to think there was a connection, was it? Could somebody have shot Charlie and then have had time to enter the house and attack Muriel before the others arrived?

She was trying hard to think, to be logical, and she was so frightened she could scarcely function. Janie reached out to try the front door and found it locked. The window—she knew she should try all of them, to make sure no window could be opened without being broken, which would alert the household.

She went around turning on lights everywhere, leaving them on behind her. Through the parlors, the dining room, the kitchen, the pantry; she didn't go down into the basement, instead sliding the little bolt that locked it from the kitchen side. Everywhere on the ground floor except in Neva's and Aunt Bea's rooms. Should she disturb them to ask about their windows? It was unlikely that either had left anything open; even if they were, the windows were the kind that could be opened a few inches and secured by a bolt. No, better not to disturb the old women and unnecessarily alarm them.

The house was ablaze, yet it didn't make her feel any safer. Janie went back to the phone and stood looking at it. What would she say if she called the police?

There had been no sign of forced entry at the time Muriel had been attacked; Jeff had made the rounds and checked. Charlie had been shot at St. Andrew's within minutes of the time the bingo games had ended, say about ten-fifteen. It had been much later than that when she'd returned home with Jeff to find the ambulance there. The oldsters had found Muriel only minutes earlier, having been considerably delayed because they'd gone to the hospital with Charlie; there was no way of telling exactly when Muriel had been hurt. So there was nothing in the time sequence to prove or disprove any connection between the two assaults, and there was no similarity between shooting a victim and hitting one over the head, except that both were violent.

Outside of hitting Muriel brutally over the head, what crime had been committed this last time? Nobody had reported anything stolen, unless Sylvia's sweater and shoes might fall into that category.

Uncle Addison's valuables? The things she'd sold to pay for the furnace and the water heater? Yet if anyone had known about those things, why wait until the house was filled with people to attempt to take them?

Well, of course the house hadn't been full that evening. It was a Wednesday, and anyone who knew the household would have been aware that they would all be at bingo at St. Andrew's. And Janie had been out with Jeff Carey.

Why had the intruder entered the house? And how?

Talk to Jeff, she thought. He wasn't on the Homicide squad, but he certainly knew more than she did about such things.

Her finger was almost steady as she dialed 911.

And then she didn't know what to say, how to say it, so that the dispatcher would take her seriously. In the end she gave her name, address, and phone number and asked that Officer Carey call her. She didn't get into any long explanations, which she sensed might work against her because so much was speculation. Sounding incoherent—and she *felt* incoherent, trying to sort it out in her mind—might make the dispatcher write her off as one of those kooks Jeff had talked about.

The female voice assured her that Officer Carey would get the message. The dispatcher did not think it necessary, since the young woman caller sounded reasonably calm and had not asked for immediate assistance, to inform Janie that Officer Carey, along with every other available police officer in the district, was busy at the scene of a derailed train carrying explosive materials and that he could expect to be tied up there for hours.

Janie replaced the receiver and wiped her sweating palms on her jeans. What now? Sleep was impossible, she knew that. She decided to draw all the shades that were not already drawn, leave the lights burning and to hell with the electric bill, and wait for Jeff to call or come around. She'd try to read, or maybe watch television. If she kept it turned very low, probably it wouldn't disturb Neva or Bea.

The house seemed cold. She turned up the thermostat she had only just turned down, got a sweater and a lap robe to put over her legs, then settled into a corner of the couch, waiting for the phone to ring.

It was eleven-thirty. Teddy looked at the clock and shoved it back under his bed. "They ought to be asleep by now," he said hopefully. "Those old people go to bed pretty early and get up the same way. Come on, let's go see."

As soon as Janie had gone, they had taken off their pajamas and donned jeans and shirts. They carried their footwear, in case even those thick-soled running shoes should make sounds that would give them away.

Teddy eased open the door at the foot of the attic stairs. A faint glow filtered up from the ground floor, as he'd expected, although he had a flashlight to use once they'd reached the outside.

"Crazy," Joe said.

Teddy looked around at him in the dimness. "What's crazy?"

"Living with so many old people. I only live with my grandma, who's old, and she drives us all crazy. My old man especially."

"These don't. I like them," Teddy said. "They pay me for running up and down stairs, and Aunt Bea makes great cookies."

"Yeah, my grandma does, too, but she don't let nobody have any of 'em," Joe said.

"She must let somebody have some sometimes, or why does she make them?" Teddy wanted to know.

"Only at meals," Joe said, disgusted. "She don't think anybody gets hungry between meals."

"We better be quiet now," Teddy warned. "In case Janie hasn't gone to sleep yet. Sometimes she reads for a while after she goes to bed."

They tiptoed with exaggerated care past closed bedroom doors and the open ones to the bathrooms. The light grew brighter, and a scowl formed on Teddy's face as he reached the head of the stairs.

"What the heck's going on? There's lights all over down there. Somebody's watching TV, for crying out loud!"

"We can't go down that way," Joe said, "they'll see us."

"Yeah. OK, we'll use the other stairs. Be careful, they're steep. You could break your neck."

They used the flashlight there, letting themselves out into the back part of the house, twisting the button that unlocked the night latch on the rear door.

"You gonna lock it behind us?" Joe asked, hesitating.

"No, we'd have no way to get back in. What if we get hungry during the night and need more food?"

Recalling the supplies waiting for them in the tree house, they laughed softly. They put on their shoes and went down the creaking steps and across the yard to the maple tree, where the ladder climbed to their hideaway.

Saturday night was a terrible night for watching television. Janie twisted the dial from one channel to another, vainly seeking something that would take her mind off what her mother had told her and give her some way to pass the time until Jeff contacted her.

Garbage on all channels, she thought disgustedly. Late movies that hadn't been any good when they were made twenty or thirty years ago and certainly hadn't improved in the meantime. The people who picked the programs must think everyone was doing something entertaining on Saturday nights, so there was no point in spending good money for a decent movie on TV.

She switched it off in disgust, then wondered what else there was to do. She couldn't read, she was sure of that. If only Jeff would call!

She walked to the doorway of the parlor and stood looking at the obstinately silent phone. Of course, the best thing would be if Jeff simply came in the police car. Maybe what she should have done was report a prowler. Then they'd have sent him here at once, wouldn't they? For all she knew, there *was* a prowler. She felt as if eyes were watching her from what few dark corners remained.

Suddenly, Janie stiffened, heart racing. "What was that?"

She asked it aloud, though there was no one to answer. It had sounded like a door closing.

Reluctantly, she moved toward the kitchen. Maybe someone had gotten hungry and come down for a snack, though with all they'd eaten earlier it didn't seem likely.

The lights she'd left on banished shadows. There was no one in the kitchen. Janie stared around her, unable to dismiss the memory of that small sound and the fear it had aroused.

Automatically, as she'd already done several times, she began to check the locks on the windows, and then on the back door. It opened under her hand.

Incredulous, Janie sucked in a breath. How could that be? She'd left it locked, after everyone else had gone to bed. She couldn't have made a mistake. Could she?

She pushed it shut, hearing the very sound that had brought her off the sofa a few minutes earlier, and twisted the lock, then reached for the sliding bolt above it, ramming it into place.

Please, Jeff, come soon. Her mouth was dry and her heart beat so loud that the sound pounded in her ears.

Once more she made the rounds, checking everything, then fell into a corner of the sofa and wrapped herself in the robe. She waited.

It was a great lark, putting one over on Janie.

They curled in their sleeping bags, giggling over the pictures in the magazine Teddy'd found in the trash. They'd taken so much food upstairs that neither of them was hungry. "We can have it for breakfast," Joe said, and Teddy agreed.

"Maybe when it's summer they'll let us sleep out here every night," he proposed.

"You know, I'm kinda sleepy," Joe said.

"Yeah. We worked hard today." Teddy sighed deeply. "Good night, Joe."

He'd thought he was sleepy, too, yet sleep was slow in coming. Teddy lay there listening to the leaves of the maple as they rustled in the night breeze. There was a rising moon; its pale beams found their way between the branches, probing through the unglassed windows.

Teddy's head was at the opening of the doorway. There was still a light showing from the kitchen, which was peculiar. He hoped it wasn't because Aunt Bea or any of the others were sick. He liked them; it wasn't the way he'd imagined it would be, living with a lot of old people. Mr. Jacoby helped him with his homework when he needed it. Aunt Bea made even better cakes and cookies than his mother, and she had time to make them almost every day. Miss Neva teased and kidded with him and was generous with the dimes for running errands. And Miss Sylvia had ever so many interesting things in her room which she explained to him and let him handle.

There was a collection of elephants carved from many different kinds of wood and a small one out of jade. He'd always thought jade was green, but the little elephant was closer to white, and beautifully detailed. "That one is rather valuable, I think," Sylvia had told him.

Teddy had been fascinated. "Where did you get these? Did you travel a lot? This one says it was made in India. Have you been to India?"

"No, but my brother went everywhere," Sylvia had told him. "I have a scarf from Peru, and baskets from Mexico. Somewhere, maybe in that box, there are wooden shoes from Holland."

She showed them to him, her small treasures, and told him stories about them. "Donald loved to go everywhere and see everything, and he always wrote to me about the places he went."

"What happened to him?" Teddy wanted to know.

"Oh, he died in an air crash a year or so ago. He was ninety-two, and he still was traveling—imagine."

Teddy considered the legal age of twenty-one too far away to comprehend, let alone ninety-two.

He lay now in the tree house, feeling the breeze ruffle his hair, and tried to imagine being ninety-two. His skin would wrinkle and turn pale, and his eyes would get bad, and he'd have to have false teeth like the ones that Charlie used to leave in the bathroom.

Yuck, he thought. He'd hate to have false teeth. He wondered what they would feel like. Before he figured it out, he was asleep.

He woke, feeling that not much time had passed. The moon was still in almost the same spot among the treetops, touching the leaves with silver.

There was a sound below.

Teddy lifted his head ever so slightly, peering down through the thick branches of the maple. At first there was nothing, and then the sound came again: the crack of a stick beneath an incautious foot.

He was on his stomach, well hidden in the foliage, and he rose on his elbows, feeling goose bumps form when he came out of the end of the sleeping bag.

Was there somebody down there? Walking around in the backyard in the middle of the night?

Quite suddenly, Teddy had a vivid memory of Cora Cottler sprawled in the field behind the theater, blood drenching the front of her dress, her mouth open so that the fly could walk in and out over her lip.

He was cold all over. What if Janie was right? What if it wasn't safe to be out here? What if The Sniper, who had killed that woman and the others, who had shot Charlie, was here in his own yard?

He twisted, craning his neck to see better, straining his eyes.

There, something surely moved along the hedge on the far side of the yard, as if it had come around the other side of the house. The shape was impossible to identify until it came to one of the silvery places in the moonlight.

A figure in dark clothes moved quietly, then stepped upon another stick and disappeared once more into the deep shadow of the hedge.

Fear gripped his bowels until he almost cried out with it. Beside him Joe slept soundlessly. They'd left the door unlocked, and Janie was in there, and the others, the old people. The Sniper killed old people.

What had he done?

Teddy was breathing through his mouth now; he had to in order to get enough oxygen. He couldn't see the figure anymore; he wriggled farther out of the sleeping bag, hanging dangerously over the edge of the tree house platform.

He saw nothing, but he heard the back steps creak. And then the figure disappeared beneath the porch roof, out of Teddy's sight, shutting off most of the light that had streamed forth.

What could he do if the man went into the house? Start yelling? Would a killer go away if you yelled? Or would he just start shooting?

The figure stayed out of his sight for several long moments, while Teddy agonized over what to do. Did he hear the knob turning in that unseen hand? He couldn't be sure.

The door didn't open, though. Maybe, he thought in wild hope, Janie or somebody had noticed it was unlocked and relocked it.

In the stillness there was a muffled oath. Then the figure retreated from the door, and Teddy heard the small sounds as the intruder walked around the near side of the house, vanishing into the shrubbery.

Joe turned in his sleep, letting an arm flop out so that it struck Teddy's shoulder. Teddy would have fallen over the edge of the platform if he hadn't already been hanging on for dear life.

Teddy turned and put a hand firmly over Joe's mouth, whispering harshly into his friend's ear. "Shhh! Don't make any noise, just wake up!"

"Mmmfff! What—"

"Be quiet," Teddy hissed, and removed his hand. "There's someone down there."

"What? Who?" Joe asked groggily.

"I think," Teddy said, "that it's The Sniper."

Joe had never awakened so quickly and so thoroughly before in his life. He rose on his knees, peering over the edge into the patterned black and silver of the yard below.

His whisper was no more than a croak. "Whatta we gonna do?"

"Somehow," Teddy whispered, "we have to tell Janie. Only somebody locked the door."

"Over the roof, then," Joe suggested.

Of course; he'd forgotten the roof. "OK," Teddy agreed. "Wait just a minute, to make sure he doesn't come back."

They crouched in silence, listening.

And then, just as they were getting to their feet, before making their way out on that overhanging limb toward the roof, they heard the intruder returning.

Teddy desperately gripped the flashlight, wondering if he dared to turn it fully on the figure that had come to a halt below them. Beside him, Joe groped in blackness and picked up the only thing of any weight that came to hand: a full, icy bottle of Pepsi.

Because the figure was looking up now through the branches. In their terror they could not have described the face that was touched here and there by the cold moonlight. They only knew that whoever stood below them was aware of the maple tree as a means of gaining entry to the house.

Whether or not he was aware that the tree house was occupied they could not tell. All they knew was that as they watched, the figure began to climb the ladder toward where they crouched with their pathetic weapons.

25

Incredibly, she had slept.

Janie jerked upright when the key scratched in the lock, the lap robe sliding to the floor as she scrambled to her feet. She felt drugged, exhausted, yet with adrenaline gushing as she remembered why she was here on the couch instead of in her own bed.

It was Ernie Layton. He manipulated the button to relock the door, then stared at her in surprise. "Is something wrong?"

Her throat was dry, aching. "I was . . . waiting for a call. What time is it?"

Her watch had stopped; she'd forgotten to wind it. Ernie consulted his. "Twenty past two. Do you want me to leave the outside light on?"

"Yes," Janie said, "please."

"Nice moon tonight," Ernie offered, in one of the few spontaneous conversational gambits he'd ever come up with. "It's a beautiful night."

Janie muttered something inane, echoing his good-night as he went past her and up the stairs. She noticed that the fourth step creaked when he put his weight on it.

Janie began to fold up the lap robe. Maybe she'd better go to bed after all, she thought.

The figure came up the ladder, almost soundless except for the rasp of breathing with the effort of the climb.

It was too late to make a dash for the big branch and the roof. They would be detected at once, and both boys were convinced that the climber had a weapon, the same one that had killed the woman they'd found dead in the field.

A beam of moonlight lay across the edge of the platform on which the tree house was built. They had withdrawn from this light, into the comparative safety of darkness. Teddy thought briefly of a nightmare he sometimes had in which he tried and tried to scream but could not utter so much as a squeak. In the dream he always knew that if he could scream, the grip of the nightmare would be loosened, and he would waken free of the terror.

This time was the same, except that this time it was real.

A hand grasped the edge of the platform.

Sick with fear, they stared at it. A man's hand.

Seconds later, the mate to it appeared, crazily patterned in darkness and silver light.

There had been no opportunity to consult with each other, no way to plan. Yet they acted in concert. Joe brought the Pepsi bottle down on the hand nearest him; at the same moment Teddy struck with the flashlight and all his strength.

There was a howl of protest and pain. The hands vanished and they heard the tearing of leaves and small branches as the would-be intruder fell heavily to the ground.

They didn't stick around to listen. Joe was on the edge of the platform, searching out the right limb, then making his way, monkeylike, along it to drop onto the roof.

Teddy was right behind him. For a moment he teetered on the limb, then scrabbled along it in Joe's wake. The roof, perhaps slick with dew, was harder to walk on than it had been in daylight. Even barefoot, they slipped and slid, and in their panic they could not slow their frantic flight even though no one pursued.

Behind and beneath them there was a flurry of movement, then nothing. No indication of pursuit, yet they felt the murderer's scorching breath on the backs of their necks, and their flesh cringed awaiting The Sniper's bullet.

"Damned window's locked," Joe sputtered, and Teddy changed course for the next one along. Heedless now of noise, he hammered on it with his fist.

"Janie! Let us in! It's me, Teddy!"

No lamp came on inside, and he changed course again, this time finding refuge through an open window.

In the bed Mr. Jacoby sat up with a muffled grunt of alarm. "What's going on? Who's there?"

The light clicked on beside the bed in time to keep the boys from breaking their necks or at least their toes.

"He's out there," Teddy said, teeth chattering, goose bumps all over his exposed flesh. "The Sniper! He's in the yard!"

The officer who came in response to Janie's call was the one Jeff had introduced her to, Max Upton. He looked competent and assured, and he didn't hesitate to stride through the house and out the back door. He had a flashlight that looked as if it might be used as a weapon as well as for illumination. It had exceptional lighting power; when he swung it upward along the trunk of the maple, they could see where small branches and twigs had been torn loose when the intruder had slid downward without benefit of handhold.

Max shone the light over the area where the man must have landed. "The ground doesn't seem soft enough to retain much of an impression, but we'll look at it again in daylight. Don't anybody walk around out here, OK?"

That was something they could agree on unanimously. The entire household was awake by this time; even Ernie Layton joined them when they assembled in the parlor while Max Upton took various statements.

"Do you know where Jeff is?" Janie asked. "I left a message to call me with the dispatcher hours ago. After my mother told me she remembered what had happened the night she was hurt."

"I suppose he's on duty with that overturned freight on the edge of town. They called me in after I'd already done a full shift because they were shorthanded. As a matter of fact," Max told them wryly, "I'm into the third shift period for the day, and nobody's offered to relieve me yet. Let me make sure I have all this information correct, all right?"

While he was reading back their statements, Janie looked down at Joe standing beside her. There were what appeared to be blood spatters over his hand and arm.

"Joe, are you hurt?" she asked, dropping onto the edge of the couch for a closer inspection.

Joe looked at the spots, too. "Nah. That's gotta be *his* blood. I hit him with a full Pepsi bottle, and it broke and musta cut him."

"He ought to have some bruises, too," Teddy said. His confidence had come back once he'd reached Janie, light, warmth, and a police officer. "I whacked him with the flashlight. I guess I dropped it, then; it's probably broken."

Max closed his notebook and stuck his pen in his shirt pocket. "Well, I expect you scared him off for good. He won't be back. You can go to bed and go to sleep. I'll make another pass by here before I go off duty, just to check things out; I don't think you have any more to worry about, though."

"It was The Sniper, wasn't it?" Teddy asked. "The one that's been shooting everybody?"

Max grinned. "Everything that happens now is blamed on The Sniper. He didn't shoot at you, did he?"

"No, but he didn't know we were in the tree house. It *was* him, wasn't it?"

Max winked at Janie over Teddy's head. "Probably not. The guy they call The Sniper shoots at people, he doesn't try to break into their houses. Or their tree houses."

To her astonishment and growing indignation, Janie realized that he wasn't taking this very seriously. He was going to leave, and nothing had been solved; she felt no more safe than she had felt before.

She went with him to the front door, stepping outside so that she could speak without being overheard by the boys. "You don't think this had anything to do with The Sniper, do you?"

His gaze was frankly admiring, which somehow only increased her ire. It wasn't masculine admiration she wanted from him, it was protection. "No, Janie, I don't think it's The Sniper. Every criminal has an MO—a modus operandi—which means the way he works. A guy who has been going around taking shots at people isn't very likely to suddenly start breaking into tree houses and scaring little boys."

"He wasn't breaking into the tree house. He was using it to gain access to *this* house," Janie pointed out. "He didn't know the boys were there."

"So he was a burglar. He'd have gotten in if he could and made off with the silver, or robbed your purse, or whatever else came to hand. He must have had a hell of a scare, being attacked by somebody he couldn't see. He's probably in a tavern somewhere right now, having a stiff drink and wondering what happened. Take my word for it, he won't be back. Go to bed and go to sleep and forget it. He didn't get anything, and he won't try again. Not here, he won't."

She stared after the police cruiser when Max Upton pulled away. Were the police always so blasé about things like this? Of course, they encountered crime on a daily and impersonal basis, but . . .

He was wrong, Janie thought. She knew he was wrong.

Still, she tried to smooth the matter over when she'd gone back inside. She sent the boys on to bed, and advised the others to turn in again, too.

"I don't think I can sleep right away," Sylvia said. "I wonder, wouldn't it help if we had a cup of hot tea?"

There was a concerted movement toward the kitchen. Janie was the only one who was fully dressed, except for Ernie Layton. He hadn't had time to take off any more than his shoes and his suit coat before the boys had come storming off the roof. His red tie had been loosened and now dangled askew. He joined them with no special invitation, which was unusual, Janie noted.

Could Ernie Layton possibly have been the one who tried to come in over the roof at the back of the house?

Timewise, he might have been. He'd come in and spoken to her only moments before the boys had burst through Mr. Jacoby's window making enough racket to waken the entire household. Yes, there could have been time for him to fall off the ladder, pick himself up, and come around to the front door. He'd even looked a bit more rumpled than was customary.

Why should he have, though? When he had a key to come in the front door? The only thing she could think of was that he'd wanted to be inside the house without anyone knowing he was there. Only to do what?

Janie moved with the others, getting down cups while Bea put on water to heat and Neva brought lemon and milk and sugar. Neva looked quite fetching in a pink silk dressing gown over a paler pink nightie; her small feet were encased in fluffy matching mules that did more to exhibit her feet than to keep them warm.

Sylvia and Aunt Bea wore flannel gowns. They'd belted warm robes over them and wore fuzzy slippers.

Mr. Jacoby, in dignified tailored pajamas and an elegant maroon robe that Janie guessed had been selected by Rachel, followed Janie's gaze toward the young roomer, and then took the aggressor's stand.

"I think, Mr. Layton," he said in a voice that defied the sort of tactics Ernie had been employing with Janie, "that we must have some information about you. For the peace of mind of all of us."

Ernie looked startled. "About me, sir?" For some reason he flushed.

"Yes. You know that a murderer is loose in our streets, and that has put most of us on edge. And now someone has tried to break in, and it's frightening to us."

"It scares me, too," Ernie said. He pulled his tie back into place, as if that might give him confidence in the face of this verbal assault.

"Then you won't mind telling us who you are. What you do. Why you want to live in a single room in a house with a lot of senior citizens?"

There was something about Mr. Jacoby, an air that compelled compliance. "In a time such as this, we have a right to references, I believe. To relieve our fears."

Now Ernie had gone pale. "You aren't saying . . . you're afraid of *me*, are you?"

"We are afraid," Mr. Jacoby said gently, "of *everyone*. How are we to know whom we can trust?"

Ernie stood with his hands thrust into his trousers pockets, yet his stance was no longer casual. "You think *I* had something to do with the . . . the violence?"

"Did you?" Neva asked sharply.

"No, of course not."

"Where were you last Wednesday evening, when Charlie was shot?" Sylvia asked.

"Wednesday night? I was with"—again color touched his face—"my fiancée. I spend all my free time with her. I was with her tonight."

"And why do you want to live *here?*" Mr. Jacoby probed insistently.

"Why—why, because it's close to where I work. I'm trying to save money to get married on, so I wanted something inexpensive. I didn't care who else lived here, as long as I didn't have to pay car expenses and had a place to sleep. I didn't intend to spend much time here, just sleeping."

Since Mr. Jacoby had paved the way, Janie finally got out the question she'd been trying to have answered for days. "Where do you work, Mr. Layton?"

It was as if someone were turning a light off and on behind his rather pale skin; he kept alternating between hot and cold. It seemed that he visibly drew himself together. "I'm employed at Chalmers, Halvorsen, and Montgomery," he said. "Mr. Chalmers is going to be my father-in-law. He'll attest to my presence at work and also at his home almost every evening."

"The funeral home? But why were you making such a secret of it?" Janie asked, bewildered. "You kept doing all those fool things to keep from telling me that . . ."

He met her gaze with more openness than before, displaying as well a touch of defiance. "Did you ever try admitting to anyone that you're a mortician? Sheila is the only one my own age I've ever met who didn't back away from me as if I had some incurable disease. And that's because her father's owned a mortuary all her life. I can't stand it, the way they look at me, as if I were . . . unclean. It's a perfectly respectable occupation. I'm not ashamed of it, I just don't . . . like other people's reaction to hearing what it is."

Neva patted him on the arm. "Of course it is. We understand perfectly. Come along, everybody, get your tea and let's sit down with it. It'll be time to get up before we go to bed if we don't get on with it."

Janie sipped her own tea, needing the warmth of it, listening to the ebb and flow of conversation around her while hearing almost none of the actual words. She didn't care what Max Upton thought, she was convinced there was something more sinister than a burglary intended by the man who'd climbed to the tree house.

Who in his right mind would have attempted to break into a house blazing with lights from every ground-floor room? Was that why the "burglar" had attempted to gain entrance through the second-floor windows?

"I'm so grateful that dreadful creature didn't get inside," Sylvia said. "Grateful enough so that I think I'll go to church tomorrow and give thanks. I'll call Alfred first thing in the morning and see if he won't take me on his way to play golf. Surely I can find someone there who'll give me a ride home, or I can call a cab. Why don't you come with me, Bea?"

"Well, maybe I will. This has been most distressing, but how much worse it would have been if I'd been here alone." Bea gave them a tremulous smile. "I'm so glad you're all living here, too."

"What if he'd gotten in upstairs?" Sylvia speculated. "He might have robbed us all. I cashed my Social Security check on Friday, and I have most of it in my purse. What would I have done if he'd stolen it?"

"You have Alfred," Bea pointed out. "He'd see that you had what you needed."

"Yes, I suppose so. He's a good boy, even if he does insist on being on the golf course every Sunday instead of in church. I *always* took him to Sunday School when he was a child. I don't know why he won't go now; he could play golf in the afternoon."

Mr. Jacoby tapped his watch. "Anybody noticed what time it is? We're a tired bunch, by the look of us." He rose, resting a hand on Ernie Layton's shoulder. "I hope we didn't offend you, young man, but these are dangerous times. It wasn't a matter of prying, and I'm sure no one condemns your profession."

There was a murmur of assent as they all rose and carried teacups to the kitchen. Janie surrendered hers to Bea and headed for the stairs.

She felt drained, exhausted, and overwhelmingly disappointed that Jeff hadn't called. She hoped the work he was doing with the overturned freight wasn't hazardous.

She hoped, too, that she'd be able to sleep. It was nearly 4 A.M.

26

Though she had slept badly, tormented by dreams of being pursued by a faceless man with a knife, and of moving through the house where a killer lurked in the shadows, Janie was up by ten on Sunday morning.

She felt tired and hung over, yet compelled to try to function. Even a shower didn't restore much of her energy.

She put on running clothes, knowing that sometimes hard physical exercise could help. If Jeff hadn't worked all night, a double shift, he might have run with her. Everything, she reflected, was better when Jeff was with her.

He wasn't likely to show up today, not after the night he must have put in. She hoped he'd call before he fell into bed, though. Even that would ease her mind, just hearing his voice.

Everybody else was obviously up ahead of her. The others were having a leisurely breakfast of sourdough pancakes with real maple syrup (from Addison Hamer's private stock, nearly as valuable as his liquor supply), with tiny, succulent sausages. Janie wondered how well they'd continue to eat when Uncle Addison's supplies ran out and was grateful that she didn't have to worry about that at the moment.

Bea, Neva, and Sylvia were all dressed in their best; nothing dowdy about any of them, Janie marveled. Neva wore a smart navy suit with a red scarf that matched her pumps and purse. Bea was resplendent in a flowered print with a jacket, and Sylvia was quite stylish (except for what Teddy called "old lady shoes") in a brown wool dress.

With the simple dress, she wore a medallion that made Janie lean over to examine it more closely. "It's beautiful! Where did you ever get it?"

Sylvia patted the large golden circlet where it hung at the end of a chain. "My brother Don brought it back from Central America on one of his trips. He went everywhere, you know. I've never worn this before because it's so *huge*, it seemed inappropriate for an old woman. This dress sort of calls for something, though, doesn't it? Because it's so plain. I think the thing is Aztec, or maybe it's Mayan, I can't remember. It's a replica of a calendar of some kind, if I recall correctly."

They all agreed that it was stunning. The three of them, it turned out, were going to church together, since Neva's friend wouldn't be picking her up until later.

"We've called a cab," Sylvia informed Janie. "Alfred couldn't come. He'd planned to play golf with a friend at Cedarcrest today, as usual. And we've arranged for a cab when we get out after services, too, so we should be all right."

Janie didn't find that totally reassuring. They had been waiting for their cabs after bingo when Charlie had been shot. Still, they couldn't be expected to play permanent hostage to The Sniper.

Mr. Jacoby left about the same time the women did, walking in the opposite direction. His daughter had offered to come over and pick him up, but it was such a nice day he preferred to walk.

"Be careful," Janie said to him, meaning it, and he gave her that smile she'd become so attached to in the short time she'd known the old man. "That sniper, he can't be after everybody in our household," he told her. "So I ought to be safe for a Sunday morning stroll of a dozen blocks. You be careful, too."

Janie stood in the doorway looking after him. *The Sniper can't be after everybody in our household,* he'd said. The words lingered in her mind after she'd closed the door and walked through to the kitchen, where she began to clean up after the boys, who had eaten and vanished back to the attic.

Was it possible that The Sniper was after *one* someone in their household, if not all of them?

She couldn't put the idea out of her mind. She'd never been directly touched by serious crime before, and now, in a matter of a few weeks, she seemed surrounded by it. Even discounting the earlier murders of women she had not known (though Bea had seen several of them; was that significant?), Janie felt overwhelmed by the things that had happened. Teddy and Joe had found one of the bodies. Charlie had been shot. Her mother had been hit over the head and knocked unconscious. And last night someone had tried to enter the house.

Coincidence, as Max Upton thought?

No, Janie thought, closing the dishwasher door and rinsing her hands at the sink.

Yet what was the thread between the incidents, the connection? The Sniper, they said, was irrational, shooting at random, leaving no clues to his identity. Was it random, though, when even a tenuous connection existed? Or was it only that no one, so far, had recognized what the pattern was?

The music flowing softly from Bea's radio over the sink was interrupted by a newscast to which Janie half listened as she finished wiping up counters, putting away cereal boxes, and eating a leftover sausage.

It was only with the final item of general news that she paused to pay attention. "Fifty families evacuated from their homes in the north end last night because of a derailment of several cars carrying hazardous materials have been allowed to return to their dwellings this morning. The cars have been righted without serious injury to anyone, though several railroad employees were treated for inhalation of toxic fumes and released from General Hospital. Streets in the area are again open to traffic.

"And now a word about sports. On the local scene, the fifth annual Cedarcrest Classic got underway this morning with over one hundred competitors for the—"

Janie reached up and switched it off. She hoped Jeff hadn't been among those affected by the toxic fumes; though they'd said railroad employees, she knew the media often made mistakes about such details. At any rate, Jeff must be off duty by now. Should she call again? Just to make sure he was OK?

No, she decided. He'd call her when he was up to it. Instead, she called her mother.

Muriel sounded better. "My head doesn't hurt so much this morning, unless I try to get up. Then it's awful, but they say the pain will be decreasing from now on. Janie, did you talk to the police?"

"Yes." Janie had already determined not to add to Muriel's concern by telling her about the attempted burglary last night, nor her own distress brought on by Max Upton's attitude. "They'll take it from here, I think. Mother, have you remembered anything more about the night you were hurt? Anything about the person who did it?"

"No. I didn't hear a thing, except that step on the stairs when I was still on the second floor."

"What about smells? Did you smell anything? I mean, like tobacco, or shaving lotion, or anything like that?"

"Nothing," Muriel said.

"Did you have any impression of size? A big man, a small one?"

"Strength," Muriel said. "He hit me very hard, that's all I know. I'm sorry, honey, there just wasn't any warning, and I didn't know a thing except that I blacked out. Oh, there is some good news to give to everybody."

"We could use some," Janie told her. "Are they going to let you come home soon?"

"Ken—Dr. Trent—says it will probably be a few more days at the earliest, and then only if he makes house calls for a while."

Janie noted the use of his first name and would have been delighted had she not been so concerned with more serious matters.

"No, it isn't me," Muriel was continuing. "It's Charlie Silvers. They've moved him out of ICU. Not very far out, actually, just into a ward down the corridor, so the ICU crew will be available if there are any setbacks. They tell me he's feeling better, though, and is stronger. They don't think the bullet is doing any further damage, so they're simply going to leave it alone."

"Wonderful! I'll tell everybody. They're planning a great party for when he comes home."

"I'll send him a message. How's Teddy?"

"Teddy's fine, having a good time with Joe and the trains," Janie said evasively. What would her mother think when she found out the truth about last night?

They talked for a few minutes more, and Janie hung up.

If the police wouldn't listen to her, wouldn't consider the strong possibility (in her own mind, the certainty) that all these crimes were connected, what on earth could she do?

She flopped down into a chair and picked up a pen to doodle on a pad of paper left near the phone to write messages. After a moment she realized she had written a list of the murders, her mother's assault, and the tree house intruder. Consciously then, she began to add other things.

Bingo, question mark. Did the fact that several of the victims had been bingo players at St. Andrew's mean anything?

Were the attack on Muriel and the incident last night related? Either to each other or to the murders?

Why should anyone have hit Muriel over the head? If they'd wanted to steal something from the house, what could it have been? Nothing, so far as she knew, was missing or even disturbed.

How had the intruder known about the tree house? It had been hidden in the trees, unknown to the occupants of the main house, for years until the boys had recently uncovered it, so it wasn't common neighborhood knowledge. Joe hadn't known of it, and she suspected that what Joe didn't know about the area wasn't known to much of anybody.

So, someone who'd been around since the tree house was revealed by the pruning?

Had Muriel's assailant been frightened off and returned last night to complete whatever his mission was?

"What in hell could it have been?" Janie asked aloud. "Nobody here is rich. We have the usual collection of watches and pay or pension checks, Sylvia has that collection of elephants which are probably worth a little, though certainly not a fortune, and who knows about them anyway?"

There was simply no connection that she could see between the murders of the unknown women and the people in this household. Except that Teddy had found one of the bodies. And that the body he found had been Alfred Bonnard's landlady.

Janie sat very still. She could hear the ticking of the grandfather clock and a car moving past in the street.

She didn't have it yet, but she felt that she was getting close to something. What, damn it, what!

Until Charlie the victims had been strangers, except that Mrs. Cottler was Alfred's landlady. The Sniper had fired into the small group of bingo players *from this house* and injured Charlie, though not fatally. It was the first time The Sniper had failed to kill his victim. Why?

It was like a puzzle to which she must find the pieces. They were all there, she was convinced of that, if only she could see them. And when she put the pieces together, the puzzle would be complete, the answers revealed.

The phone shrilled, propelling her out of her chair, almost falling toward the instrument. "Yes, hello?"

"Janie?"

He sounded wiped out, yet as glad to hear her voice as she was to hear his. "Listen, I just got your message. I worked all night—"

"I know, Max told me and I heard about it on the radio, too. You didn't get any of that toxic fumes stuff, did you?"

"No, though I got enough of a whiff of it to be glad my duty was keeping traffic rerouted and looters and idiots out of the area. I'm going to take a shower and then come over for a few minutes before I sack out, if it's OK."

"Of course it's OK. I've got a lot to talk to you about."

"Well, I don't know how long I'll stay conscious; if I quit moving, I'll probably pass out. But I . . ." His tone changed, dropped to a more intimate note. "I need a fix, Janie. I'm getting rather attached to you."

"Good. The feeling's mutual. I'll be here when you get here," she told him, smiling.

After she'd hung up, though, she reverted to her previous train of thought. If she could organize the ideas so that she could convince Jeff of her own conviction that all these incidents were related, maybe he could convince his superiors, and they'd do something about it.

Where had she been? The Sniper firing into the bingo players from this house. Charlie had survived, though up to now The Sniper had been very accurate.

Chance? Chance, too, that Charlie had been the first *male* victim?

Or had The Sniper intended to shoot someone else? One of the women?

That took a few moments' thought. If that were the case, had The Sniper been shooting at random, at *any* woman, or had he been shooting at a *particular woman?*

Suddenly, as clearly as if it were being said to her now, Janie recalled something Sylvia had said.

I had won a twenty-dollar gift certificate from the deli, and I dropped the envelope it was in. When I bent over to pick it up, there was this shot, and Charlie cried out behind me, and everybody was screaming.

What if, Janie speculated in a creeping horror, Charlie had not been the intended victim at all? What if The Sniper had intended to shoot *Sylvia*, who had escaped injury because she bent over at the crucial moment to retrieve the envelope, and the bullet had hit Charlie, who had been *behind* her, by mistake?

Now there was a connection, though still tenuous, Janie thought, between the earlier victims and this household. For Alfred's landlady was the fourth victim, and Alfred's mother had nearly been the fifth victim, and Alfred's mother lived in the household where Muriel had been attacked and which had been scheduled for another intrusion last night.

Right now Alfred's mother was presumably safe in church (safe until she came out, though that was by no means a certainty) and Alfred was playing golf . . .

It was as if her mind moved in slow motion, pulling together the tiny threads, sifting the relevant from the irrelevant. It was like one of those tests they give for color blindness; every ingredient, all of the picture was there, but for one who is blind to certain colors, the numeral or the letter cannot be seen.

Janie's fist pounded gently on the arm of her chair as if by so doing she could force her brain to produce the answers.

Alfred was playing golf. Yet his mother had said he was at Cedarcrest . . . and on the radio the announcer had said there was a tournament there, with over a hundred entries . . .

Would they allow anyone else to play the course while there was a competition taking place? Janie knew very little about golf, but she was reasonably sure that a tournament would close the golf course to anyone who wasn't a participant.

She reached for the phone book and ran her finger down the C's . . . there it was, Cedarcrest Golf and Country Club. She dialed and waited until a pleasant female voice responded.

"Can you tell me, is there a Mr. Alfred Bonnard registered in the tournament today?"

"Bonnard?" The voice was dubious. "It would be difficult to reach any of the players. Is this an emergency?"

"Yes," Janie said firmly. "It's an emergency. Can you tell me if he's playing?"

"Just a moment, please."

It was an eternity before the silence ended. "Ma'am? I'm sorry, Mr. Bonnard is not on the registered list of competitors. Of course, he could be among those watching the tournament. I'm afraid I have no way of reaching him, however."

"I see. There's no chance he's playing, other than in the tournament?"

"Oh no, not today."

"Thank you," Janie said, and hung up. Hadn't Sylvia specifically said that Alfred was playing today with a friend?

She looked at her watch.

Sylvia, with Neva and Bea, would be getting out of church within the next quarter of an hour.

Even if their taxi was waiting, if they didn't have to stand on the curb until it arrived, what guarantee was that of safety?

None, Janie thought, suffocating. None whatever.

What was the name of the church? She'd heard them say it—what was it? All Saints Episcopal? Yes, the one just beyond Teddy's new school.

She found the number, dialed it, and listened to it ring. She cursed under her breath.

"What's the matter?" Teddy came up behind her, curious.

"I'm trying to get a message to Aunt Bea at the church, but nobody answers. They're having services right now, for heaven's sake, why don't they answer?"

"The phone's not in the church part," Teddy said with perfect logic. "It's in the pastor's office, in the other building, probably, like in our church. Nobody's there during services."

Janie hung up, immediately looking for another number. She knew Jeff's address by this time, though she hadn't memorized his phone number. Again, the ringing went on and on. Too long for her to take it for granted that he was still in the shower; anyone but the most dedicated bather would have stepped out to answer the phone by this time. Maybe he was already on the way over, only how could she be sure of that, or that he'd come directly here, not stopping for anything?

"What's going on? What are you upset about?" Teddy demanded.

Twelve minutes now until the old women would be out of church. She prayed that the sermon had been a long one, that there would be a delay. She had nothing but her own intuition to go on, but she felt compelled to hold them in the church, not to let them come out into the spring sunshine, unsuspecting, vulnerable.

She made up her mind. "If the phone rings, answer it. If it's Jeff, or if he comes here, tell him I've gone to the church over by your school, All Saints Episcopal. Tell him it's an emergency and to meet me there as fast as he can. Don't tell anybody else anything, no matter who they are, understand? And don't unlock the door for anyone, and don't go outside. I mean it, Teddy, do just as I say."

He was staring at her in consternation. "Is it The Sniper?"

"Yes." She was jerking on her sweatshirt, not bothering to zip it.

"Janie, why don't you call the police?"

"There isn't time," she said, and dashed out the door, leaving it ajar for her brother to close.

She ran hard, dodging the few pedestrians, cutting across streets at occasional risk, concentrating on making the best time she could. How ironic, that she couldn't trust herself to explain clearly and convincingly enough, couldn't trust the police to understand and agree and come quickly enough.

What she was going to do when she arrived, if The Sniper was there, she didn't know. She only knew she had to be there before the services ended.

27

There wouldn't be another fiasco. He was determined on that score. First he'd hit that fat slob by mistake—and hadn't even managed to kill him—and then the Madison woman had surprised him when he'd been searching for the stamp album—where in hell was the damned thing?—and finally, last night. Who'd have dreamed anybody'd let those kids sleep in that tree house, knowing there was a killer loose?

He still didn't know why the house had been all lit up that way. If it hadn't been for that, he would simply have used the key he'd copied from hers and let himself in after they'd all gone to sleep. He'd substituted sleeping tablets for the vitamin she always took before she went to bed, so she wouldn't have wakened even if he'd turned on the overhead light.

It would have been so simple that way. Maybe he wouldn't even have felt the need to kill her, though after all he'd been through it would be a waste not to.

And he wanted her dead. God, how he wanted her dead.

There were no words to express how much he hated her.

No, he'd given her more than an even chance. He'd tried everything to get the album away from her, tried asking outright for something she seldom if ever used any more—the way she was always giving up new hobbies and activities, after she'd spent a small fortune on the equipment for them, was ridiculous—tried making her think it had been lost during the move, tried everything he could think of. Including outright theft, which ought to have been simple and had turned out to be impossible. Where she could have put what he sought was beyond him. She wouldn't have been stupid enough—or generous enough—to give it away. She still had it, somewhere. Maybe she was stupid enough to have given it to that kid to play with.

Well, he'd get his hands on it when she was dead. Nobody would question his right to everything in that dreadful cluttered room, all the junk she'd been accumulating for more than eighty years. He would go there, after the funeral, grieving, and pack it all back in the boxes and go away.

And then he would hand over the keys to that miserable little apartment, and nobody in this part of the country would ever hear of him again.

He hadn't made up his mind where he would go. He'd considered a lot of different places, places his uncle had talked about. Talked about, and visited, and never invited a nephew to go with him, though he could have afforded to well enough.

How much it would have meant if he'd been able to travel with his uncle. To do anything to get out from under her thumb.

Her thumb, hell, he thought now, angrily yet coldly calm, more like her foot. Right on his neck from the time he was a toddler.

He'd rebelled at one time. He could remember kicking her in the shins and leaving bruises. It hadn't done him any good; she'd beaten him nearly senseless for it. Yet there had been the satisfaction of seeing the black and blue marks the next day.

Satisfaction had been a rare commodity in his life. She had ruled him from the time he was an infant, stepping on him every time he tried to do anything on his own. Dragging him to those psychologists and psychiatrists. Even having him locked up that time, signing the papers while he'd wept and shouted and pleaded with her. Oh, he had to admit he'd seen tears in her eyes, but she'd done it all the same.

It had been a terrible place; he still had nightmares about it all these years later. Well, they'd never lock him up again. He'd see to that. With her gone, there was no one to know any of the things that had happened in the past. And there would be all the money, money that could take him anywhere, buy him anything.

Well, not anything. It couldn't buy him youth, or the love he might have had. It couldn't wipe out the memories of how she'd managed to ruin virtually every relationship that might have been meaningful. Twice he'd been on the verge of marriage, of being normal and happy like everyone else. Twice she'd taken the prospective bride aside and told her things. Things that made the young women return his rings and break the engagements.

There had been years in therapy. The thing that amused him now was that for the past fifteen years she'd believed him cured of what she considered his aberrations. She thought he had turned into a dutiful son, concerned for her welfare, patient, kind.

He hadn't done this in broad daylight before. It added a touch of danger that excited him. He had no real fear that he would be observed and captured, or even later identified. No. He'd seen what they were like when he fired into a pack of them. They screamed and milled around like headless chickens and couldn't describe anything to the police later.

Today would be no different in that respect.

What would be different was that today she would finally die.

She was running well, but she was not sure it would be fast enough. Janie wasted no time looking back or getting her bobbing wrist in position so that she could check the time. It would slow her down to do either, and time was of the essence.

She knew that because she could think of no reason why Alfred would have lied to his mother about playing golf except that he intended to be elsewhere, doing something she would not have approved. Alfred, who had had his mother's "lost" purse long enough to have made a duplicate of her door key, who could easily have entered the house and been hunting for something, who had struck Muriel to keep her from knowing he was there.

She had no idea what it was that Alfred was hunting for; last night's attempt to gain entrance again proved only that he had not yet found it.

She hadn't been running regularly enough; she was becoming winded, and the church was still a block away. There were cars parked solidly on both sides of the street, and no sign of any general exodus from the area, thank God. Thank God, too, that she'd run with Jeff recently or she'd have been in worse shape than she was now.

There were other runners out, getting their Sunday exercise. A family group approached and passed her: mother, father, two sons, all in red running shorts and sweatshirts, waving before they disappeared behind her.

There was another runner up ahead, an older fellow in gray sweatpants and top with the hood up. A weekend runner, probably a beginner; he didn't run well or easily. In fact, he slowed to a walk several times before she came abreast of him.

Janie paid no attention to him. She was concerned with the congregation at All Saints. The double front doors were swung open and the priest in full regalia stood at one side as the people began to leave the church.

Please, let them be at the front of the church and among the last to leave, she thought. She was still half a block away.

She looked among the concentration of vehicles and saw no sign of Alfred's car. But of course he wouldn't have it pinned in that way; he'd have to be able to get away in a hurry. So he wouldn't have parked it in front of the church, or around the corner.

How far could he expect to shoot with a Beretta and kill someone? Why hadn't she asked Jeff that? The night that Charlie was shot, his assailant had apparently been hidden by the trees across the street. Instinctively, Janie glanced directly opposite the church. There were two boys on bikes coming toward her, and an elderly woman walking. There could have been someone in one of the cars, but she'd already rejected the idea that Alfred would be in a spot where he couldn't readily escape.

She heard the labored breathing of the elderly runner behind her, then falling away as she put on an added burst of speed, knowing it was the last that she had.

There they were. Neva and Bea and Sylvia, shaking hands with the pastor, everybody nodding and smiling, everybody happy.

Pain cut through her flank in a searing stab, and she tried to yell. "Go back! Go back inside!"

Her voice didn't carry any distance at all. People were starting their cars, laughing, visiting, kids yelling after an hour or two of being kept quiet. Nobody paid any attention to her.

Where was he? Janie sagged against a blue Thunderbird, gasping, pressing a hand to the ache in her side, glancing around for a possible waiting place for The Sniper. He could be in any of those houses, she thought despairingly. Behind any of those windows. Hidden by a tree in any yard.

Her eyes swept over the beginning runner to a man in his undershirt and baggy shorts, mowing his lawn, and then snapped back.

The runner was Alfred.

She screamed as he raised the weapon, steadying it in both hands, aiming. "No! No, don't!"

He fired.

Wildly, Janie spun around again, looking toward the church, and so little time had elapsed that she saw Sylvia falling, as if in slow motion.

Neva and Bea had hold of her on each side, easing her to the ground.

Now there were screams from every direction. Janie didn't hear them. She had gotten a second wind, or a particle of one, and she plunged into the street after the runner in gray.

For a moment he didn't know he was being pursued. The weapon had disappeared; he was only another weekend runner, minding his own business, not standing out at all in the crowd that was quickly gathering.

Janie was beyond reasoning, beyond anything but the compulsion to stop him. She dove between a pair of teenaged girls in shorts, drawn by the noise and confusion, and yelled. "Alfred, stop! Stop!"

He turned his head and saw her, then, stumbling over the curb as he recognized her. Shock nearly knocked him off his feet, and then he redoubled his efforts, pitching back into the street in front of a car that swerved, driver cursing.

Alfred had gained the far side of the street, and Janie went after him. No one seemed to be paying any attention to them; the interesting activity was at the door of the church where the priest and several elderly ladies knelt beside a white-haired woman in a brown dress.

He wouldn't get away with it, he would not! Janie determined, and thought that she was gaining on him.

Alfred was not a runner. Janie, though not in excellent condition, was half his age and had taken pride in her stamina. She *was* gaining on him.

She saw it even as he veered along a side street, the car in which he had so generously given all the oldsters a ride to the bingo game on the night when he'd shot poor Charlie.

Alfred was a creature of habit, and one of his habits was to lock his car doors when he parked his car. He had the key out, jamming it into the lock, when Janie flung herself upon him, dragging him nearly to the ground.

He swore at her, striking out with a blow that left her seeing stars and tasting blood, yet she clung tenaciously to a leg, nearly dragging the sweatpants down as he struggled to get the car door open.

He kicked out at her, this time hard enough so that she loosened her grip, senses swimming. And then he was into the vehicle, starting the motor.

Janie scrambled to her feet and, in one final all-out effort, threw herself onto the hood as he accelerated violently away from the curb.

There was nothing to hold onto. Sooner or later she was going to slide off, and he'd probably run over her, Janie thought frantically, or someone else would.

And then Alfred slammed on the brakes, sluing sideways, as a white Granada with a wine-red top forced him over the curb and up against a tree.

Amazingly, she could run, or at least trot, back to the church, leaving Jeff to deal with Alfred. The crowd had not dispersed, though the pastor was pleading with them to draw back enough to give the lady air. In the distance, a siren rose and fell, coming closer.

Janie pushed through the onlookers, dropping on her knees beside Neva, who was holding Sylvia's hand. Sylvia's eyes were closed, but astonishingly there was no blood anywhere.

"Knocked her down and out," Neva said, unsurprised to find Janie there, "but she's breathing all right. That fancy Aztec medallion probably saved her life. Look, the bullet hit right in the middle of it. Ruined it."

Janie felt a crazy desire to laugh, or perhaps cry; she wasn't sure which. Sylvia's life might well have been saved; she had yet to be told that her son had tried to kill her.

Though Sylvia was badly bruised, her injuries were not serious. Had it not been for her age, which made the doctors decide to keep her overnight for observation, she might have gone home that same day.

Alfred had at first said nothing, glaring at his captors. And then, upon learning that he had once more failed in this effort to kill Sylvia, there had been an unprecedented outpouring of vituperation: his hatred of his mother, who had had him confined in a mental institution until he had learned how to outwit her and the authorities, to convince them that he was as sane as any of them; his desperate need to be free of her control; his conviction that all his dreams would come true if he had the money that could be obtained when he got his hands on the stamp album his uncle had left to Sylvia; his decision to use the gun that his uncle had brought back from a trip to Europe, which Alfred had discovered accidentally and appropriated for his own use.

Lieutenant Zazorian had arrived on the scene, and they would take Alfred away for formal questioning within minutes. Janie spoke quickly, before it was too late to find out for herself.

"Why did you think the stamp album was valuable?"

He gave her a look of sheer hatred but replied readily enough. Perhaps it was the need to make himself appear rational, normal in his desires. "He left her everything, Uncle Donald did, not a nickel's worth to me of any of it. Including the stamp album. She didn't really care about it, she thought the stamps were rather pretty, and she put a few more in. Just pretty pictures, of no particular value, she thought they were. I didn't know any different, either, until I read the article."

He stared around the circle of faces, attaching no significance to the tall officer making his way through the crowd from the police cruiser which had parked in the middle of the street for the lack of room elsewhere.

"It was called the Connell stamp, and the value printed on it is only five cents, but it's worth something like four thousand dollars. The article said a postmaster in New Brunswick was given the authority, in eighteen-sixty, to order a new set of stamps when the province switched from British shillings and pence to Canadian dollars and cents. On the five-cent one, he had his own portrait. The governor of the province fired him, but not before Connell bought up all five thousand sheets of the stamps. They say he burned most of them, but kept a few for souvenirs, and now they're worth a mint."

He was defiant, angry. "I read about that one and saw a picture of it, and realized there was one in my mother's book. So I looked at the album more closely and found that there were other valuable ones there, too. I tried every way I knew to get it—she didn't care about it a damn, but she'd never do anything just because I wanted her to— and finally I decided to kill her for it."

"But you killed the others, too," Janie said, nearly inaudible in her horror. "Those women you didn't even know."

"I couldn't just shoot *her,* could I? I'd have been the first one the police would have looked at. But if there was a sniper loose, killing women senselessly, why, there'd be no reason to suspect me at all. She'd have been just one more of them. No loss, any of them," Alfred ended sullenly.

Zazorian had reached the inner circle, along with two other uniformed officers. Before he could speak to issue an order, Janie asked quickly, "But you knew Mrs. Cottler."

He looked deeply into her face in a way that made her shrink against Jeff. "Yes. Is that how you knew it was me? I was afraid it was a mistake, after I'd done it. It seemed too good an opportunity to miss at the time. Meeting her there when I was looking for another victim. She was going to raise my rent again, the bitch, and she wouldn't do anything about the electricity so that I could make coffee and toast at the same time." He looked at the newly arrived officers. "Is that too much to ask? To have both coffee and toast at the same time?"

"No, sir," one of the officers said. "I'm going to have to put cuffs on you, sir."

Alfred did not resist. "I nearly made it," he said. "Didn't I?"

The officers exchanged glances. "Yes, sir," one of them agreed.
"You nearly did."

"Janie? I can't hear you very well; what's all the racket in the
background? What's going on?" Molly demanded.

"A party." Janie covered one ear so that she could hear better and
spoke more loudly into the phone. "I said it's a party. Celebrating
Charlie's homecoming. They're drinking piña coladas, and it's getting
rather merry."

"Good. I was afraid you were having another crisis of some kind. I
see they sent that Alfred Bonnard to Western State; he won't even
come to trial, will he?"

"It doesn't look like it. Nobody had any doubt that he's mentally ill
and has been for years, though he managed to cover it pretty well.
Sylvia knew it, of course, but I guess she hoped he was better, so she
didn't talk about it."

"I suppose she feels partly responsible for those other people who
died."

"I think she did, at first." Janie turned her back to the partygoers,
hoping to shut out more of the laughter. "Oddly enough, though, she
seems to have forgotten it now. And she speaks of Alfred with affection, as if he were in a regular hospital somewhere with a disease, like
TB. She writes to him regularly, though he doesn't answer. Listen,
Molly, this is a bad time to talk. It's too noisy. Can I call you back
later? Did you want something special?" She strained to hear the
answer.

"Yes, I want to talk about the final arrangements for the wedding.
You *are* going to be there, aren't you? Or have things gotten so hectic
you're no longer interested?"

Janie twisted her head so that she could see Jeff, dutifully sampling
Neva's frothy drink, and Mr. Jacoby, laughing up at him over something the younger man had said.

"Oh yes," Janie told her friend. "There's nothing I'm more interested in than how you go about planning a wedding. I think I might
have use for that kind of information before long."

Jeff turned, saw her, and grinned, lifting his glass.

"Yes," Janie said, "very soon now, I think. I'll call you tomorrow,
OK?"

She hung up and moved toward the parlor, accepting Jeff's glass to finish the drink he didn't really want. "There's some apricot brandy in Uncle Addison's cabinet in the other room," she told him softly. "Or an excellent scotch. We'd have to leave the party temporarily."

Jeff bent to brush a kiss across her nose.

"I thought you'd never ask," he said.

About the Author

Willo Davis Roberts has written nearly seventy novels, including *Act of Fear*, *The Jaubert Ring*, *Expendable*, and *White Jade*. She lives in Granite Falls, Washington, with her husband David, who is also a writer/photographer.

Date Due